# A THORN IN THE ROSE

## Also by Samantha Lee Howe

### Novels

*Killing Kiss*
*Futile Flame*
*Demon Dance*
*Hateful Heart*
*Zombies at Tiffany's*
*Kat on a Hot Tin Airship*
*The Darkness Within – Final Cut*
*What's Dead PussyKat*
*Jinx Town*
*Kat of Green Tentacles*
*Silent Sand*
*Jaded Jewel*
*Jinx Magic*
*Kat and the Pendulum*
*Posing for Picasso*
*Jinx Bound*
*Ten Little Demons*
*The Stranger in Our Bed*
*The House of Killers*
*Kill or Die*
*Kill a Spy*
*The Soul Thief*

### Collections

*Crimes of Passion*
*Legends of Cthulhu and Other Nightmares*
*The Complete Lightfoot*
*Cthulhu and Other Monsters*
*Zombies in New York and Other Bloody Jottings*

# A THORN IN THE ROSE

## SAMANTHA LEE HOWE

NO EXIT PRESS

First published in the UK in 2026 by No Exit Press,
an imprint of Bedford Square Publishers Ltd,
London, UK

noexit.co.uk
@noexitpress

© Samantha Lee Howe, 2026

A Maxim Jakubowski book

The right of Samantha Lee Howe to be identified as the author of this work
has been asserted in accordance with the Copyright, Designs and Patents Act
1988. All rights reserved. No part of this book may be reproduced, stored in or
introduced into a retrieval system, or transmitted, in any form or by any means
(electronic, mechanical, photocopying, recording or otherwise) without the
written permission of the publishers.

Any person who does any unauthorised act in relation to this publication
may be liable to criminal prosecution and civil claims for damages.
A CIP catalogue record for this book is available from the British Library.
This is a work of fiction. Names, characters, places, and incidents either
are the product of the author's imagination or are used fictitiously,
and any resemblance to actual persons, living or dead, businesses,
companies, events or locales is entirely coincidental.

ISBN
978-1-83501-334-2 (Paperback)
978-1-83501-335-9 (eBook)

2 4 6 8 10 9 7 5 3 1

Typeset in 10.8 on 13.5pt Garamond MT Pro
by Avocet Typeset, Bideford, Devon, EX39 2BP

Printed and bound in Great Britain by Clays Ltd, Elcograf S.p.A.

The manufacturer's authorised representative in the EU for
product safety is Easy Access System Europe, Mustamäe tee 50,
10621 Tallinn, Estonia
gpsr.requests@easproject.com

*In memory of my grandmother, Kathleen Hulse.
A survivor of World War II and a strong, independent
and feisty woman with a fierce sense of humour.*

# Prologue

*London, 1941*

THE AIR-RAID SIRENS STARTED AT NINE.

Melinda Greenway and her younger brother, Valentine, had just returned from supper with friends to celebrate Mel's nineteenth birthday. The evening had been a subdued affair, with Mel watching Val, and stopping the sixteen-year-old boy from drinking the black-market booze her friend Susan had somehow managed to procure. Mel wasn't much of a drinker, but she'd had a try of the stuff for the sheer devilment. It had tasted like boot polish to her, and she'd soon abandoned the glass, with the contents tipped into Susan's window plant. After that, she'd sat calmly watching the others get slowly squiffy with a slight, indulgent smile on her lips. It was difficult to celebrate any birthday these days, and that morning Mel had received *The Letter* by way of a birthday card: an invitation to enlist, much to the horror of her parents.

Val, however, was enjoying himself, and despite her efforts to thwart him had somehow managed to consume three glasses of the awful liquor. He was decidedly wobbly by the time Mel dragged him out to the taxi and they wended their way back to the Central London home her parents owned.

Travelling anywhere at night was dangerous. Taxis couldn't use their headlights, street lights were either destroyed or switched off, and all windows in every house had blackout curtains in the hope that a German raider wouldn't see them in the middle of the night.

After a hairy trip through debris-covered London streets, they got out of the taxi and Mel noted how quiet the evening was for once. So far there had been no raid. She remembered well that terrible day when London was burning and the Second Great Fire of London almost took down the city.

*But we're still here*, she thought now. *Still fighting.*

Mel dragged a staggering Val inside and helped him remove his coat before she removed hers, hanging them up in the small closet beside the door. The house was quiet; their parents were either in the snug or had retired early. Mel was relieved, as she knew her mother wouldn't approve of Val drinking and she would no doubt be blamed for not taking better care of him.

Mel often thought she and Val were a disappointment to her mother, as their father was. Arthur Greenway was a poor relation to the South Yorkshire Greenways. He was fifth in line for the Greenway title, but there was very little chance he'd ever inherit anything, since Lord Anthony Greenway and his wife Anna had three healthy boys. The family had supported him for most of his life, though, but since the war started it had become everyone for themselves, and Arthur's meagre allowance had dried up, much to his wife Bertha's chagrin. Mel heard that displeasure in every word her mother spoke to her father these days and it meant the atmosphere at home was often strained, not helped by the morning post and Mel's request to enlist.

Mel hung up her coat.

The thought of enlisting was an exhilarating prospect. Things had changed since the war, and with the men away, fighting on the front line, women were called on to fulfil the traditionally male-dominated roles. Already Mel had enquired about the possible areas she may have an aptitude for, and she was excited by the thought of trying something new and learning something that would otherwise be closed off to her.

'Get a glass of water and go to bed, Val,' she said. 'And be quiet!'

Val was too merry to listen, but half-crawled upstairs with Mel following on behind in case he fell.

*He'll have a bad head tomorrow,* she thought.

She had just got him settled in his room when the sirens started.

'Melinda? Valentine?' she heard her mother calling from down the landing.

Mel sighed. Now her parents would see Val was drunk. Even though Val was very resourceful, and so good at smoke and mirrors that Mel believed he'd naturally lend himself to a career as a magician (a comment she'd jokingly made on many occasions), she would no doubt be held to account for his current condition.

Bertha Greenway came down the hallway, pulling on her coat over her robe. Her head was covered in a scarf hiding her curlers as she rubbed the sleep from her eyes.

Arthur Greenway followed on. Mel noted how drained and old he appeared these days. Since losing their allowance, he had taken a job in the Home Office as a translator, as languages were the only thing he'd been good at.

'We need to get to the shelter,' Bertha said. 'Where's Valentine?'

'You go ahead,' Mel said. 'I'll get him.'

At that moment Valentine came to his bedroom door. 'What's all the noise?' he slurred.

Bertha glared at him, then turned accusing eyes to Mel.

'Get your coat on, Val!' Mel said, grabbing his arm. 'We have to get out of here, now.'

The sirens fell silent. Mel froze. Silence was bad; it meant the raid was imminent and there would be no time to reach the shelter before the bombs started falling. That was quick. Quicker than ever before, which meant something had gone wrong between the security forces anticipating the raid and the siren operators, who clearly hadn't received the warning with enough time.

There was a high-pitched whistling sound and a bomb landed a few streets away, going off with such a loud *crack* that Bertha yelped. The house shook and Bertha and Arthur stumbled down the stairs in a panic.

'Come on!' Bertha called. 'We have to get out of here!'

Mel pulled Val to the top of the stairs. Another sharp whistling sound echoed through the air – too close. Arthur had reached the front door with Bertha right behind.

A sick feeling roiled around Mel's stomach as though she knew what would happen next.

'No!' Mel shouted a warning, but Arthur's hand was on the door just as the bomb landed in the street in front of the house.

The front door exploded. Arthur flew backwards, smashing into Bertha, followed by a shower of wood and metal shrapnel. The house was rocked by the close detonation, and the front windows blew in. Mel lost her grip on Val's arm and he slipped forward, tumbling head over heels down the stairs while Mel fell backwards onto the landing.

Her head cracked against the oak bureau at the top of the stairs, and Mel slipped into thankful oblivion as London erupted into fire, smoke and further destruction.

Mel woke.

A fire engine siren took up a mournful call close by. Mel's body was stiff and sore as she started to move her frozen limbs. Under her head she felt the fuzzy warmth of congealing blood. She pushed herself up, her back resting against the landing wall, the bureau at her side. Her eyes were blurred and a wave of nausea surged up into her throat. Mel turned her head, heaving down onto the floorboards, even as her head felt like it would explode.

'Steady there!' said a voice.

A sturdy pair of boots and an army uniform came into view as a soldier kneeled beside her. Through her blurred vision, she could just make out the insignia of single silver, which her befuddled mind recognised as a first lieutenant.

'Don't move.'

Mel met the kind eyes of a man in his twenties as her vision began to clear.

'My brother…my parents…'

'Don't worry,' he said. 'Help is on the way.'

Another wave of nausea came but Mel closed her eyes and swallowed, pushing it away with sheer willpower. She didn't want this stranger to see her so weak, even though she couldn't do anything about it. It was all about that stiff upper lip that her mother constantly encouraged her and Val to have. She couldn't fall apart now and show the family up. It just wasn't done.

But at the thought of her family Mel opened her eyes once more.

'The door…' she said recalling the explosion. 'Are they… all right?'

'You're bleeding. I think you have a concussion,' he said as, at that moment, two medics came up the stairs.

The blue-eyed lieutenant moved aside, and Mel was laid down on a stretcher and told not to move as they strapped her on.

Then they began to carry her down the stairs, but Mel's eyes were searching among the debris, looking for her brother and parents.

She saw Val as they reached the bottom. He'd fallen at an odd angle and lay unconscious at the bottom of the stairs in a twisted heap.

'Help him! I'm fine,' she said.

The medics and the lieutenant exchanged looks.

'*Please*. He's my brother. He's only 16!' Mel said.

'We'll get you in the ambulance first, Miss,' said one of the medics. 'Then we can see to the rest.'

Mel turned her head, looking for her mother and father, and a jolt of pain whipped through her skull at the effort.

'Try to keep still,' the lieutenant said as he noticed her wince. 'You're badly injured. We need to get you to the hospital.'

Mel was loaded into the back of the ambulance.

'Please…' she said to one of the medics. 'Check my brother. My parents are there somewhere, maybe under the rubble.'

'We're on it, Miss…' the medic said.

A short time later, the young lieutenant got into the ambulance and sat down beside her. His face was sad, and he looked as though he was struggling to find the right words.

'There's nothing they could do,' he said. Then he patted Mel's hand.

'But *Valentine*?'

The lieutenant shook his head. 'I'm sorry.'

The tears came then, a weakness her mother would have abhorred, but how could she hold back amid such a horrible thing? To lose one of them would have been bad enough, but to lose all? It was unbearable.

The soldier patted her arm again. Mel found herself wondering why someone so young was still there, in London, and not fighting at the front. It was a stupid, irrelevant thought, and shouldn't have come into her head at all. Someone had to be here after all, protecting London.

The tears subsided along with the headache from the concussion, but the lieutenant didn't leave her. It was a silent act of kindness and Mel appreciated it, even as her emotions grew numb with shock.

One of the medics closed the back of the ambulance, but the lieutenant made no move to leave and remained by Mel's side as the vehicle set off for the hospital. It was a long drive, through semi-dark streets filled with debris and the bodies of the newly dead from the raid.

Mel thought she heard the screams and wails of the bereaved in the aftermath of the worst blitz so far even though the night was now silent. She reached out for the kind lieutenant's hand. He took hers gently, passing on the only comfort he could give. For which Mel was eternally grateful.

# 1

*South Yorkshire, December 1945*

MELINDA GREENWAY OPENED HER EYES. THE PAINFUL memory lodged in the front of her mind. Every day, since that awful night, she woke with the recollection of her parents' and brother's deaths, still wondering how she had managed to endure in the ruins of their home while her family hadn't. She reminded herself, as she had to every day, that the war was over. She was lucky. She'd survived when so many hadn't, and despite everything, she did at least now have a new roof over her head.

Even so, the guilt of surviving was never far away. She ran a trembling hand over her forehead as though feeling the pain of the concussion and the trauma of the event as keenly as the day it happened. So much had transpired in the years since and her world had changed, sometimes for the better, sometimes for the worst. But any change created insecurity, and Mel was feeling fragile that morning and very much alone.

She evoked the second lieutenant's deep-blue eyes again. Alive as they were with sympathy, as though he knew the pain she had felt. Mel had never felt connected to anyone like that before. Not that it had mattered much in the end.

She pushed the memory of Derrin Bradley firmly to the back of her mind, a desperate attempt at taking back full control of her thoughts and her emotions, locking them away along with Derrin's image. She hadn't seen him since he left London with no warning, not even a letter to explain that he'd been sent somewhere else. For all she knew, he had died on the front; or worse, was badly maimed. The thought brought a shudder to her, knowing that for some men this would be a fate worse than death. And Derrin, so young and vital, so full of energy and life, would not fare well in such a situation.

To distract herself, Mel looked around the room for the first time in the daylight. Yes, it was small, but no more so than the room she'd occupied in the female quarters at the army barracks for the past four years. At least here, she could personalise – if they let her stay. And that was a big *if* at this point.

She'd arrived at Avonby Hall just the night before, after weeks of letter exchanges with her second cousin, Lord Jonathan Greenway. The housekeeper had shown her to her room, telling her that Lord Jonathan and Lady Laura had already retired. Now, she realised, she had been housed in a former seamstress's room. There was still a dressmaker's dummy, a box of fabric pieces, cotton reels and a Singer sewing machine in the corner, as though they'd been abandoned just days, and not years, ago.

It was a strange homecoming, somewhat bittersweet. During the war, the previous lord, Anthony Greenway, had died in a plane crash with his wife and children, leaving Mel's father as the next in line. A title that would eventually have been passed on to her brother, Valentine. They hadn't even been told of Anthony's death when tragedy struck and Mel's entire family were wiped out, leaving her with the new title of lady, but not the rights of ownership – because of the codicils attached to their family legacy. Jonathan, as next male in line, had moved into the Avonby estate along with his new wife, Laura, taking the family title and inheritance. All the while, Mel was oblivious of the change in circumstances, because on leaving the hospital she had enlisted. She'd visited her former home only once, to rescue a few treasured items, but never since. But even had she received the notification about the change of lineage, it would have meant nothing – there was no room for meaningless titles in the war, and Mel doubted she'd use hers even now.

Post war, the Greenways had been forced to make cuts as many wealthy families did. Despite her status, Mel understood she was only at Avonby if she made herself useful. Something she planned on doing right away. Mel had a penchant for gardening, a hobby she'd picked up during her down time after she'd enlisted. She found tending flowers, and growing vegetables on the base allotment, therapeutic. As a result of this experience, she'd promised to work hard at Avonby to help restore the land, and the vegetable patch, to their former glory. This was an arrangement that pleased Lord Jonathan, particularly after the years of the house being commandeered. Now things were back to normal – almost – but with many changes and cut corners. Run with less than half the staff it once had, the estate was not as efficient as it used to be, and Anthony had been forced to sell off some of the land to pay for essential repairs on the house. The former 300 acres were now reduced to 100, which still seemed a lot to Mel, who had grown up with little more than a postage stamp garden in Central London.

Mel poured tepid water into the bowl on the dresser, then washed as best she could before dressing in her faded army jumpsuit. Working in the Transport Company of the Royal Army Service Corps (RASC), Mel had learnt many skills. She'd worked every bit as hard as her male counterparts; not least the long hours spent servicing, repairing and keeping the army vehicles running. She'd learnt to drive cars, jeeps and trucks, but also a motorcycle that she still ran and had arrived on late the night before.

She'd told Jonathan she could help in this way, too, and had offered her chauffeuring and mechanical skills first, as she loved this work the most. He'd been very circumspect about the idea, and Mel knew she'd have some proving to do before he would take her main talents seriously. The world had changed, but some sensibilities hadn't. Mel knew only too well that public opinion was foremost in Jonathan and Laura's minds, and that their outward respectability was the only thing they cared about despite everything they'd all been through. It was something Mel had never thought about until she'd found herself in dire straits, discharged from the army now the war was over, and relegated to being seen, not as a soldier any more, but as a woman.

And, ridiculous though it was, not able to get a job using the skills the army taught her, even though, in fact, she'd been better at them than some of the male mechanics.

Jonathan and Laura had paid her a visit and given her 'the talk' before they finally agreed to take her in. As a Greenway, many things were expected of her if she were to live in their home, not least that she earned her keep, but also that she was seen by society as a respectable member of the family.

'We will also,' Laura had said, 'of course, be looking for a suitable match for you.'

Mel had kept her face blank, half-expecting some reference to marrying her off – a thought that didn't fill her with joy – but she knew she could get out of it later if she made herself indispensable on the estate. She was smart, after all: smarter than they could even suspect after her feeble-woman-needing-a-home performance.

Mel had no intention of letting them down, even though their prudish ways grated on her. She was grateful to Jonathan for offering her a home and a small salary (or 'allowance', as Laura called it, because it was less vulgar for a family member to be supported than employed) and she would behave with decorum, and do her best to be as invisible as possible, blending in with the other servants even though, technically, she wasn't one of them either.

This thought made her recall that she didn't actually belong anywhere in Avonby, and for a few seconds she floundered, feeling a growing sense of panic about the newness of her circumstances. She'd been independent for so long that moving in with her family felt like a backward step, even though she had no choice in the matter.

When the small wave of anxiety fled, Mel looked down at her overalls and realised these wouldn't do at all. What if the family invited her to join them for breakfast? Thinking that a possibility, Mel slipped the overalls off and opened the one suitcase she had with her. She pulled out a plain dress that was neutral enough for her to be in the kitchen eating with the servants, or, if she was invited, suitable to wear when joining Laura and Jonathan in the breakfast room.

There was a sharp rap on the door as Mel finished dressing.

'Just a moment,' she called.

She slipped on a pair of flat, comfortable shoes and opened the door to find a young servant girl in a black uniform with a white collar standing outside. The girl made a quick curtsey.

'Sorry to disturb you, Lady Melinda. Mrs Felman, the 'ousekeeper, sent me to fetch you for breakfast.'

'Thank you,' Mel said. 'What's your name?'

'I'm Nancy, Miss.'

'Nancy. Nice to meet you. I'm Mel.'

'Right you are, Lady Melinda,' Nancy said.

'No. I mean... don't call me Lady. I'm Mel.'

Nancy studied Mel for a few moments. 'Erm... if you say so... but I... Well, this way... Lady... Mel...'

Nancy led Mel down the long corridor past the servants' stairs and towards the main staircase, which spread down the centre of the huge hallway. On one side of the staircase the walls were filled with paintings which Mel wanted to look at, but Nancy never paused as she hurried her along, as though something drastic would happen if they were late. Mel was sure these portraits were relatives of some sort, and made a mental note to come back and study them at her leisure. The other side of the staircase, framed with an intricately carved oak balustrade, opened onto a vast hallway.

As they descended the staircase, Mel saw the enormity of the house for the first time. Several doors were off the hallway, and she wanted to know what was inside all of them.

They reached the bottom of the stairs, and Mel paused and glanced upwards at the magnificent high ceiling. Nancy turned left, away from the impressive front door, and Mel half ran to catch up as the girl didn't stop even to take a breath. They passed the servants' stairs which exited onto the hallway, up from the kitchen right near the room they were approaching.

Mel observed that the house was impressive but a little worn, as though the war had taken energy out of the place. She recalled Jonathan and Laura saying how the house and land had been misused by the army. The Greenways' heritage was within these walls, and she couldn't get away from this overwhelming sense of history, even if she barely saw any of the furnishings or rooms as Nancy rushed on, as though gaining speed in her gallop for the imagined finish line.

At last, Nancy paused by one of the thick, tall oak doors, raised her hand and made a short sharp tap.

'Come,' said a voice beyond, and Mel recognised the clipped tones as Laura's before Nancy opened the door and led her into the dining room.

Laura and Jonathan were already seated and being served as Mel entered. They were at one end of the huge table: Jonathan seated at the table's head, and Laura on the side next to him, facing the door. Opposite her was a further, unoccupied, place setting.

Mel floundered, not knowing what to do as neither of them offered her a seat at the table. Instead, both Laura and Jonathan stared at her. Mel thought they were dismayed by her old, faded dress, or maybe by the fact that she was there at all. She became aware of someone else in the room and saw a tall, smartly dressed man in a butler's uniform. The butler approached and pulled out the chair opposite Laura.

'Lady Melinda,' he said, bowing low to her. 'I'm Williams.'

Mel thanked him and scurried forward; she'd never felt more awkward and less at home as she took the seat and gazed, with some obvious embarrassment flushing her face, at her second cousin and his wife.

Jonathan made a sound in his throat, somewhere between a gasp and a cough.

'I trust you had a good night's sleep?' he said.

'Thank you, yes.'

'And the room is to your liking?' Laura said.

Mel noticed a small contemptuous smirk flirt across Laura's lips, vanishing almost as soon as it appeared. She tried not to analyse it and moved her attention to the table and the food – an excessive amount of fruit and bread for three people – that lay before them. She wondered now if the Greenways were not subject to ration coupons like everyone else. Was it different if you were wealthy aristocracy?

Mel had never thought about that until now, because the line from the government was always that *everyone* was rationed.

'Egg, bacon and sausage, Lady Melinda?' asked Williams even as he put a laden plate down in front of her.

Mel couldn't remember the last time she'd eaten an egg, and now there were two fried ones with two bacon rashers and two sausages before her. Her stomach growled loudly, reminding her that she hadn't eaten since the morning before when her journey from London had begun, following the small removal truck carrying her meagre possessions – her mother's writing bureau, a trunk full of clothes (some her mother's that she planned to repurpose), personal items she'd rescued from the house and her mechanic tools – as they travelled along potholed roads to Avonby.

'Please eat before it goes cold. We don't advocate waste in this house,' Laura snipped.

Mel picked up her knife and fork and ate, reaching for some bread to mop up the egg yolk, much to Laura's horror.

'Good Lord, she has brought the barracks with her!'

'I am so sorry!' Mel said, dropping the bread back down onto her plate. 'It's been a long time since I was in any polite company.'

She saw a look of sympathy on Jonathan's face, but Laura's lips stretched into a thin line.

Mel finished the food with more decorum, remembering how horrified her mother would have been to see her behave this way. She almost heard the echo of her voice reaching her from the grave.

*Really, Melinda, there's no excuse at any time for bad manners, even during wartime…*

After breakfast, the overseer, a gruff man in his late forties called Paddy McMahon, came to take her for a tour of the grounds. As she left the dining room with Paddy, Mel couldn't help overhearing Laura's shrill comments. 'She is feral, Jonathan. What on earth are we to do with her? And that awful dress…'

Jonathan's mumbled reply was too low to hear as Mel and Paddy walked away, but she was plummeted into a deep depression as her future lay in the balance and the hands of two people she really didn't know.

After a drive around the estate and gardens, which Mel observed needed immediate attention to bring them back to anything approaching their former glory, they ended up at the back of the house where the greenhouse and vegetable patches were located.

'That's the back door, Miss, which leads into the boot room and then to the kitchen. When you've finished looking about the plants and veggies, I reckon you might find some more congenial company there – if not such excessive food,' Paddy said.

Mel found herself smiling at Paddy. She knew then she would make friends at Avonby, even if it wasn't with her own relatives.

'I reckon you're right,' Mel said.

Paddy took his leave, and Mel went into the huge greenhouse to assess the damage.

Inside, she found a little man and woman who were working in the potting area, repotting some plants that had grown beyond shoots.

'I'm Mel,' she said. 'I think we are going to work together.'

The woman gave a gummy smile and the man nodded.

'Right you are, Miss. I'm Joseph and this is me wife, Rosa. We've worked the gardens here since we were both potty trained... Oh beg your pardon... Miss.'

Mel laughed. 'That's okay. I'm not shocked. And I'm Mel, not Miss, and definitely not Lady. Let's see how I can help you.'

# 2

*June 1946*

'You've got to admit she has been useful,' Jonathan said.

'I suppose,' said Laura. 'But why invite her to the garden party? And have a dress made for the occasion? It's bad enough having an extra mouth to feed.'

They were sitting at an ornate mosaic table on the lawn in the grounds of the Avonby estate. It was a bright and warm summer morning. Jonathan, seeing the unusually mild weather, had suggested they take advantage of it, even though Laura had insisted on being under the awning for fear of freckles marring her English rose complexion.

Laura picked at the fresh chicken salad luncheon, unaware, Jonathan thought, of just how privileged they were.

'Don't be ridiculous, Laura. Mel's restored the gardens! Look around you. I could never have reinstated the garden party tradition with them in their previous state. Plus, since Mel's been here, productivity has increased on our own vegetable garden. We're now no longer buying extra from the grocers – except for special occasions. That's food rations we can use elsewhere. And money that I was able to spend on new hens. All are laying eggs now, too. Which means we are effectively feeding ourselves and the servants some of the basics from our own land again. Just like the old days.'

Laura looked around at the garden as though noticing the difference for the first time. She reached for the glass of ice-cold lemonade that sat on the table beside her plate and sipped.

'Well, it is improved. I will grant you that. But all this talk of productivity... You are beginning to sound like her. It is so *common*. She is not one of *us*, Jonathan, despite her lineage. It is like the war has... tainted her somehow.'

'Darling, I know it's difficult for you having another woman in the house, but Mel barely intrudes on us, and she works hard all day. She could have been different. Difficult. You know that. Her family were... I really *was* obliged to take her in regardless. But she's not being awkward. There hasn't been a mention of her rights or entitlement. She's really deserving of so much more than the meagre salary I pay her. I suppose she has been changed, but maybe it is for the better? The chauffeur even told me she helped him fix the car. Reading between the lines, though he would never admit it, he couldn't solve the problem, but she knew what to do. We must respect some of the things Mel has brought with her, even if she did learn it in the army. She's useful. We both know it. And, since Paddy retired, she has filled the gap, and that means one less salary a year. So many savings, Laura! What harm is there in letting your seamstress make her something half decent to wear? It's the least we can do for her. Anyway, I thought your plan was to marry her off as soon as possible. There's no chance of that if all she wears is those awful army overalls and boots.'

Laura sighed. 'I suppose you are right. And of course I didn't mind Cynthia making her a dress for the party. But please, no more talk of her doing mechanics – it is just so inappropriate.'

Jonathan took the win for the moment even though Laura begrudged it. He'd had a word with Cynthia himself, and made sure that Mel had several dresses for future functions, since such things were becoming possible again. And new shoes – those awful boots had to go! Even so, it was difficult to spar with Laura as she had such strong opinions on class and station. Opinions that had been somewhat shaved away by his own time serving as an officer and working with the Foreign Office to bring home the wounded and often badly broken soldiers from the front. Jonathan had learnt how to humanise those of a lesser class than himself for this reason, even while Laura had held onto her values with staunch fanaticism.

She hadn't seen what the war did to people, though he had, but he couldn't blame her for closing her eyes to it. Sometimes he wished that all he had witnessed could be washed from his memory and they could return to innocent times, or at least normality. But normal post-war was very different than normal pre-war, and there was no getting around that, no matter how much Laura pretended nothing had changed. He supposed this was her way of coping, after all, and everyone survived the experience in different ways.

As for Mel, Jonathan had grown fond of her but kept his distance. She was not, as Laura had said, *quite* one of them, but she was a relative and she had proved she was willing to earn her keep, and for that he couldn't object to her many quirks. She was, after all, a very interesting personality with many traits you'd never usually find in a woman of her breeding. Qualities Jonathan couldn't help but admire, despite himself, which was why he always insisted she joined them for supper, even when she avoided meals with them at other times. He found her company quite stimulating compared to Laura's often judgemental attitude. Despite Laura's misgivings, it was time, he believed, that they did reintroduce her to society as part of this respected family. After all, the neighbouring aristocracy would expect it and there were among them a variety of suitable bachelors to introduce her to, which would please Laura. Though Jonathan secretly hoped she wouldn't like any of them, Mel being married would take away some of the guilt he had at taking an inheritance that should really have been hers.

Even as he thought this, Jonathan couldn't help observing how Mel had stepped up. Taking on the role of overseer, she was a natural, and he'd had so many fewer issues with the farm tenants and workers ever since. Though he didn't have a clue what she did to appease everyone, things were running more smoothly on the estate and he no longer heard gripes from anyone. That alone made her worth her weight in gold to him, as the stresses of taking on Avonby had been exacting their toll.

A scream echoed across the lawn, breaking their peaceful luncheon.

Out of instinct, Jonathan leapt to his feet and ran towards the sound, along with Williams and the serving maid, Daisy, right behind him.

Jonathan rounded the house to find Mel hugging Nancy.

'What is it?' he asked. 'What's upset the girl?'

Mel glanced over Nancy's shoulder towards the rose bed. Jonathan gasped as he saw a human hand and arm protruding from the soil.

'I was weeding,' Mel said. 'Nancy brought me some water just as I made the discovery.'

Jonathan saw the dropped tray and the water glass on the lawn. The soft grass had prevented the glass from smashing. He bent and picked both items up, and handed them to Daisy to take back inside.

'Take Nancy inside, please,' said Mel, handing her over to Williams. 'She'll need some strong tea. Two sugars. For the shock.'

Williams led the hysterical young woman away around the back to the kitchen entrance.

'What the devil,' Jonathan said once they were out of earshot.

'A body. Female, judging by the fingernails and the slenderness of the hands,' Mel said. 'Dead a few months I'm guessing.'

Mel was observing the arm with an inscrutable expression as she spoke, and Jonathan understood, in that moment, he didn't know his cousin at all.

Mel was still by the roses when the police arrived a few hours later. The main station was some distance from Avonby's rural village, and it had taken time for the police to send the appropriate people. During that time, Mel hadn't wanted to leave because she'd been worried about any further contamination of the site and the spoiling of any potential evidence she'd seen. Now she stepped aside as a young uniformed officer began to cordon off the area. She watched him, making sure he didn't step anywhere he shouldn't, aware that other officers were searching around the grounds, trampling over the lawns, and some of the flower beds, with little care or respect.

She turned and watched as two plainclothes officers came around the side of the house. The sun was behind them, and she squinted as they approached. There was something familiar about one of the men, but she didn't recognise him until he was a few feet away.

'Lady Melinda Greenway,' said Williams in his best formal tone, 'this is Inspector Bradley and Sergeant Wakeman.'

'Mel,' said Derrin Bradley. 'I didn't expect to see you…'

There was a moment where his words lingered and Mel almost finished his sentence for him, but surprise at finding him there, on Avonby land, almost took her voice away.

'Derrin,' she said finally. 'Nice to see you again.' She spotted Jonathan approaching and made the appropriate introduction to cover the awkwardness of the moment.

'Has anyone touched anything?' Derrin asked.

'No. I've been here the whole time,' Mel said.

Derrin nodded, moving in to take a closer look. He hadn't changed much in the last two years, and Mel found herself falling in beside him like she had in the old days when they'd been working on something.

'I found her. I was weeding. I stopped as soon as her hand and arm were revealed,' Mel explained.

'I'm so sorry, Lady Melinda,' said the sergeant. 'No woman should have to see this. Do you need anything? Can I get you a doctor?'

'I'm not the one in need of a doctor,' Mel snapped. 'I've seen worse.'

'Wakeman. Go and take statements from Lord Greenway and the staff,' Derrin said. 'Lady Greenway can stay with me and tell me what she knows.'

As Wakeman hurried to comply, Derrin realised Mel was looking at him, her expression serious, and there appeared to be an unasked question on her lips.

'How are you?' he asked.

'Surprised to see you,' she said. 'New career?'

Derrin nodded. 'The police seemed the right move when I was demobbed, especially after my experience.'

Mel glanced around to make sure they weren't overheard. 'What experience are we talking about?'

'The Military Police work. I was moved across. I wrote to tell you,' he said.

'I never received any letters,' Mel said, but there was no accusation, just a polite statement of fact.

'You never got my letters?' Derrin repeated, processing this news as if it was the most important thing he had heard all day.

Mel shook her head.

An awkward silence fell between them for a few seconds, but it felt even longer to Mel because, for once, she was lost for words.

'So, you're a "lady" now?' Derrin said, changing the subject.

Mel glanced at the house. 'My father would have inherited instead of Jonathan if he'd… lived. Or Valentine would have if he'd survived. I was always going to have the title either way.'

'I'm sorry…' said Derrin. 'But surely that means you…?'

'No. Family custom. The estate was passed down to the next male in line.'

'Stupid custom,' said Derrin.

Mel cracked a smile. 'You've always had a way with words.'

'Obviously.'

They smiled at each other: more than old friends reunited.

Derrin looked away first, and to avoid any further awkwardness he glanced down at the crime scene. Silence followed as his eyes made a thorough examination of the site, in much the same way that Mel's had. They'd both had much practice, after all.

'What do you see?' he asked now.

'Pardon?'

'The crime scene. You've always been observant… What do you see?'

'It's a woman,' Mel said.

'How do you know?'

'Delicate bone structure. Tiny wrist. The ring finger shows an indent where she may have been wearing a ring. Engagement or wedding?'

'And?'

'Some broken nails.'

'Fingernails break…'

'Her others are well-manicured. Perfect… She put up a fight. Plus, soft looking, no calluses. She wasn't someone who did any consistent hard labour.'

Derrin turned his gaze back to the hand and studied it for a while. 'What else?'

'A very shallow grave. So, she was buried in a hurry… or…?'

'Or?' Derrin pressed.

'The killer wanted her to be found,' Mel concluded.

'I apologise in advance for the roses…' Derrin said. 'We have to dig her out.'

'Under the circumstances… you're forgiven.'

They exchanged a look, both expressions guarded, and Derrin found himself wondering if he was being forgiven for more than the roses, even though he probably didn't deserve to be.

Mel took herself off to her small bedroom to think while Derrin's team moved in to comb the crime scene and extract the body. She didn't need to see more, though a part of her wanted to. She was drawn in by the death and began to wonder what was wrong with her that she would be so interested, so morbid. But it wasn't the dead body that was attractive, more the reason for why the woman was there, and Mel really wanted to know the answer to that question.

By nightfall the police were moving out with everything they'd found. Mel watched them go from her bedroom window. She was left with a series of questions and images that she went through in her mind. She had watched from a distance while a photographer recorded the scene. The images were graphic in her head, clearer perhaps than when she had been standing there, absorbing every detail to examine later, like she had captured those images herself. And now she put together the pieces as though they were part of a puzzle, or parts of the engines she so loved, clicking them into place.

She saw the occupants of the household and the estate, too. All like shadowy pieces waiting beside an empty chessboard, poised and ready to be moved, but their faces and places remained a mystery to Mel because she didn't know the start position of any of them.

'The key to this whole mystery,' she murmured.

There was always an opening point. Just as there was when you were taking apart or putting together an engine. Anything practical could be learnt, but Mel had brought other skills into the equation, ones that she found difficult to explain, but her powers of observation were a factor. She saw things – minute details that sometimes others didn't notice because they were looking too much at the whole picture. But if you dissect a whole, what you sometimes got was much more detail than the overall view gave. It was the reason she excelled in a job that had previously been designated for men only. The instructors hadn't expected her and the other women to do so well, but they had been successful because they wanted to prove something to themselves as well as to their teachers.

*All skills*, Mel thought, *are transferrable*. But that wasn't true; some skills came naturally from another place that Mel herself didn't understand. Some might call it a talent. Derrin always had…

She brought her mind back to the overview of the murder, shutting down the brief slip of her thoughts into another direction.

The killer might be among them. During their day-to-day routine, and looking at the people who worked and lived in Avonby, she hadn't observed anything irregular. However, now that the body had been found, the killer might reveal themselves by suspicious behaviour, but she thought it unlikely – for this person had some intellect, some finesse, some motive for what they had done, and that was the thing that wasn't clear. That was the thing that might expose the truth.

*Why?*

The answer might lie in the identification of the victim, of course. Mel knew that murders were often committed by those closest to the victim. It was unlikely to be a random killing. There was always a reason.

But first – who was she?

# 3

There was whispering in the halls of Avonby, and Mel's acute awareness of it made her feel uncomfortable, as though the murmurs were about her. An old feeling of paranoia seeped into her subconscious. That feeling had never left her, even though she pushed it down and aside as much as possible. She hadn't been wanted at Avonby; despite Jonathan's offer, she knew he was just doing his duty. Guilt-ridden, maybe, that this place shouldn't have been his at all. But he'd been kind to her, nonetheless, though Laura was always distant, treating Mel as though she were a servant with a few more privileges than the others. Mel felt that way, too. As if she wasn't one of the family, but she wasn't one of the serving staff either, and it was a hard position to sit in because you were never quite comfortable wherever you were.

After her first week there, she had taken breakfast in her room because she couldn't sit comfortably with Laura and Jonathan. She had tried to join the serving staff in the kitchen, but they clammed up when she was around. Even so, as she oversaw the horticulture on the estate, she'd built some relationships and had forged a few alliances among those she worked with. It wasn't easy at first, as the old gardener, Joseph, had thought she was interfering with her new-fangled advice and the extra machinery that she brought in to speed up the work. The conflicts between them resolved, though, when Mel realised that Joseph was happiest when he was left to potter among the gardens rather than having to deal with the more practical side of running the estate and food production, which just didn't appeal to the old man, who loved the plants and flowers and had always been about the aesthetic of Avonby's grounds. Mel let him have autonomy in this area, with occasional tweaks and by bringing in a team of gardeners on a casual basis to help when there was need. In the last six months she had delegated jobs to those who were best at them, a key factor being a passion for their roles. Once she'd figured out this side of the job she'd been given, the gardening aspect of running the estate had become effortless and all the gardeners worked in harmony.

Mel wasn't meant to be in the rose garden that day, as it was Joseph's domain, but one of the casual gardeners had been called away because his mother was sick. Mel had fallen in to bridge the gap. The weeding had to be done as the gardens were being prepared for Jonathan and Laura's summer garden party in a week's time. There was no one else to do the work.

It was one of those circumstances that led to Mel finding herself in the middle of another mystery. An unhappy accident, you might say.

Her mind flashed back to another night, some four years earlier.

She had been called out to fix an army truck, only to come face-to-face with Derrin again. By then she had been in the RASC for a while, after first joining the ATS, and despite losing everything in the Blitz she was forging a new life. During that time, she'd learnt to drive and fix cars and bikes, but she was still new to mechanics even though she clearly had a knack for it.

On the night she'd met him, Derrin had disappeared as soon as they had unloaded her into the emergency room – embarrassed by the emotional display, no doubt. She'd thought about him a few times since, wondering what his name was. She had wanted to thank him, but time had galloped on, and other, more pressing, things had taken precedence. She hadn't found out his name until much later. *That* night, in fact, and he hadn't been the one to share it; someone else had.

She had arrived with her superior to fix the car. There had been a collision, caused by a bomb landing nearby, and Derrin's vehicle wouldn't start even though the surface damage didn't seem much.

He had a driver, and the man was slightly injured with a minor head wound that was being treated. But Derrin needed to get somewhere and so it was important to get the car moving.

Mel's sergeant looked under the bonnet at the engine and scratched his head. He checked the usual things: the alternator, the radiator, the battery connections.

'I'll have to take your vehicle,' Derrin said.

'Look, Lieutenant Bradley, I can't let you have my truck it's...'

'Try it now,' Mel said. 'No choke.'

The sergeant looked back at Mel delving into the engine. She had a small canister of fuel in her hand. The mechanic frowned, wondering what she was doing.

Derrin climbed into the front seat and turned the key. The engine fired immediately.

'What did you do?' asked the sergeant.

Mel shrugged. 'The car's an Austin 10 – I drive one. Sometimes mine won't start when the engine's still warm, so I shoot some fresh fuel into the carburettor. Usually sets it right again.'

The mechanic looked shocked. 'I didn't teach you that. How did you know?'

'I noticed the carb was empty – the fuel had evaporated because of the heat,' Mel explained. 'So, it was obviously the problem.'

'I need a driver. You're coming with me,' Derrin said.

'But Lieutenant Bradley, she's just a trainee mechanic,' objected the sergeant.

Derrin gave the sergeant a look. 'The student just taught the master,' he said. 'You happy to come with me?'

'Yes, Sir,' Mel said.

'Let's go.'

Mel's mind returned to the present. The body, and Derrin's presence, had disturbed the peace she had begun to find at Avonby. She'd built an affinity with her ancestral land and home. She had a mission: the estate needed her, and Mel didn't want any distractions. Especially a disruptive influence like Derrin Bradley.

Now that the police had gone, Mel undressed and climbed into her bed. She was out of sorts and a little bent out of shape, as she always was when her old life intruded into the new.

Getting under the covers, Mel turned off her bedside lamp and closed her eyes. But her thoughts of Derrin had taken another painful turn. When he had disappeared from her life without a word, Mel thought that she would never see him again. At the time, she had been bereft and confused. Now, after their brief exchange that day, she knew he hadn't lied about writing to her. Derrin would have told her where he was going and that he had been moved on. She hadn't received any letters, which probably meant that someone had blocked them. *But why?* Who would care? The war had changed things for men and women in the army. For a time they were equals, and Derrin had never treated Mel as though she was anything but that. When he disappeared overnight, she was left without her one true ally. Soon after that, as the war came to an end, Mel and others in her troop had struggled when their roles changed back again. It felt like they had been relegated, and all the hard work they had put in over the years meant nothing and wasn't even appreciated. Mel, like so many women, had to carve a new life for herself, one that made her feel valued and significant still. Not an easy task when everything they did in the war years was important.

She stifled a yawn, but rubbed the sleep from her eyes, forcing her mind to remain awake with a huge effort.

She had once known her place so well. Now, the lines had blurred, and Mel didn't want things to go back to the way they were before the war. That was, she now understood, a time of innocence, and once innocence was lost it could never be regained. Plus, she liked who she had become, despite the reason for the change.

She pushed thoughts of Derrin away as her mind drifted to Valentine and her parents. That was the moment when the unfelt spin of the Earth missed a beat and the bottom fell out of her world. She had suffered, grieved, felt unfathomable loneliness. Even in a barracks full of women and the friendships that had been forged, there was still a hole inside her that couldn't be filled. Mel had distracted herself with the work, and army life had become her new obsession. But she had been freefalling nonetheless, and it had taken Derrin to make her understand that it was okay to feel out of control sometimes. She didn't regret a thing. Mel's feelings for Derrin had always been complicated and that hadn't changed with time. But the distance had taught her one thing: she was alone, always. Derrin, despite sending a few letters she'd never received, hadn't come to find her to see why she hadn't responded. That action alone spoke volumes about where their relationship sat in his priorities, and that perhaps it had been time to end things anyway. After all, a wartime romance wasn't like a real relationship. It probably wouldn't have stood the test of time in the normal world, without the pressure and fear they had all lived under each day. Though, Mel thought now, she might have wanted to see if it could.

# 4

The staff of Avonby were subdued when Mel entered the kitchen, despite Mrs Weston, the cook, showing her best cheery face. That morning, Mel came downstairs at her usual time. Not having slept much because of the previous day's events, she'd stayed in her room for as long as she could, so that it wasn't too odd for her to appear before the day was due to start. By now, Avonby's staff were accustomed to sharing a table with Mel sometimes at lunchtime, which had become a practical necessity, since she couldn't just take food up to her small bedroom during the working day. As they grew used to her presence, they had begun to chat naturally around her, treating her, with some exceptions, just like one of them. Although Mel had always been aware of the whispered conversations that hushed when they became mindful of her company, up until she had found the body, she hadn't felt there were very many secrets kept from her.

Mel noted that some, but not all, of the servants were present and finishing their breakfast in silence. There were many levels of duties at Avonby, and some started sooner than others. Among this group were some downstairs as well as upstairs staff, all on the later morning shift because – other than Mrs Weston, who always rose early with her kitchen maids – the early shift was often occupied by a stable hand and whichever chambermaid was on fire-lighting duty that day. Sometimes there was also Lady Laura's personal maid, Hettie, who helped her dress in the morning when she had an early start, which wasn't often. As a result, Mel was faced with the main day staff now, and she knew that word of what she said here would spread out to those not present.

'We need to talk,' Mel said as she sat down at the huge kitchen table which served not only as a place to sit and eat, but also as a working surface on which Mrs Weston and her kitchen maids could prepare food for all levels of the occupants at Avonby, and for those party days, soon to return to their world. 'As I'm sure you're all aware, a body was found on the grounds yesterday. A woman. The police took her away but we need to be as helpful as we can be.'

'What 'appened to her, Miss?' asked Nancy, who still refused to call her Mel.

Mel turned her gaze onto the housemaid and noted the rings around the girl's eyes which indicated a lack of sleep. She worried about Nancy, who on the surface appeared to be such a strong personality, but who in the face of death had crumpled completely – which suggested to Mel that some wartime trauma must still be affecting her. Something she understood better than most people.

'I haven't been told yet how she died, but the fact that she was buried, without proper respect, is suspicious.'

A murmur of concern erupted around the table.

'Now, Lady Melinda!' Williams said with his usual measure of respect and authority. 'There's no good panicking everyone like this. You'll upset the sensitive souls of these young girls, who've never seen the like.'

Mel suppressed a smile at Williams's concern, which was punctuated with a loss of his usual formal speech and a lapse into colloquial terms. Williams, who always adhered to formality and had never called her anything but 'Lady Melinda', still struggled to balance her position in the household – which was understandable, given that in the evenings he served her, along with Laura and Jonathan, in the formal dining room. It was a juxtaposition that Mel found difficult to align, and she appreciated why Williams would have difficulty with it as well.

'I really don't mean to cause panic at all, Mr Williams,' she said, addressing him as the other servants did, and not merely 'Williams', as her cousin and his wife did. 'But you know I'm a practical person by now?'

'Yes indeed, Lady Melinda,' said Williams.

'We need to know who she is – was – to help the police. And one of you *must* know something.'

Mel's eyes went around the table and found no one willing to meet them.

'Well, I think it's exciting,' gasped their newest arrival, Daisy, whose duties ranged between scullery, chamber and sometimes kitchen maid. 'A real-life murder! Right here!'

'Good grief!' said Mrs Weston. 'This isn't a romance novel, girl!'

'Sorry, Mrs Weston,' Daisy said, suitably scolded.

Mel put her hand on Daisy's arm. 'It's okay to be interested. It shows you're alive,' she said. 'And after the… past few years… that's a good thing. But don't get ahead of yourself, no one knows what happened yet. Though I'm sure we will find out.'

'Righto,' said Daisy, gazing at Mel as though she was some higher being that understood how the world worked more than a girl of her station ever could: a misconception that Mel planned to straighten up over time, for she'd worked with girls from similar backgrounds to Daisy in the RASC. All of them had been intelligent and capable mechanics by the end of the war, holding no less ability than Mel did. They didn't, however, have the same education as Mel had, and she was very aware of her privilege on that score, and didn't see it as making her any more worthy of adoration than anyone else.

'Right, you lot! Off to work!' said Mrs Felman, coming out of the small quarters she had off the kitchens.

Without argument the remaining household staff of Avonby dispersed to their respective areas, leaving Mel, Mrs Weston and Mrs Felman alone.

'Perhaps we need a word, Lady Melinda,' said Mrs Felman, then she turned and walked away towards her small office.

Mel had built a rapport with Mrs Weston over the last few months, as the cook had a great deal of empathy for her confusing position in the household; now they exchanged a look, from which Mel derived that the cook was on her side.

'I'll have some breakfast for you when you're finished,' Mrs Weston said.

'Thank you,' Mel said, then she turned to follow Mrs Felman into her small office, which was positioned under the stairs and just off the kitchen, but down a corridor that led to her personal quarters.

'Please take a seat, Lady Melinda,' Mrs Felman said as Mel closed the office door.

Mel sat down by Mrs Felman's desk, half expecting to receive a reprimand; but as she looked at the housekeeper, she discovered the woman was crying.

'I think I know who she was,' she said.

'Tell me,' Mel said.

'She came to us from one of the agencies we use from time to time. She was from Sheffield, I believe. She was a good chambermaid. Never had any complaints from Lady Laura... who can be... well you know how Her Ladyship can be. Anyway, she was with us for about six months, then just disappeared. Overnight.'

'Did anyone look for her?' Mel asked.

'Girls come and go all the time. It's hard to look for any of them. We wait a respectable time to hear from them, but they rarely explain why they leave. I did contact the agency and they said they hadn't heard from her. Daisy was her replacement, when we realised she wasn't coming back,' Mrs Felman explained.

'Can you tell me anything else about her? Who was she friendly with among the staff?'

'Well, she was a quiet one, to be honest. I never heard any gossip come from her mouth, or anyone else's about her. She shared a room with Nancy. They were friendly enough. But when I questioned her, she didn't know anything either.'

'I'll speak to Nancy,' Mel said. She stood up and walked towards the door. 'What was her name?'

'Ruby. Ruby Lewis.'

Mel's hand paused on the door handle. She experienced a brief flashback of the hand in the rose bushes and the indent on the finger that suggested a wedding or engagement ring.

'One other thing. Was she engaged? Married? Perhaps a widow?'

'Oh no,' Mrs Felman said, 'the agency only sends us single girls. And I never heard any mention of any men where she was concerned.'

'Don't talk to anyone else about what you know, or what you think you know, until I investigate further.'

'Why?' Mrs Felman asked.

'Because it's very likely this wasn't a natural death,' Mel said. 'And someone here knows something about it. May have even been involved.'

'You mean, someone we know might have… killed her?' Mrs Felman said.

Mel knew that person, whoever they were, was very dangerous, but she didn't want to panic Mrs Felman.

'Well, it could have been an accident,' she said, softening the blow. 'But it wouldn't be wise to appear too curious or to reveal you know anything, either way. Just as a precaution.'

Mrs Felman nodded her understanding.

Mel opened the door and said semi-loudly, 'Of course, Mrs Felman. I didn't mean to upset anyone.'

'I'm glad you understand, Lady Melinda,' the housekeeper said quickly, realising what Mel was doing. 'As Mr Williams said, some of these girls are very naïve and can be easily shocked.'

'Indeed. Anyway, we must all get on with the day,' Mel said.

# 5

Dressed in her overalls and work boots, Mel found Joseph by the destroyed flower beds.

'It's a reet mess,' he said.

'I know,' said Mel.

'His Lordship wants it fixing for this party.'

'I have a few ideas on that score,' Mel said. 'Let's crack on, shall we?'

They began to tidy up the chaos, removing the destroyed foliage and salvaging what they could, but it left a gap in the rose bed that reminded them that a terrible thing had happened there. It was hard for Mel to think of anything else, even after they had fixed the other damage.

'Reet business,' said Joseph, leaving Mel no doubt that he couldn't either.

Joseph had been in the service of the Greenways for years. Unlike some of their younger footmen, he had been too old to be enlisted at the beginning of the war. If there was any gossip, surely he'd know about it? But Mel had to tread carefully – after all, the body was found in the rose bed that he planted. Mel wondered now how he could have missed it there when she'd found it so easily.

'I wonder who she might be?' Mel said.

Joseph rubbed his chin with the back of his hand to avoid smearing dirt from his soil-covered fingers onto his face.

'I'm sure the bobbies will find out, Miss,' he said.

Mel watched Joseph through the corner of her eye as he stood up and viewed their handiwork. There was no nervousness or guile, only a kind of accepting sadness about the whole sorry business. She thought herself a good judge of character, and so she didn't have any real suspicion that he might be involved. Even so, she thought he may still know who might be.

'I bet you've seen many things in your time here,' Mel said.

'Yes, Miss. Lots of coming and going among the young, too. Girls come. They wed. Then they leave to take care of their own. It's the way of things in service. Me and the missus, though, we met here, we stayed. Avonby's our home.'

Mel knew this was the case for most of the long-serving members of the household, Mrs Felman and Mrs Weston being a case in point, as both women were now in their fifties. It occurred to her that she'd never asked either woman when they joined Avonby's service; it was a given that they'd always been there. Like the aged gardener and his wife who were nowadays old retainers.

'I don't suppose you have any idea who the woman might have been?' Mel asked.

Joseph shook his head. 'Don't have much to do with the insiders. She could be any of 'em that's come and we thought gone.'

'That's what I thought,' Mel said.

Joseph and Rosa lived in the cottage by the estate gate, which would once have been occupied by the gatekeeper, back when Avonby Hall was at its best. As a result, they didn't eat with the house staff and rarely socialised with them. Joseph and Rosa always seemed to Mel to live a very private, quiet life, away from gossip and any drama that might be a factor in the main house.

'Well, if you think of anything, let me know,' she said.

Mel brushed the dirt from the knees of her overalls and looked around to see Williams approaching.

'Lady Melinda? A police officer is here to see you,' Williams said. 'I've put him in the drawing room.'

'Me? Really?' Mel said, surprised. 'Can you offer him some tea? I'll go and change into something more suitable.'

She said goodbye to Joseph and then went back into the house via the boot room. After leaving her mud-encrusted boots there, Mel washed her hands and then slipped off the overalls, throwing them into the wash basket. Underneath she was wearing a pair of slacks and a sweater, which were better than the overalls, but still would be frowned on by Laura if she was seen in them.

Mel used the servants' stairs to avoid being seen. On the second floor, she headed along the landing to her room, went inside and quickly pulled out a dress, stockings and some plain black shoes. She was almost ready when someone knocked at her door.

She opened it to find Nancy.

'Miss,' Nancy said, dropping a quick curtsey, which Mel found frustrating but didn't say anything about.

'Did Mr Williams send you? I just need to put on my shoes.'

'No, Miss. It's about what happened. Yesterday.'

'Come in,' Mel said.

Nancy came into the room after a quick look around the landing to make sure she wasn't observed.

'Mrs Felman said you wanted to speak to me,' Nancy said.

'Yes, I did. Firstly, how are you?'

'Bit shocked, Miss.'

'Of course you are. Do you have any idea who it might be?' Mel said.

Nancy shook her head. 'How could I know?'

'Do you think it could be Ruby?' Mel said.

Nancy's face blanched white when she heard the name.

'Ruby? Why would anyone think it was…?'

'Ruby left suddenly and no one heard from her again,' Mel said. 'Is it possible she was the woman we found?'

'Oh no, Miss! I couldn't think it!'

'All right. If you don't think it was her, do you know why she left?' Mel asked.

'She just left one day. That's it. I don't know nuthin' else.'

'But you shared a room with her. She didn't tell you anything? You didn't notice anything? Something small? How was she behaving a few days before?'

'I don't know! We didn't really talk. She was a quiet one…' Nancy said, but Mel's barrage of questions overwhelmed her. 'It couldn't be Ruby! It just couldn't!' she said again, head shaking in denial. 'What a horrible thought!'

Nancy was so jittery and acting so oddly that Mel started to believe she was lying. The girl knew something more than she was saying, but how to get her to admit it when she appeared so afraid? Mel wasn't sure whether she should question her right then or not. She remembered a similar situation when she was in the army. One of the other girls had sneaked out in the night to meet with a soldier she was seeing. No one was supposed to go off base at all that night, as they'd had an intelligence warning of an impending air-raid attack. The missing RACS mechanic was caught in the raid and killed, but her roommate swore she didn't know she'd left the base. Mel had seen the lie then too, but, not wanting to get a fellow soldier in trouble, had kept her own counsel. After all, their friend was dead, and shopping the other girl for helping her leave the barracks wasn't going to help anyone.

But Nancy's denials were important. There was a potential murderer in play at Avonby. This made a lot of difference to what action Mel might have to take. Even so, she thought that tact was the best policy. It was early days, and a hard questioning might make Nancy clam up further and make her avoid conversation with Mel later; whereas, if she pretended to take her word at this point, Nancy may well slip up later.

'That's fine then, Nancy,' Mel said. 'It probably isn't Ruby. But if you do remember anything about her leaving, let me know, as this could potentially rule her out.'

Nancy's face flooded with blood, and the girl had gone from white to bright red, which again showed Mel that she had some guilt associated with Ruby. She was determined to find out what that was. But for now, she let Nancy go. Relieved, she exited Mel's room after checking the corridor outside.

Mel sat on her bed and slipped on her shoes, fastening them while contemplating Nancy's behaviour. The girl had been messing with her throat as though she were scared that Mel would choke the truth from her. She now wondered what had spooked the maid so much. What did Nancy know about the body? Was it Ruby Lewis, or not? And, more to the point, who did she fear would see them talking? All these questions ran around in Mel's head unanswered as she worked on putting together this puzzle. Right now, she was beginning to place Nancy on her invisible chessboard – but was she a pawn or a main player?

Pulling a cardigan over her dress, Mel left her room and headed downstairs via the main central staircase.

The door to the drawing room was closed and she pushed it open, only to find that Derrin was there alone. He was sitting on the sofa with a tray in front of him containing tea and scones, on a small oak coffee table that Mel knew had been bought years ago by one of her ancestors.

Mel paused, realising he hadn't seen her yet as his attention was focused on the large window, looking out to the huge lawn. It was a particularly lovely view, and Mel herself had often sat in the same spot, appreciating her own handiwork in bringing the landscape back to its former glory.

Watching Derrin now, Mel couldn't help but remember why she had always found him so appealing. Not only were his eyes an incredible blue, but his fair hair was thick and glossy. He looked kind, and Mel knew he could be, but he could also be fierce, a fact that was not obvious in the way he sat with great composure.

'Derrin!' she said at last.

As soon as he saw her, Derrin stood and came forward.

For a moment, Mel thought he was going to offer his hand for a formal handshake, but instead he hugged her. They held each other for a few seconds then parted, though Derrin didn't fully release her. Instead, he placed his hands on her forearms and held her away from him so he could look at her.

'I'm sorry I couldn't do this yesterday,' he said. 'It would have been unprofessional under the circumstances. But that is how I should have greeted you, as an old friend.'

'Is that what we are now?' Mel said. 'Friends? And *old*?'

Derrin laughed. 'Still keeping your sense of humour, I see.'

Mel smiled but then grew serious. There was a tension between them that came more from what was unspoken than said.

'Have you any news on the victim?' Mel said, trying to alleviate some of the atmosphere.

'We don't know who she is as yet, and none of your employees could tell us anything yesterday.'

Mel nodded, 'There's a suspicion she is a former housemaid known as Ruby Lewis. From Sheffield originally.'

'I had a feeling you'd have learnt more from them than I could,' Derrin said, his smile returning. 'You always have been someone to confide in.'

'I was planning to reach out, but hoped to learn more for you first,' Mel said.

'This is an excellent lead, though. Thank you, but I don't want you to get more involved. This could be dangerous,' Derrin said.

'I can handle myself,' Mel said. 'You've seen me in action.'

'I know. But those days are gone. We're back in the civilian world now, and you shouldn't have had to go through all of that back then, let alone deal with a murder now, on your own land. It's bad enough you found the body.'

'So, she *was* murdered?'

'Mel! Let it go. I told you, you can't be involved in this,' Derrin said.

'Well! I'm hardly some feeble-minded socialite!'

'I don't mean to offend you, you know that. But times have changed and—'

Mel pulled away from him and crossed her arms.

'Yes, times have changed, Derrin, and you can't undo the past nor return to it. Even if I wanted to go back to the way things were before the war, I couldn't. I'm not the same person and neither are you. None of us are. The truth is, I don't want to be the old me. The old me would never have met you, and except for the circumstances, I don't have any regrets.'

Derrin stared at her. It was obvious that he hadn't expected her outburst and didn't know how to respond to it. She waited for him to speak, but the silence between them grew until it was painful and she couldn't stand it any more.

'I'm never going to be the type of woman who stays at home and has a team of children,' she said. 'I'm not Lady Melinda, despite the label. I'm Mel. I'll always be just Mel now. And Mel is a mechanic, she rides a motorbike, she works hard and has calluses on her hands to show for it. She doesn't have a useless title that gives her no security anyway.'

'I know,' Derrin said. He reached out and took her hand again, forcing her to uncross her arms. He looked at the calluses and ran his fingers over them.

A tingling response leapt up inside her and Mel withdrew her hand. They couldn't go there again, despite her feelings of the previous night. As he said, things were different now. That didn't stop her still feeling something, though, and she supposed those emotions would never go away. Not unless she started something with someone else, and the likelihood of that was zero to none.

'Are you going to tell me what happened to her?' she said. 'You said it was murder... Could it have been an accidental death?'

'Strangled,' Derrin said.

'A violent ending. No doubt, then, that the intent was to kill?'

'One doesn't strangle someone with your bare hands by accident or without commitment,' Derrin said.

'To merely silence someone, you shoot them. It's quicker and there's less contact. But to strangle... it's personal,' Mel said, summarising his thoughts before he'd fully shaped them himself.

'I hadn't quite thought of it that way, but yes. It does seem personal and requires strength and determination to see it through.'

Mel saw the perpetrator in the back of her mind, in conjunction with the rose bed. She re-enacted the struggle, all with a face for Ruby Lewis she hadn't seen and a blank one for the killer. The pieces of what had happened were so fragmented, yet she knew something of it, by some dark instinct inside herself that she couldn't explain.

'She wasn't killed there,' she said.

Derrin perked up with the idea of discussing possibilities with her, even though he was resistant to it.

'Why do you say that?' he asked.

'There wouldn't have been time for the killer to hide the damage. There would have been a struggle. Noise of sorts, for sure, even as he silenced her. I'm sure someone would have heard or seen something on the estate. They would have had to, and then come to her rescue. No, she was already dead before that.'

'I believe you're right,' Derrin said. 'And no one has admitted seeing anything. Or at least, they aren't coming forward if they did. But I agree with you, she didn't die there. She was put there afterwards, and as you observed, in such a way as to be eventually found.'

'I can help you,' Mel said.

'I shouldn't even be discussing this with you,' he said. Derrin sighed. 'I can't put you at risk. This could be perilous, Mel.'

'Yes, it could be. But there is a killer on the loose and it could be someone here. Who's to say they won't kill again?'

At that moment, Laura came into the drawing room. She took a small step back when she saw Derrin and Mel standing close together, as though she sensed their intimacy.

'Inspector Bradley,' she said. 'Williams just told me you were here. Melinda, you should have sent for Jonathan and myself.'

Mel's back stiffened at Laura's use of her full name, because she knew that Laura used it to get a rise from her. Jonathan always respected her wish to be referred to as 'Mel'; Laura didn't.

'That's fine, Lady Laura,' Derrin said. 'I asked to see Mel, we are old friends. We were in the army together. We had some catching up to do.'

'Oh!' said Laura. 'Indeed. We do not like to be reminded of Melinda's army days. We know she did what she must, but... she is *Lady Melinda* now, Inspector.'

Derrin nodded, then turned his attention back to Mel, completely shutting down the intrusion as if Laura hadn't come in at all.

'We'll be in touch when we know anything more. And of course, if you or your staff have any further information, we'd like to hear about it. Nice to see you again, *Mel*,' he said. 'Lady Laura.'

With that Derrin left, showing himself to the door.

'Well, really!' Laura said. 'Obviously the army took his manners as well. What was he? A private?'

'First lieutenant,' Mel said.

'An officer? I thought only gentlemen became officers,' Laura said.

'Derrin is very educated,' Mel said, fighting to keep the annoyance from her voice. 'He may not have a title, but is more gentlemanly than most who have.'

'What connection did you have with him in the army, then?' Laura said. 'Maybe there is some conflict. Perhaps someone else should deal with the case?'

'You want to know what my connection to him is? He was the person who *found* me. When the house was bombed. When Mother and Father and Val *died*!'

Laura's lack of empathy sent Mel into a complete spin. Anger flared up inside her, and she pushed past Laura and ran out of the drawing room before she said something she regretted. She wished that Derrin hadn't felt the urge to leave because of Laura's presence and rude attitude. She wanted to apologise to him, but as she reached the front door, she saw his car wending its way down the long driveway and out through the estate gates.

She took a deep breath and let it go in a long sigh, already regretting her outburst. She relied on Laura and Jonathan's generosity, and no doubt Laura would be upset with her now and tell Jonathan some tall tale about how she still belonged in the barracks.

*Stupid! Stupid, Mel!* she thought.

'I believe the inspector was here?' said Jonathan behind her.

Mel didn't turn because she didn't want her cousin to see the flush colouring her cheeks and misread it. She had to keep her emotions in check if she wanted to keep a roof over her head.

'Yes,' she answered, keeping her voice neutral. 'The girl was murdered. Awful business. I hope they find the culprit.'

'Indeed,' said Jonathan.

Mel only turned around when she was sure Jonathan had moved on.

There would be repercussions for her temper, but for now, she pushed the worry of it aside. There was much to think about, and many scenarios of how the woman came to be there, and who might be behind it.

With all this in mind, Mel returned to her duties, a prevailing melancholy following her around for the rest of the day. Derrin's reappearance had only highlighted her profound loneliness. Part of her wished she hadn't seen him again, and that she hadn't found that cursed woman, or 'thorn in the roses' as she was coming to think of her.

# 6

THE GARDEN PARTY WAS JUST ABOUT TO start when Mel escaped her preparation duties and was able to go upstairs to change. She had kept her head down for the past week, working long days to make sure everything would be perfect. Outside on the beautiful lawns was a large marquee, and an art deco-design bar had been positioned inside; its mirrored glass inlaid with black and gold declaring the opulence of the Greenways. Laura had wanted to make a statement to the local gentry, and this event was certain to do that.

Around the inside of the large tent were multiple flower arrangements, which Mel and some of the maids had put together using the blooms from the gardens, although her ancestors would have bought in such adornments. Laura had no concept of what it took to bring such an event together and not have it cost a fortune, but Mel was still about saving where expense was unnecessary, and had focused a lot of energy on this aspect. Jonathan, on the other hand, was privy to these saving measures, as Mrs Felman often told him what Mel did and how useful she was.

While Jonathan had spent the week fielding Laura's complaints about Mel's attitude, Mel, for her part, had done her best to stay clear of her cousin's wife for fear of an irreconcilable argument on top of her brief eruption. Laura wasn't the sort to let things go lightly, and in this instance, Mel didn't want to apologise. Laura had been insensitive. She always was and Mel believed that Jonathan knew it, which was why he hadn't approached her about the conflict, and why he was even now trying to placate Laura without imposing any kind of sanction on Mel.

Back in her room, she found it difficult to switch off from the party prep and found her mind's eye still overseeing the marquee. She saw it now: the tables being covered with white linen cloths, scattered with rose petals, and the backs of the chairs adorned with big tulle bows. The flower centrepieces had thick white candles in silver candelabras, which Mel had found stored away in the basement, hidden from the thieving fingers of the many army soldiers who'd occupied the house during the war. But all of this wouldn't be so perfect if the estate handymen hadn't cobbled together a wooden floor to stand everything on, and also provide a dance floor for after dinner.

It was beautiful, Mel thought, and well constructed. Everyone was going to have a great time, including herself if she relaxed enough and stopped worrying about what might go wrong. The likelihood was that nothing would.

Mel looked at the long, pale-blue, simple but elegant dress, and new shoes and stockings that Jonathan had made sure she had. She'd even let Laura's handmaid, Hettie, put pins in her hair, creating natural waves when she now removed them and ran over a soft brush to bring out the shine. Hettie had left some bits of make-up for her to use, too, and she applied some rouge to her cheeks and lips, and a little kohl around her eyes based on how Laura wore hers, which she knew was the fashion.

When she was ready, Mel was shocked to see herself. She had forgotten what it was like to dress for an evening event because she hadn't done it for years. The woman looking back at her through the dressing table mirror was indeed feminine. Seeing herself like this brought a round of insecurity and a wave of memories that she didn't care to revisit. That night, on her nineteenth birthday, out with friends and her brother Valentine, was the last time she'd looked even remotely like this.

She was leaner now than then, her teenage puppy-fat long gone, and her figure was honed by the physical work she did. Her arms, rarely seen bare, held some muscular definition. Even so, the dress, hair and make-up softened her, and she knew she looked attractive, even though she was unaware that she was always naturally pretty.

'I guess clothes do make a difference,' she murmured.

As the dress had a sweetheart neckline, her neck was too bare. She didn't have a scarf that was suitable to tie around it – and then she remembered. Her mother had some simple jewellery that she'd kept along with the other salvaged items from their home. She opened the chest containing these few things and her heart leapt when she saw, on top of the trunk, a photograph of her and Valentine when they were young. A distant memory of the two of them running along the house corridors, both under ten years of age, squealing with delight. Such innocent times, knowing nothing of the devastation that would follow years later.

Mel's hand trembled as she picked up the frame. The photograph reminded her why she had no personal items on the walls of her small room. It was still too raw, still too painful. Even after all these years and so much water under the bridge. Would the grief ever go?

Mel recalled other nights when, after her family was gone, she'd shaken and trembled with the memory, reliving the shock and pain as though it had just happened. On some of those nights, Derrin had been there; he'd taken her in his arms, held her until the tremors disappeared and then kissed and soothed her until she was back to herself. She'd always appreciated how he'd done this with silent care, never asking her anything, as though he understood already what was happening. Many soldiers came back from the front with some sickness of the mind that no one wanted to talk about, but the knowledge of it was common among the soldiers. Derrin would be aware of it for certain, but there was a firm belief of 'stiff upper lip', and 'being British' meant you had to be strong. Even so, Mel was sure Derrin didn't see these episodes as a weakness. Sometimes she wondered if he had his moments too, but hid them when he did.

Of course, such feebleness would be frowned on by the new guardians of Avonby, and Mel did her best to keep those moments private and away from her family and the servants on the estate. She'd become so good at hiding them, excusing herself when she felt the familiar moments of disassociation come over her. Being female meant she could claim a headache whenever she needed time out. Not something she did often, but an excuse called on when she had to use it. The truth was, Mel rarely got any ailments. She was stronger than she appeared.

It was fortunate that her episodes were rarer these days and only occurred in moments of stress, which she still found challenging to deal with. To be reminded right then of everything she'd lost was enough to cause an onslaught of those awful terrors.

She considered crying off from the party despite wanting to see her efforts realised. She couldn't fall down, showing up Jonathan and Laura, right at the height of their return to society. The only sensible thing to do was to not go.

Mel caught sight of herself in the dressing table mirror and her back became rigid. Laura would love her not to be there. And, although she never actively looked for conflict with her cousin's wife, she also cared as little for Laura as Laura did for her. Stiffening her resolve, Mel put down the photograph and rummaged through the chest until she found the black velvet jewellery case that had once belonged to her mother.

She pulled the case from the bottom of the chest, took it over to the dresser and placed it down. Steeling herself for more memories, she lifted the lid.

Inside were a few necklaces of fine gold, with paste gems, but one item stood out as perfect for her dress: a thick gold choker, with a rich-looking sapphire on it. Mel took it out and held it against her neck. She didn't remember her mother ever wearing the necklace, and for that she was grateful. The jewel wasn't paste, or at least, if it was, it was very well made, because the gem caught the light from her lamp and glimmered like the real thing. She put the necklace on and it was a perfect match with her clothing. Then she added a gold hairclip to one side of her hair, lifting it away from her face, while the other side flowed down in waves.

Like the old days, when she put on her soldier's uniform, Mel experienced the same sensation of donning armour, and it would fortify her in the coming hours, which were bound to be difficult as she was sure she would be socially inept. The difference between her uniform and the dress, though, was that for once she didn't feel invisible.

A loud knock on her door brought her back to the immediate present.

'Miss... Lady Melinda... Guests are arriving.'

Nancy was wearing her best uniform for the occasion, as she'd be called on to serve drinks alongside the young footman, Toby, as well as Williams that night. Her hair was pulled back into a tight bun and she looked very smart and prim.

'Wow, Mel!' Nancy said. 'You look... oops, sorry, I mean Lady Melinda. You look very beautiful, Miss.'

'Nancy, that's the first time you've called me Mel and I thank you for it,' Mel said. 'Do it more, please.'

'I'll try... but I daren't let Lady Laura hear me, we're all on strict instructions to be formal with you, especially tonight.'

Mel gave a small laugh and Nancy giggled.

'Sorry!' she said, looking around again with that same guilt she had exhibited just a few days earlier, and Mel thought maybe she'd misinterpreted Nancy's behaviour then, after all. The guilt might be her fear of being overly familiar with Mel, and Laura catching her.

'We must go, Miss,' Nancy said again. 'Lord Jonathan wants you to greet everyone.'

Mel took a breath. She had forgotten this simple etiquette – if she'd even known it in the first place. As the lesser member of the family, she would be expected to do the job of welcoming everyone at the front door. Making sure they had drinks and canapés. Then, Laura and Jonathan would make their dramatic entrance as the hosts.

Mel hurried towards the servants' staircase.

'Oh no, Miss!' said Nancy. 'You gotta do the main stairs. There's already some people waiting.'

# 7

Walking down the main staircase with the huge hallway filling fast below was Mel's worst nightmare. She hadn't expected everyone to be so prompt, and as she stood at the top of the stairs looking down, Mel was overwhelmed to see more than sixty people already gathered, with more coming in.

Williams had taken care to instruct his staff well, and already coats had been taken, drinks were being served and trays of canapés were doing the rounds. Everyone was smiling, including Avonby's staff and the few waitresses they had hired in for the evening, who were all taken with the glitz and glamour of the occasion. Guests would soon be led outside to see the magnificent gardens and the marquee, but not before their hosts greeted them.

Mel took another deep breath and, holding the handrail to steady herself, began the trek down to be among the guests, planning to obtain a glass of champagne to steady her nerves as soon as she reached the bottom. Halfway down, she paused, almost losing her courage. At the same moment, all heads turned and Mel found the majority of the guests looking up at her. Whispers took up among them, as though they didn't recognise her and were speculating on who she might be.

Torn between flight or fight, Mel froze on the spot until Williams, recognising her discomfort, stepped forward and announced very loudly to everyone: 'Lady Melinda Greenway.'

Mel had no choice but to start walking again even though her legs trembled. As she reached the bottom of the steps, she was swamped with people coming to introduce themselves to her: they were very interested in this secret and distant member of the family who they had no doubt heard rumours about but hadn't yet met.

'Lady Melinda,' said a woman who was introduced as Lady Spedman, 'is it true you were in the army?'

Mel was about to answer when Williams interrupted by announcing Lord Jonathan and Lady Laura Greenway.

Mel turned to look at her cousins coming downstairs, only to see the barely concealed rage in Laura's eyes. She was left wondering what she had done wrong this time, but as the guests now surged towards the lord and lady of the house, Mel was able to lose herself among them. She backed away, bumping into someone who was standing behind her.

'I'm so sorry!' she said, turning to apologise.

'Lady Melinda, I am Lord Richard Stanley, and I believe your cousin is annoyed because she feels upstaged. And I am not surprised because you did make a very magnificent appearance.'

Mel blushed. 'Oh no. I didn't mean to.'

'Of course you didn't,' he smiled. 'Some things just come naturally.'

Stanley cut a very dashing figure, and Mel's cheeks remained warm as he continued to heap praise on her. To cover her embarrassment, Mel looked away and found Laura and Jonathan in the thick of their guests. Laura was wearing the most ostentatious gown, which was in keeping with the 1920s theme of the party and was covered in sequins in both black and gold. She was stunning with her fair hair piled up on her head in an elaborate coiffeur, and the smile that now lit up her face showed she was happy with the attention she was getting. Mel relaxed as the moment of Laura's wrath passed.

'I couldn't pull that off,' Mel said, smiling at Lord Stanley.

'That, my dear, is fancy icing on a very dull cake,' Stanley said.

Mel couldn't help but grin at Stanley as he made himself something of a conspirator.

'So, you're a friend of Jonathan's?' she asked.

'Old school friends,' Stanley said. 'But this is the first time I have been to Avonby.'

'Really? Why is that?' Mel asked.

'Jonathan hadn't inherited the estate back then, of course, and didn't know he was going to. And we only reconnected a few months ago. But I'm sure to be a regular visitor from now on!'

Reading between the lines, Mel wondered if they had been more acquaintances than friends before Jonathan had inherited Avonby. Now that he was a much more appealing friend, Stanley was keen to be around him. She was tempted to stay and talk to him a little longer, but his flirty smile was a concern, because she didn't really want to encourage him for fear of being misunderstood.

'It's very nice to meet you, Lord Stanley,' she said. 'I have duties to attend to so I must go, but I do hope you enjoy the evening.'

'Hopefully we will talk again,' said Stanley.

Mel gave a polite nod and went outside to check on the final appearance of the marquee, even though she already knew everything was perfect and there was nothing more she could do.

Once all the guests were seated, Mel placed herself at the end of the family table so she could leave to take care of anything she needed to. Concerned that Laura was still displeased with her, she kept herself as far away from her and Jonathan as she could. Between her and her cousins were some friends of theirs, and Mel was happy to chat to them instead.

Even though she'd done the seating plan herself, there was a man sitting next to her whom she didn't know. He was sullen, in his early thirties and Mel disliked him on sight. He reminded her of the arrogant officers she'd dealt with in the army – privileged upperclass men with titles but no real talent for the officer roles they'd been promoted to because of their birthright. Despite being born into such a family, Mel could see the flaws. It would be just like Laura to have placed a potential suitor next to her. She was pleasant to him, being careful to hide her displeasure and suspicion, but the whole evening was torture, and it was a relief when dinner was over and the band started to play. Primed with generous measures of alcohol, some couples got up immediately and took to the dance floor. The man beside her began to fidget. Fearing he was preparing to ask her to dance, Mel used this opportunity to excuse herself on another organising pretext and left the marquee.

In the garden, she took a seat on a bench inside one of the small gazebos and looked out at the sunset, which was just beginning to drift down on the horizon. The sky was lit with golden and red hues. The sight of it was soothing, and Mel enjoyed being alone again as she wasn't keen on crowds of people these days. She sighed with relief, letting all the tension of the day go, happy with her own company.

'There you are!' said Derrin, appearing in full dinner suit like all the other male guests.

'I didn't know you were here!' she said.

They looked at each other appreciatively for a few seconds, and for once Mel was pleased with the effort she'd put in and that Derrin was there to see her like this. It made a change from her overalls, or boring day dresses.

'Lord Jonathan invited me,' Derrin said, unaware of Mel's thought. 'He came into the station yesterday.'

'I didn't know that,' Mel said.

'He's naturally concerned about our Jane Doe,' Derrin said. 'May I join you?'

Mel nodded.

Derrin took a seat beside her and Mel found herself feeling relaxed for the first time all evening.

'You're sure I'm not imposing? You looked quite content on your own.'

'Of course not. You're always good company.'

'You look beautiful,' he said.

Mel got a small thrill from his words but covered her pleasure by returning the compliment.

'Thank you. You scrub up well yourself,' she said, and then to hide their mutual admiration she asked, 'Anything new?'

'I was going to ask you the same thing.'

'I have nothing to tell you. I wish I did. No one is talking about what happened, unless they are but just not around me. I think it's because we've all been so busy with this party, and perhaps Laura has banned the servants from discussing it. There is not even a whiff of gossip. So, I'm surprised Jonathan came in to see you, to be honest. What were you able to tell him? Only he's unlikely to share the information with me.'

'I'm sorry to hear that. Are things not going well here?' Derrin asked.

'Oh, it's fine. It is just, I'm not really one of them. I could be, but…'

'You don't want to be?' he said.

'Something like that. But never mind all this. Tell me where things are with the investigation.'

'So that's how things are with us now?' Derrin said. 'It's all about the murder.'

Mel gave a sad smile. 'Perhaps.'

The light in the garden was slowly turning darker and Mel's blue eyes were shining in such a way that Derrin wasn't sure if she was on the verge of tears. He didn't want to see her cry, feeling a sense of guilt because he might have been the cause of it. Looking at her that night, dressed beautifully and for all the world a Greenway, even when she said she didn't belong, Derrin was aware of the intense divide between them. He had always thought she was too good for him, and when the opportunity to leave London had presented itself two years ago, he had taken it with barely a qualm. Although he hadn't lied about writing to her, Derrin hadn't tried too hard to keep in touch. It had seemed at the time, with the war almost over, that their relationship had come to its natural conclusion.

Now, as he found himself once more in her company, Derrin regretted his cowardice. He had let her go, rather than fight for her – rather than see if they could work outside of the war, in more normal times.

'We haven't found Ruby Lewis, but I've been able to rule her out,' he said, answering her question.

'It's not her?' Mel said. 'I'm surprised.'

'The woman we found was in her thirties. Lewis was only 18 or 19. Our Jane Doe was also… pregnant.'

'Good grief!' Mel said. 'But… who was she?'

Derrin shook his head. 'We still don't know.'

'Do you think she was killed to silence her… as to who the father might be?'

'It is interesting that your mind went there, as mine did. It's possible,' Derrin said, and he couldn't help being impressed with her. Mel's mind had always been attractive to him. She was also capable of seeing the possible reasons why a crime might happen. Not an easy thing to explore, but Mel did it better than most police officers he knew. 'Hard to imagine any man doing that to a girl he's been involved with, but if the father of the child is involved, then we have to wonder why he couldn't do right by her. Maybe he is married?'

'Something to consider. They would have something to lose or something to gain by her death and disappearance, I suppose. How far on was she?' Mel asked.

'Three months. Probably didn't show. So, her condition wouldn't have been common knowledge,' Derrin said.

'Maybe another employee left that fits the bill,' Mel said. 'I could…'

'No. I'll be in tomorrow to ask some hard questions,' Derrin said. 'Like I said before, you need to distance yourself from this, Mel.'

'You did. But you also just asked me if I'd heard anything else. So you expected me to have done some investigation, didn't you?'

'I know you too well,' he said. 'But I'm not going to encourage you.'

Mel smiled; she was happy and relaxed around Derrin. It was just like old times in many ways; even though the change in their statuses put them worlds apart, their mutual past would mean they would always have a connection. They sat in comfortable silence as the final drifts of sunset turned burnt orange and petered out until the sky was black ink.

As full dark arrived, the lights around the marquee appeared to burn brighter and cast light over their seating area so that anyone could see them if they came outside. Mel didn't expect anyone to do that, though, as the band was in full swing and music echoed out over the lawns. It was joyous and celebratory, which was what she had expected it to be, even if she only appreciated it from a distance rather than being fully immersed.

Mel fought the urge to touch Derrin's hand, to further share the moment. She was pleased to be around him, and part of her wanted to turn their conversation back to their earlier mutual approval, even though she had been the one to steer them away with her curiosity about the murder. She now placed her hand down on the bench beside his in a subliminal invitation. He mimicked her movement and their hands slid closer, like magnets pulling against an invisible force.

'Am I interrupting anything?'

Mel looked up to see Lord Stanley approaching. He was holding two glasses of champagne as though he knew she would be outside, but had expected her to be alone. Perhaps he had got the wrong idea earlier after all.

Mel felt a change in the atmosphere as Derrin tensed up beside her and moved his hand away. For once, she wanted to know what he was thinking.

'Oh, Lord Stanley this is First Lieutenant… sorry… I mean Inspector Derrin Bradley,' Mel said, making the introduction.

'Ah yes! Now I recognise you. You are investigating the murder,' Stanley said.

'How do you…?' asked Derrin.

'Lord Jonathan is a close friend,' Stanley said. 'And as for you, Lady Melinda, you have been working way too hard all night. I know Laura is taking all the bows for organising this event, but some of us have noticed it is you that has done all the work. I brought you this. You can relax now; everyone is having a great time. I am sure the inspector will understand that you need to not be talking about grim events tonight.'

'Of course,' Derrin said, standing up. 'I'll leave you to relax.'

'No, it's okay. I'm perfectly happy…' Mel said, also standing up.

The three of them looked at each other, and Derrin frowned at Stanley but still managed to retain a professional air.

'If you'll excuse me,' he said. 'I ought to be going.'

'Good man,' said Stanley.

Derrin's frown deepened, but with a final nod towards Mel, he took his leave without another word.

Mel's mood plummeted as she watched him go. She wanted to call him back and ask him not to leave, but the words choked in her mouth. She was frustrated by how easily he gave up and left when she was sure their former closeness was on the verge of being opened up again.

She considered calling Stanley out for his rudeness. How dare he presume to interrupt them like that? He had behaved as though Derrin was totally beneath him and that he had no right to be socialising with her. She was disgusted, and now she questioned her earlier appreciation of the man when she had thought him flirty and slightly amusing. He was a snob, like most of Jonathan's friends.

Stanley held out the champagne glass and smiled, turning on the charm, but Mel noticed that the smile did not quite reach his eyes and wondered why she hadn't picked up on his artifice earlier, when she was normally so observant. She held up her hand in polite refusal, but inside she was seething and didn't want to spend any further time with the man than was necessary.

'I think I'll retire and leave you all to your fun,' she said. 'As you said, my work is done, and therefore I'm no longer needed. Goodnight, Lord Stanley.'

As Derrin drove away from Avonby, he felt an overwhelming sense of disappointment. He had accepted Jonathan's invitation on the pretext that he might observe the occupants of Avonby when they let their hair down. Now he wondered if it had been a mistake attending. He had seen Mel coming down the stairs, and the surge of emotion her appearance brought made him feel unsteady for the rest of the evening.

She hadn't seen him there as he'd deliberately lost himself among the other guests, wanting to observe her in what he believed to be her natural habitat. But things had changed when he saw Lord Stanley talking to her. They had been flirting, Derrin could tell from the exchange of smiles and the slight flush in Mel's cheeks. He found himself wondering if she'd had any relationships since they'd parted two years ago – casual or serious – and he realised he didn't know. Not knowing had been fine until Lord Stanley was there – a handsome man, and on the level that Mel deserved. Derrin hadn't been prepared for seeing her with someone else and how that would make him feel.

The only thing he could do was bow out gracefully when Stanley appeared to follow up on their earlier connection.

*In the end*, Derrin thought, *if Stanley is right for Mel, then she will be grateful for me leaving.*

# 8

Mel was head down in the engine of the family's silver Rolls-Royce when she heard the approach of a car coming up the long driveway. She'd given the engine its yearly overhaul, and had just finished the oil change, much to Henry the chauffeur's annoyance, because he had wanted to take the car out to a garage to get the service. With the work done, Mel picked up the rag she'd been using and began to wipe black oil from her fingers, before slamming down the bonnet of the car.

'It'll need a wash now,' Mel said, handing the rag to Henry. 'But first start her up?'

Henry got behind the wheel and started the car. The engine purred and Mel, satisfied that it was running better, turned her attention to the approaching Jowett Javelin car, which she recognised now as Derrin's. Remembering his comment about asking hard questions of Avonby's occupants, she was not too surprised to see him. She was pleased he was there, though, as the investigation needed to move forward. Even though he hadn't said so, she had a suspicion that Derrin had been holding back out of respect for the family's summer party plans. He'd even left his arrival to a respectable time, knowing they had all been up late the night before.

Derrin parked the car beside the Rolls and got out. In the passenger seat was a young constable who climbed out of his side, closed the door and came round the car, following closely in Derrin's footsteps.

'Mel,' Derrin said. 'This is Constable Jennings.'

Mel was more than a little self-conscious at being caught in her overalls, but you could hardly do mechanics in a dress.

'I'm here in an official capacity,' Derrin said.

'Of course you are. I'll take you inside,' she said.

Derrin and the constable followed Mel up the stone steps to the large double front door. Mel was conscious of her oil-stained fingers as she opened one door and led them inside.

'Where do you want to start?' she asked.

'Downstairs?' he suggested.

Taking them down the servants' stairs to the kitchens, Mel was running through her thoughts as to where to the interviews should take place, and it was obvious that Mrs Felman's office needed to be utilised. She wanted to talk to Derrin about the night before, and their rude interruption too. She wanted him to know she wasn't interested in Richard Stanley, because his behaviour suggested he thought she was.

In the kitchen, Mrs Weston and Daisy were prepping for lunch. Mrs Weston looked around when she heard Mel arriving with Derrin and Constable Jennings.

'Lady Melinda,' she said, being formal because of the police presence. 'What can we do for you?'

'Mrs Weston, could Inspector Bradley and the constable get some tea, please, while I have a word with Mrs Felman?'

'Get to it, Daisy,' Mrs Weston said. 'Please take a seat, officers, unless you'd prefer it brought to the drawing room.'

'Here is fine, Mrs Weston,' said Derrin, while Daisy rushed around filling the kettle and setting it on the stove to boil.

'You can use Mrs Felman's office for the interviews,' Mel said, returning after speaking to the housekeeper. 'She's in there now waiting for you, if you want to speak to her first.'

'Stay here,' Derrin said to the constable before he went to see Mrs Felman. 'Get names and details of any of the staff that are available now for interview.'

Jennings took out his notepad and started with Mrs Weston and Daisy, who both looked worried by his presence.

'There's no point in speaking to Daisy,' Mrs Weston said. 'She hasn't worked here very long and won't know anything.'

'Even so,' said Jennings, speaking for the first time. 'The inspector will want to speak to her. He wants to talk to everyone, he said.'

Mel helped Daisy make the tea, then sat down at the table to be on hand if she was needed.

There was an air of anticipation in the kitchen as Mrs Weston and Daisy continued to prepare lunch for upstairs and for the employees at Avonby. As lunchtime approached, and various servants came in for food, Jennings made a note of their names and began to give out time slots for them to come back during the day.

Getting word from Williams that the inspector was there, Laura sent for Mel, and so she found herself once more in the drawing room with Laura discussing Derrin.

'Why is he here again?' Laura asked as Mel entered.

'He's interviewing everyone,' Mel explained. 'To see what they know.'

'I thought this dreadful business was finished.'

Mel found herself staring at Laura in shock. Surely she didn't think that by removing the body the matter would just go away? *Laura really doesn't live in the real world*, Mel thought, but she kept her own counsel.

Jonathan came in, sparing her any more of Laura's bizarre conversation.

'I guess this will keep happening until they find the culprit,' Jonathan said. 'How many has the inspector interviewed so far?'

'Most of the downstairs staff. I think Williams is in next,' Mel said. 'I doubt he'll get through everyone today, though.'

'What is he asking them?' Jonathan said.

'I don't know. All the interviews are private,' Mel explained. 'But I'm keeping an eye on everything, so you've no need to worry.'

'Perhaps you should change?' Laura said, eyeing up Mel's oil-smeared overalls.

'Of course, Laura,' Mel said, keeping her voice even and neutral. 'I just haven't had a chance to, since I was doing the service on the car when the inspector arrived.'

'Servicing the car…?' Laura said and shuddered as though the idea horrified her.

'Yes. And saving the estate more money by doing so, isn't that right, Mel?' said Jonathan.

'Engines are interesting to me,' Mel answered. 'I'd better get back downstairs.'

Mel left them, but as she closed the drawing room door she paused, deliberately eavesdropping.

'What does he want from us?' Laura said. 'And why did you invite him to the party?'

'It doesn't hurt to keep the inspector on our side. Besides, he's a decent sort of chap,' Jonathan said.

*You're a decent chap, too*, Mel thought as her fondness for Jonathan grew when she heard him defending Derrin.

'But all this prying… what if they find out?' Laura said.

Mel's ears pricked up.

'Why should they? There's nothing to tie me to all that. You know I covered my tracks.'

The colour drained from Mel's face on hearing Jonathan's words. Could he possibly have been involved with the woman in the roses? Surely not!

Movement from inside the room indicated that one or the other of them was heading towards the door. Mel hurried away to avoid being caught, taking the servants' stairs back down to the kitchen.

When she reached the room, she found a corner to sit in away from everyone so that she could observe but not be watched herself. It was a small nook by the fire that had a comfortable chair. Mel saw Mrs Weston sitting there sometimes, taking herself away from the others for a short break.

Mel was feeling shaky, and her nerves were more than a little frayed. All of which irritated her so much because she was stronger than this and she knew it. Mel had been affected more by the dead body than she'd been prepared to admit at first. At the time, she had gone into that protective state of shutting down her emotions and using her analytical skills to focus her thoughts and help her deal with what had happened. But the shock had finally hit home and, with the arrival of Derrin back into her life, Mel was reminded of all the good and the bad she had experienced over the last few years. She had been focusing on the good until now, believing that although Laura was difficult, her cousin Jonathan was supportive of her and a nice person. But having overheard a suspicious exchange between them, she was freefalling, wondering if she could read people at all. Second-guessing herself in a way she hadn't done for years. She had good instincts and had learnt to trust them during the war, but now, she wondered if she'd lost her edge. Gone soft.

Did she need constant threat to be alert all the time, she wondered?

Late in the afternoon, Mrs Weston went in to see Derrin. To keep her mind occupied, Mel was timing how long each of them was in, suspecting that the longer the interview, the more the person was revealing to Derrin. Perhaps they were even relieved to tell all they knew. Mrs Weston wasn't the longest, but she was in with Derrin for almost forty minutes. Enough time, Mel thought, to show she knew more than most. Or perhaps because Derrin thought she must know more and worked on her for longer.

When she came out, Mel got up and poured the cook a strong cup of tea and opened the biscuit jar, placing some shortbread on a tea plate.

'Are you all right?' she asked, sitting down opposite her.

Mrs Weston looked shaken. 'I hope they find this person soon.'

'Were you able to help?' Mel asked.

'I shouldn't think so,' Mrs Weston said, but something in the way she averted her eyes suggested to Mel that she had brought new information to the police. She didn't ask her anything more, because just then Toby came down to go and have his interview with Derrin, and she didn't want him or anyone else to overhear their conversation.

'We're finished for today,' Derrin said, leaving Mrs Felman's office at five o'clock. 'But I'll be back early tomorrow to continue. Thank you for letting me use your office, Mrs Felman. As it will be the remaining upstairs serving staff tomorrow and the family, I think it would be best to use the drawing room, so you can have your office back.'

'Thank you, Inspector,' the housekeeper said. 'We'll have refreshments brought to you upstairs tomorrow.'

Mrs Weston didn't glance at either Mrs Felman or the inspector, so focused was she on a large piece of beef she had placed in the oven.

Mel came back out of the nook by the fire on hearing their voices and walked up the servants' stairs to the hallway with him.

'Would you both care to stay to dinner?' she said to Derrin, as she was dreading having dinner alone with Laura and Jonathan.

'Why thank you, Miss,' said Jennings, 'but my mother will have dinner ready for me.'

'Another time, then,' Mel said.

'I have plans, too,' said Derrin. 'Perhaps you can see us out, Mel?'

Once outside, Derrin sent the constable to wait for him in the car before he said to Mel, 'You look tired.'

'It's been a long day,' Mel said.

'Are you coping?' he asked.

Despite seeing her attacks, Derrin had never broached the subject of them with her, and Mel almost didn't answer and sought a way to change the subject. But before she could find another topic, Derrin's sincere expression made it easy for her to be frank.

'I'm better these days. Now the war is well and truly over,' Mel said.

'I'm glad to hear that,' he said.

'Derrin... about Lord Stanley...' she began.

'Mel. You don't have to explain your relationships to me. He's single and so are you.'

Mel was so shocked by his assumptions that she didn't know what to say. To deny there was anything between her and Stanley now might look like protesting too much. Equally, she didn't want him to remain under any false illusion.

'Did you learn anything today?' she said instead.

'Not much more. Just that most of your staff don't enjoy working for Laura and Jonathan. Which surprised me in his case, as he seems personable.'

'Mmmm. Surprises me, too. But he's probably been tarred with the same brush as his wife. They never express their dislike to me, naturally.'

'You're very respected, Mel. There was a wish that you were in charge around here,' Derrin said.

'Strange interviews you've had today, then?'

Derrin smiled. 'General chitchat helps relax people.'

'And?'

'A few things were said that I need to investigate, but for now I don't want to share,' Derrin said.

'I'm under suspicion too?'

'Of course not. But you have an interest here, and until I get to the bottom of what I've learned, I'll be keeping those conversations to myself.'

'I understand,' Mel said.

'Thank you.' Derrin smiled.

'What for?'

'For facilitating everything today, and for being easy to deal with,' he said. 'I doubt things would have run so smoothly otherwise.'

'I want to get this solved as much as you do,' she said. 'This is an awful thing to have hanging over us.'

'No matter where it leads?' Derrin said.

Mel kept her expression guarded. 'So, you have suspicions?'

'The beginnings of some, but not any evidence to back it up.'

Mel let this information sink in. She wondered how she could help him learn more without interfering too much. Perhaps some more eavesdropping would be appropriate?

'Derrin, about Lord Stanley…'

Derrin closed off as she mentioned Stanley again.

'I should expect that you would be in a relationship…' Derrin said.

Mel laughed. 'I only met him for the first time last night. I wanted to apologise for his rudeness. Some of these people…'

Mel stopped and glanced back at the house, realising she was 'some of these people', at least in part.

'I know it's ludicrous, me saying that,' she continued. 'Anyway. I'm sorry about his behaviour.'

'You have nothing to apologise for, Mel. I'll see you tomorrow,' Derrin said. 'Goodnight.'

# 9

Mel pondered on Derrin's words as she turned back to the house. After what she'd overheard, she speculated if someone had accused Jonathan – and if they had, who that might be. She had been watching all the servants as they'd gone into the office, and paid careful attention to their behaviour post-interview. Williams had been much the same going in as he was coming out, and his interview had been almost as short as Daisy's, because he, like her, hadn't worked at the house for long. In fact, while he was talking to Derrin, Mrs Weston commented that he'd only started at Avonby a couple of weeks before Mel's arrival.

At the time, Mel had wanted to question her about it, but the moment wasn't right. She hadn't known Williams was 'new' to Avonby because he gave off an air of being part of the fixtures and fittings. As she returned to the house, she had planned the perfect excuse to see Mrs Weston: she was going to ask to eat in her room again that night. She would take the cook aside for a few minutes when she did and follow up on this, asking questions about her interview with Derrin.

'Ah, Mel, there you are,' said Jonathan, coming out of the drawing room as she was crossing the hallway. 'I wanted to talk to you about Inspector Bradley.'

Mel's guard was up as soon as Derrin's name was mentioned.

'Come into the drawing room,' Jonathan said.

Mel followed him inside the room. Jonathan closed the door behind them.

'He'll be back tomorrow, to talk to everyone he didn't get to today,' Mel said, heading off the expected question.

'Yes. I thought he would be,' said Jonathan. 'Laura tells me you have history with him.'

Mel pushed her hands into her overall pockets but didn't answer.

'Well, if you have any clout with this chap,' Jonathan continued, 'perhaps you can help smooth things out. The servants are in a tizzy and Laura is very upset about the whole thing. As you know, she is a sensitive soul and doesn't have the experiences of war that you and I endured.'

Mel remained quiet while she studied Jonathan. Was his behaviour towards her different from this morning? He was less controlled than usual, wearing a frown that did not normally sit on his usually congenial face. She was still comparing her feelings about him before that day to now when she thought he was hiding something.

'Anyway... If you can help. It would be appreciated.'

'I think Derrin is just following all lines of enquiry,' Mel said at last, 'as he should do, with due diligence. They need to discover who the woman is, and then maybe they will know who killed her.'

'Of course,' said Jonathan. 'And we will help as much as possible.'

'Do you have any idea who she was?' asked Mel. 'Only, it would help if you did.'

Jonathan was taken aback by her direct question, and his eyes focused on her and became intense and alert.

'Why would *I* know anything?' he said.

Mel noticed a small bead of sweat popping up on Jonathan's brow.

*He's afraid about something*, she thought. *Or guilty*.

As if reading her thoughts, Jonathan dashed away the perspiration.

'It is so hot in here. I really must open some windows,' he said to cover his discomfort.

Then he made much of doing just that, and stood by the open window as if the best breeze were wafting in.

'That's better,' he said, but the air was still and the temperature inside the room hadn't changed at all.

'Jonathan, if you know anything at all, I urge you to speak up. Derrin is a very good investigator, I know this because I worked with him several times in the army. He's very observant and he's like a dog with a bone when he's onto something.'

'You worked with him? How?' Jonathan asked. 'I thought you were a mechanic?'

'I am,' Mel said.

Jonathan's curiosity was piqued by Mel's lack of further explanation. Just looking at the way she was standing, alert but not tense, told him further questions wouldn't be answered.

'Well, I will speak with him tomorrow no doubt, since you aren't willing to assist us,' Jonathan snapped.

'I never said that I wouldn't help. But he won't be swayed and can't be manipulated. He's a good man and he'll be professional.'

'Professional is all we can ask for,' he said.

'Indeed. Now, I need to wash up.'

'Oh do! Laura won't be pleased if you turn up to dinner like that. We have a visitor tonight, too. So, wear one of the new dresses we got you. Not too formal, a cocktail dress. Drinks at seven.'

Mel fought the urge to sigh. Her one opportunity to be alone tonight, which she needed, was gone. She couldn't refuse to join them now, especially since Jonathan was showing signs of being too interested in her past. Besides, Laura would be more pleasant if there was someone else present other than themselves, so she knew it wouldn't be such an ordeal. Perhaps it would even be fun.

Mel made her way upstairs to the bathroom. Once there, she ran a hot bath and got in. Dinner was a couple of hours away, and as much as she had hoped to avoid Laura and Jonathan tonight, it didn't look as though she would be able to after all.

Lying in the bath, her mind was full of Jonathan's plea for her to help them with Derrin. She hoped it wasn't some admission of guilt on her cousin's part. There was nothing she could do, anyway. Derrin was his own person and always had been.

She thought back to when she had worked with him the first time, when she realised right away that he was different to anyone else she had known. It was the night when he had commandeered her to drive for him because his driver was injured.

*London, 1941*

As Lieutenant Bradley's chauffeur, she drove through the dark London streets, taking him down shortcuts to his destination near the Victoria and Albert Museum.

'How are you?' he asked almost as soon as the journey began, even though they hadn't discussed that fateful night when he rescued her from the rubble of her house.

'Keeping busy,' Mel said.

'Best thing.'

'So, what's at the V and A?' she asked.

'A meeting.'

Derrin's blunt reply made it clear he didn't want to discuss what he was doing, so Mel clammed up and didn't ask anything more. She kept her mind on the road; wending her way through pitch dark streets with no lights on was treacherous, even when you knew those streets well. At any given point a previously clear road could have been hit and could now be impossible to pass through.

As they drew closer, he asked her to stop in a street near the museum.

'Stay here. I don't want you to be seen. I shouldn't be long.'

He left her in the car, going the rest of the way on foot. Mel watched him turn the corner of the next street, wishing she could have gone with him instead of waiting. When he failed to return after half an hour, curiosity and boredom got the better of her and she got out of the car and wandered in the direction he'd gone. She had a bad feeling as she approached the street corner, and not for the first time a prickle of intuition made the hairs on the back of her neck stand up. She was swamped with a feeling of impending disaster, not unlike those small seconds before the bomb had hit the streets and killed her family.

She heard raised voices and sped up, hurrying to reach Derrin, but at the last moment she remembered his instructions and stopped. She hid behind a parked car and peered down the street, careful not to be seen.

It took a few seconds to understand what she was seeing because of the darkness of the street. Derrin had his hands up because a man was holding a gun on him. The gunman had his back to Mel, and therefore was unaware of her. She waited and listened, snooping when she had been told to stay away, but she couldn't help who she was. She had always been overly inquisitive and her keen observation skills were often brought into play at the wrong moments.

'You couldn't keep your nose out, could you Lieutenant?' said the man.

His voice was a grating cockney, and Mel recognised him for the thug he was and knew Derrin was in grave danger. She weighed up her options. There was no time to go for help: she had to do something, or this kind lieutenant was going to die.

Mel ran back to the car, opened the boot, and pulled out the torque wrench.

As she hurried back, she found Derrin had been forced to his knees. Mel was correct in her assumption: the man was preparing to execute him. Being as quiet as possible, she slipped forward, raised the wrench, and struck the thug full on the back of the head. The thug fell forward as Derrin leapt to his feet and wrestled the gun from his fingers – not difficult because Mel had hit him hard, and the man was out cold.

'Well done!' Derrin said.

'We should get the police...'

'This is army business. Get the car.'

As Mel pulled the car into the kerb, Derrin went around to the back and opened the boot. Getting out, Mel saw him tying up the unconscious man with a length of rope he'd got from the back of the car. They bundled the now bound would-be assassin into the trunk, locking him in.

As Mel got back into the driver's seat, her hands begun to tremble and she was out of breath from the exertion. She took some calming breaths to level herself out before Derrin saw her. It was nothing more than adrenaline, and for the first time since that fateful night when she'd lost everything, Mel began to feel alive again. She experienced a rush of excitement, followed by a feeling of euphoria making her aware that, up until then, she had been walking around numb with shock, functioning on autopilot.

Derrin took his time getting into the car, as he searched the street for something the man had dropped during a previous tussle. When he found what he was looking for, he stuffed it into his uniform jacket inside pocket and then got in the car beside her. Mel noticed it was a bulging envelope – it crossed her mind that it might contain money, but she tried not to think about what that meant.

'Where to?' she asked.

'Back to barracks,' Derrin said.

'You live on the base, in the barracks? I've never seen you there.'

'No, I don't. But someone there will take care of what needs to be done. Let's get moving, any minute our sleeping beauty is going to wake.'

The journey took over an hour because of the state of the roads and the lack of street lights, but during that time, Derrin remained silent and pensive as though gathering his thoughts. Mel was happy not to talk as she concentrated on the drive. It was late and she was tired after the routine early mornings in the barracks. Plus, she hadn't had a decent night's sleep since enlisting.

It was after midnight when they finally reached the barrier. The soldier manning the checkpoint booth was dozing as Mel pulled the car up and he jerked awake, pretending to be alert.

'I need to speak to General Bowman,' Derrin told him.

Getting out of the car, he presented his papers. The checkpoint soldier recognised Mel, and he gave her a nod to say she was cleared to go in.

'Where now?' Mel asked.

'Over to the back of the base. There are some warehouses,' Derrin said.

Mel glanced at him before she followed his instructions. She had always thought those large buildings stored food and clothing, and had not suspected anything else was going on there.

By the time she reached the warehouses, two soldiers were waiting for them. They dragged Derrin's would-be killer from the back of the car and took him inside one of the buildings via a side door.

'Go back to your barracks,' Derrin said. 'You'll be interviewed tomorrow, so get some sleep now while we deal with him.'

Mel was exhausted by then, but despite going straight to her room, she couldn't sleep. Her mind was full of questions that she knew she couldn't ask, because she was new to the army and was intimidated by the hierarchy and rules she was still learning to adhere to. But she still wanted to know who the man was and why he had tried to kill Derrin. She came up with only one answer to her unasked questions: from the way it was being handled, the incident had to be related to national security.

She began to experience a post-adrenaline crash. Her nerves were frayed and she felt cold. Shivering, Mel pulled the rough wool army blanket around her. Then the flashbacks started. She saw herself lifting the wrench, smashing it down on the gunman's head with an awful *crunch*.

The tremors took her. Shaking, hot and cold alternately washing over her as though she had a fever. She found herself plummeted back in time to the night of the Blitz – triggered, perhaps, by the scare of almost witnessing Derrin's murder. But the vision she had of what happened on that night was changed, for, in her delirium, she wasn't knocked out cold. Instead, she was walking downstairs in her destroyed house. Mel saw Valentine lying oddly at the bottom. She could perceive every detail as though it was imprinted on her mind, and she knew without being told that his neck was broken. Val was dead. As were her parents. The traumatised Mel looked around the debris, seeing only parts of them, including the hand of her mother, sticking out from under the rubble. Bloodied, lifeless fingers smashed, nails torn, as though she had physically fought the blast and lost.

*South Yorkshire, 1946*

Mel jerked awake, realising she had fallen asleep in the bath and with awful clarity had relived the two very dramatic incidents. So real was the dream, she wasn't sure if she had been hallucinating or just replaying it all while she dozed. But no, she hadn't seen her mother's hand that night, that was something her subconscious had created and she linked it now with the dead woman found in the roses – the hand she'd imposed onto Bertha Greenway was that of the murdered girl.

Shaking, she pulled herself up out of the bath, wrapping herself in a towel before pulling on her robe. She was clean now at least, but she was sure she was late for pre-dinner drinks, and the thought of crying off was still there, so that she could stay upstairs and nurse her mental wounds alone. But no, Jonathan had been clear that he wanted her at dinner – and when her stomach rumbled, reminding her she'd not eaten all day, Mel thought dinner was definitely a good idea.

# 10

Dressed in a lilac cocktail dress, Mel reached the drawing room at ten minutes past seven. She fell into her old habit of listening before entering. At the door, she could hear Jonathan talking and Laura laughing, happy for a change because there was company to entertain. Mel pushed open the door, curious who their guest was, because they hadn't spoken at all while she was stood outside. She regretted coming in as soon as she opened the door, and if she could have backed away unseen, Mel would have. Lord Stanley was looking handsome in a white shirt, cravat and a blue velvet smoking jacket, standing by the piano with a cocktail glass in one hand and a cigarette in the other, but Mel was dismayed to see him there.

'Ah, Mel!' Jonathan said.

'Melinda,' Laura corrected, nodding in her direction as though their relationship wasn't strained and they were on good terms. Mel reacted with a small friendly smile to keep the mood light and took the offered drink from Jonathan's hands.

'I'm sorry I'm late,' she said. 'Engine oil is quite difficult to get out from under your fingernails.'

'Oh, you are such a hoot!' Laura said, filling the room with a peal of fake laughter.

'You look enchanting,' said Stanley as Mel sipped her drink.

The strong vermouth and vodka drink hit her palette, reminding her of the heavy hooch she had tried on her nineteenth birthday. Mel was more sophisticated these days, and she didn't grimace at the taste. Instead, she took a second sip and began to enjoy the warming feeling of the alcohol.

'I was just saying what a wonderful evening it was last night,' Stanley continued.

'Indeed,' said Jonathan, 'and a large part of that was Mel's amazing organisation skills. She thinks of everything. While Laura here adds all the glamour!'

Laura giggled but Mel took the compliment without comment or reaction. She placed the cocktail glass down on the coffee table, because the alcohol was already going to her head and she preferred to keep her wits about her around her cousin and his wife. Plus, Stanley was on the charm offensive again tonight and she found herself discreetly observing him and his interactions with her cousins, suspicious of his motives.

'Well, now that things are finally normalising, we will do much more socialising, won't we Jonathan?' Laura said.

'Of course!' Jonathan said. 'And look, we hardly see you in the last several months and now twice in one week!'

Stanley laughed. 'You'll be sick of me before long.'

'Are we ready to eat?' Mel said. 'I'll ring for Williams if we are.'

Laura nodded. 'Yes, Melinda, if you would.'

Mel pulled the bell cord by the fireplace and Williams appeared right away, as though he'd been waiting for the call, which Mel knew he had. Dinner would be ready as soon as they wanted: it always was.

'May I?' said Stanley, holding out his arm to Mel to lead her to the dining room.

'Thank you, Lord Stanley,' she said.

She took his arm to be polite.

'Oh, I think we are on first-name terms now, surely Melinda. Please, call me Richard.'

She nodded but did not ask him to call her 'Mel'. Somehow, she knew that would be letting Stanley in, when she didn't want to. She was already put out by his over-familiarity and didn't want to encourage more of it.

In the dining room, Mel was placed next to Stanley, and Laura and Jonathan were positioned opposite so they could all talk together and with less formality on the huge table.

Williams and Toby came in, each carrying two bowls of soup which they placed down before the four of them. The soup was a thick broth, made from the fruits of the gardening team's labour. Mel was hungry but she paced herself and acted just as Laura did, something she'd been practising over the last few months. It was less embarrassing to fit in rather than stand out, sometimes. But while she sat with the family, she didn't feel at all like herself and experienced again a sense of dissociation, as though she were watching the scene unfold, but wasn't a part of it.

'Melinda?' Laura said. 'Have you finished?'

Mel came back to herself and noticed Williams standing next to her, waiting to take her dish. She hadn't been following any of the conversation, and she'd only eaten half the soup.

'Yes. Thank you, Mr Williams,' she said. 'It was lovely. Just saving myself for the main.'

'I heard you have been fielding Inspector Bradley's questions today, Melinda,' Stanley said.

'No. But I'm sure I will be interviewed tomorrow.'

'So, what has he found out so far?' Stanley continued.

'I really don't know,' said Mel.

'She won't be drawn on Bradley, Richard. They are old colleagues,' Jonathan said.

Stanley turned and looked at Mel, studying her for too long and without being subtle about it.

'Colleagues?' he said.

'They were in the army together,' Laura said. 'Though Melinda is learning to live up to her title again. Dreadful days meant that needs must for her. But she is back in the fold with family now, and we are taking care of her needs.'

Mel was taken aback, as Laura's words implied she was Mel's rescuer, reminding her that she'd had to throw herself on their mercy after being demobbed and struggling to find work.

'I have lots of abilities,' Mel said. 'Sadly not recognised by our male-dominated world.'

'And the gardens look spectacular,' Stanley commented. 'All down to you, I believe.'

'Indeed. With Mel overseeing their restoration, we have seen massive improvements,' Jonathan said. 'And of course, Laura has been in charge of house renovations, which are due to begin next year.'

Laura smiled at Jonathan: he was well versed in bringing any conversation and praise back to his wife.

Mel didn't mind the subject being changed as Laura launched into her plans for the house. She was happy to be quiet as Laura talked. Meanwhile, Williams began to serve them the roast beef that Mrs Weston had been attending to earlier. Mel's stomach groaned, but if anyone heard it, they didn't mention it.

After dinner the men retired to Jonathan's study for brandy and cigars. Mel found herself alone with Laura in the drawing room, but Laura poured herself a sherry and picked up a magazine, flicking through it as she ignored Mel.

'Would you mind if I went to bed?' Mel said.

'What about Richard? I thought you would want to talk to him some more,' Laura said. 'They'll come back in soon.'

Mel considered her answer before speaking. 'Have you known Lord Stanley long?'

Laura put aside the magazine, 'He knows Jonathan. From their school days. He has an estate just outside Sheffield. Big place, I believe. If you played your cards right, you could be happy there.'

'What?' said Mel.

'He likes you. And he is single, Melinda. But I think some of these rough edges of yours would have to go. I doubt he would want Lady Stanley fixing the car and driving around on a motorbike.'

'You're trying to marry me off to him? That's what this dinner was about?'

'Oh, just offering appropriate options, my dear. As I promised I would,' Laura said, but the meanness was back in her voice now that there were no witnesses to hear it.

'I think I *will* retire,' Mel said. 'It has been a long day, and the inspector will be back early in the morning. Do give my regards to Lord Stanley.'

Laura picked up her magazine again but she flicked through the pages much faster, snapping them open one at a time until Mel left the room. Laura was annoyed, but at least Mel had avoided an all-out argument with her. It was the best she could do under the circumstances.

As Mel passed Jonathan's study, she was tempted to spy on the men's talk, but she was aware of Williams still hovering as he waited for Stanley to leave. She didn't want anyone to know about her habit, because she was planning on doing so much more of it in the coming weeks if Derrin didn't get the servants and family to speak up first.

As she walked up the main staircase, her mind went back to the Jane Doe, as it often did, and her body lying in the dirt like discarded rubbish. It was a horrible ending, and Mel had an intense urge to be part of what happened to the woman next. She'd have to be interred with dignity once they found out who she was and if she had family. She would even try to convince Jonathan to pay for the funeral as a goodwill gesture.

Mel recalled the indent on her finger for a ring that wasn't there and hadn't been found. But where was it now, and did it adorn a different hand? And why did the killer take it? Could it be the ring itself that was a motive to why she died? Only time and revelations would tell – but first they had to find out who she was. Someone at Avonby had to know.

She remembered, then, that Jonathan had still not divulged to her that he'd visited Derrin at the station. She wondered if Laura knew, and if, when he visited, Derrin had told him what he'd shared with Mel. Somehow, she thought not. Derrin was very good at keeping secrets, but why had he shared the information with her? Did it mean that he knew she wouldn't tell Jonathan? Or was it because, despite his protestations that she should keep out of it, he secretly hoped she wouldn't? Mel knew she had useful skills beyond her gardening and mechanics, and so did Derrin. She could help him. She was useful and she wanted to be involved in catching the killer. But this mystery was a tough one, because the murder had happened before she had been part of Avonby's life, leaving the trail somewhat cold. As she had considered many times: the killer could be one of them, but conversely they could also be long gone. Right now, she had no way of knowing which was the case.

# 11

THE NEXT DAY, MEL JOINED DERRIN IN the drawing room after making sure that Nancy brought in tea and sandwiches.

'These are particularly good,' Derrin said, taking a bite out of one.

'Our own cucumber, grown in Avonby's vegetable patch,' Mel said.

'Lovingly grown?' Derrin said.

Mel smiled.

'Well, I suppose you want to interview me today?'

'You already told me everything I needed to know on the day you found the body – and more! No, I wanted to talk to you about your cousin, Jonathan.'

'I see. What do you want to know?'

'How's his marriage?'

'That's a strange question. He and Laura are very happy together. He dotes on her.'

'Mmmm. Well, rumour has it he was seen with another woman.'

Mel was surprised to hear his words. It wasn't something she'd ever think Jonathan capable of. She meant what she said: Jonathan adored Laura, and made all kinds of allowances for her snobbery and sometimes self-centred behaviour. Mel couldn't imagine him looking for love elsewhere because Laura took up so much of his time. Mel would even swear that he was happy. Happy men didn't cheat on their wives.

'And where did this rumour come from?' Mel asked.

'I can't reveal the source at this point, but the timing fits.'

'Timing?'

'Yes. I have a date, time and place where this happened.'

'I think whoever told you this was mistaken,' Mel said. 'There's no way he is straying.'

'They were positive it was him,' Derrin said. 'I have a full statement.'

'So, even if it is true, what has this got to do with the investigation?'

Derrin picked up another sandwich and bit into it. Mel could tell he was trying to keep a lot of information close to his chest, but you couldn't come out with something like this without a reason. There was no smoke without fire… She began to question all she knew about her cousin, having only met him for the first time a couple of weeks before Christmas the previous yearr.

'I'm still failing to see the point here,' she said again. 'So give me something.'

'The woman fits the description of our Jane Doe. She was seen with him, going into a hotel room.'

'Okay. That's very specific. When and where did this happen?'

'I'm telling you this much because I want to know if you have any suspicions about him. You live in the same house, and I know you're observant.'

Mel walked over to the drawing-room door and opened it. The hallway was empty with no sign of anyone loitering.

Derrin had arrived early, and so far Jonathan and Laura hadn't surfaced.

Mel closed the door and came back to sit not opposite, but beside Derrin. She leaned in close to speak to him.

'I have been known to accidentally pick up on conversations.'

Derrin gave a small smile. 'You're still doing that, then?'

'Old habits die hard. And I wouldn't be surprised if others had the same traditions,' Mel said. 'I did hear part of a conversation between Laura and Jonathan, but I have no way of knowing if it meant anything.'

'What did you hear?'

'Jonathan is not a cheat,' she said again. 'I've seen nothing to suggest that.'

'Not since you've been here, but what if it was six months ago and he was caught out?'

Mel mulled this over: the devotion Jonathan showed to Laura could be to make amends for some past indiscretion, it all depended on history. A history Mel didn't share or know about. There was a discrepancy in their relationship and Laura was the one pulling most of the strings, but having said that, Jonathan did plenty of things against her wishes too. Mel had always thought him very much his own man. But Jonathan and Laura had discussed a secret, and Mel's instincts had made her suspicious of what it meant. She had always trusted those instincts, too. She remembered now his words about there being nothing to tie him to 'that business'. What 'business' had he meant?

'Mel? What did you hear?' Derrin asked again.

Jonathan was brought into the drawing room to be interviewed next. Mel was sitting near the window behind him, so that she could observe Jonathan's reactions. She knew some of her cousin's tells, and was sure that she would know if he was lying to Derrin.

'I've asked Mel to stay,' Derrin said, 'as support for you as a close family member. I've ruled her out where the murder is concerned, because she was nowhere near Avonby at the time of the victim's death and couldn't have known her. Other things we know: there were finger marks around the victim's neck, which were large, and we believe they were made by a man.'

'She was strangled, then?' Jonathan said. 'I didn't know that.'

'Yes. And there would have been a great deal of force used. The coroner discovered broken bones in the neck. Her larynx was crushed. What we also learned was that she was in the first trimester of pregnancy,' Derrin said.

Mel kept her face straight as Derrin talked, and she watched Jonathan's face twist with emotion at the somewhat brutal and blunt description the inspector gave of the way she had died. His reactions were human and sympathetic, showing no signs of guilt that she could see.

'Good Lord,' said Jonathan. 'Dreadful. I can't believe this happened here.'

'She will have suffered. It would not have been pleasant. Did you know her, Lord Greenway?' Derrin said.

'Erm... no... why would...?'

'I ask you to think carefully. If this woman was known to you, then you may be implicated in her death.'

'I could never do such a thing!' Jonathan said.

Mel saw his outrage and shock just as surely as Derrin did. She wanted to believe he wasn't a killer and that he was faithful to Laura, despite Derrin's suggestion that he might have had an affair in the past.

'Where were you the first week of December?' Derrin asked.

'I don't know. Probably here... I'd need to look in the estate diary. It will be in Mrs Felman's office.'

'Do you remember being in London around that time?'

Jonathan shook his head. 'Not specifically. Except, I did go to meet with Mel in December. Laura was with me,' Jonathan said.

'That was the second week in December,' Mel confirmed.

'That was the only visit that month. I'm sure of it,' Jonathan confirmed.

'I have a witness who saw you with a woman fitting the description of our Jane Doe, the week before that.'

'Me?' said Jonathan. 'Absolutely not!'

Mel had been watching Jonathan with such intensity that her eyes began to sting, until she remembered to blink. Jonathan's ruddy cheeks showed he was upset, perhaps even guilty. She was torn. Derrin hadn't accused him yet, but he might be on the verge of doing so, which was enough to make anyone feel guilty, even if they weren't. Was he lying and or just afraid of the allegation? Even so, she didn't intervene. She let Derrin follow his line of questioning, because Jonathan would either crack under the pressure, or he wouldn't, and if he was somehow involved with the woman then the mystery might be solved sooner rather than later. But she hoped he was telling the truth and he hadn't known her.

Mel tried not to think what it would mean for her – and for Avonby, which had to stay in family hands, no matter what – if he were guilty of murder. She pushed these worries aside and brought her attention back to the present as Derrin barraged Jonathan with question after question. She was somewhat proud of how her cousin handled it: Jonathan didn't break. Instead, he recovered his composure and the embarrassed flush left his cheeks, returning his skin to its normal tone as he pulled his nerves back together. He was a true Greenway, tougher than he appeared and with so much character that Mel couldn't help but admire him.

'And who accuses me of being unfaithful to my wife, who I'm devoted to? Mel can tell you that! I'd like this person to say it to my face,' Jonathan said.

'Mel did confirm your devotion,' Derrin said. 'But I won't be revealing my sources just yet. I need to check out this diary and any alibis you have first. I will also talk again to your housekeeper, and see if she remembers anything. In fact, Mel, would you bring Mrs Felman up when I'm finished with Lord Greenway?'

'Yes,' Mel said.

The interview had been a surreal experience for her, with some of the information Derrin had been given used to rattle Jonathan. Despite his resistance to the interrogation, she had the feeling he was hiding something, purely based on what she'd overheard. Even so, she wasn't convinced he was a killer.

'Have you finished with me, Inspector?' Jonathan asked.

'For now, but I'd like you to go to your study and remain there, without speaking to anyone in your household for the moment. Constable Jennings?' Derrin called.

The young constable, who was outside the room making sure that no one was listening, now came in.

'Yes, Inspector?' he said.

'Take Lord Greenway to his study and remain there with him, please.'

'Well really!' said Jonathan, offended by the idea that he couldn't be trusted in his own home. Then he turned on his heel and left with the constable.

'What do you think?' Derrin asked Mel when Jonathan was out of earshot.

'Although I think we are all capable of violence in the right circumstances, Jonathan is not a killer,' she said. 'I've never even heard him raise his voice.'

Derrin nodded in subconscious agreement.

'I don't think so either,' said Derrin. 'How frustrating. But he's hiding something. Maybe he does know this girl?'

Mel didn't confirm or deny Derrin's opinion, as she knew it was based on the same things she'd observed.

'Perhaps you should let me speak to Jonathan alone?' Mel said. 'I might get more out of him.'

'I'd like you to do that, but not yet. Let him stew a little first, wondering what Mrs Felman and others tell me. I'd like to talk to Lady Laura, too.'

'I'll get Mrs Felman,' Mel said. 'And last year's diary. That may clear the whole thing up.'

As Mel left Derrin, she was distracted. Her mind was elsewhere, exploring past times and memories when she'd seen Derrin interrogating someone else. It had been a whole different ball game that time. Jonathan may have been intimidated today, but he hadn't really seen a bad side of Derrin. The onslaught of memories burst over her. She fell back into her thoughts of the thug she had almost brained to save Derrin. A fierce act that she still did not regret for, as she had just said to Derrin, they were all capable of violence in certain circumstances, and especially when life or death was on the line.

# 12

*London, 1941*

The next morning, when she was brought in to be interviewed about the incident, Mel had been introduced to General Bowman. Mel took in the tall, imposing man, with his handlebar moustache and rotund frame. He was rather a cliché as generals go, but there was something about the man that suggested he had seen and done things that someone of his status wouldn't as a rule, which made her realise he was anything but what he appeared to be.

'Take a seat, Private Greenway,' Bowman had said. 'Lieutenant Bradley tells me you were very useful last night.'

'I only did what I thought was right,' said Mel.

'A lot of people wouldn't think to get a wrench and hit someone over the head to save someone's life,' Bowman said. 'You put yourself in peril doing that.'

'I didn't really think about the risk. I just knew if I didn't act, he might die,' Mel said.

Derrin and Bowman exchanged a glance that for once Mel couldn't read.

'The lieutenant was on a mission last night. We'd had intelligence that an exchange was being made.'

'The man we caught was running a black-market ring, which we'd turned a blind eye to for some time,' Derrin had explained.

'I see. Because black markets are helpful in these times?' Mel said. 'It makes people feel they can still get some luxuries? And even though it is against the law, this crime doesn't really hurt anyone? At least, that is how people view it.'

'You're a very smart girl,' said Bowman.

'I had a source who told me an information exchange was going to take place. Last night, thanks to you, I got there before that could happen,' Derrin explained. 'When I arrived, I found Jake Nesbitt and another man. I threw myself on Nesbitt, the other man was spooked and ran, then Nesbitt pulled the gun on me.'

'So, that envelope you pocketed was information for the Germans?' Mel said.

'I told you she was observant,' Derrin said to Bowman. 'And yes, it was. I knocked it out of his hands during the fight.'

'What else did you see, girl?' Bowman had asked.

'As we drove away, I saw someone run out from a hiding place in one of the doorways in the rear-view mirror. He went off down the street in the opposite direction from us. I'd have mentioned him if I'd known there was another man involved,' Mel told them. She didn't add that she wouldn't have shopped a normal person just for being out after curfew.

'Did you notice anything about them? You said "he"?' Derrin asked.

Mel slipped her mind back into the moment around that very brief glance, consciously using a skill she'd always had of being able to play back things that she had seen in her mind's eye.

'It *was* a man. He was wearing a thick wool overcoat. There was something about the way he ran. His leg. One was slightly shorter than the other, or an injury that made him limp. Not an obvious limp, but there.'

'Incredible,' said Bowman.

'It does sound like the man I saw briefly. He must have sneaked back in the hope that Nesbitt would finish me off and they could complete their deal,' Derrin said. 'Now we have to discover who he is.'

Mel was able to determine from the stern set of Derrin's jaw that this was something he didn't relish.

'I'd like you to watch while we interview Nesbitt,' Derrin continued. 'You won't be in the room but behind a two-way mirror.'

'Me? Why?'

'Lieutenant Bradley thinks you have skills. And it is clear to me that you have. He also believes you might have the stomach for some extra work we could offer you,' Bowman explained.

'I'm a mechanic,' she said.

'Yes. And during the day you are going to continue your training. But on occasion, you'll have some extra duties. Top secret duties. Are you interested?' Bowman said.

'Yes,' Mel said without hesitation. 'When do I start?'

'Let's talk after the interrogation,' Bowman said.

Mel was led to a room, and she saw the man they called Nesbitt sitting at a table. There was dried blood in his hair and smeared down the side of his face, which Mel knew was from the injury she had inflicted. She explored her feelings around that, but there was no guilt, and she knew she'd do the same again in similar circumstances.

The interrogation started with some intense questioning led by Derrin. But when they didn't get the answers they wanted, another man came into the room. He placed a pouch down on the table and opened it, revealing several brutal-looking instruments. Nesbitt was grabbed by two soldiers, who tied him to the chair. Then Mel witnessed a different type of interrogation. She tried to shut her brain off from the violence of it, remembering she was supposed to pick up on something. Meanwhile, what she noticed most was Derrin remaining cool and unruffled as Nesbitt was tortured by the other man. He kept his face emotionless, as though he was switching himself off to the vileness of what they were doing too. Mel understood that the soldiers saw this as a necessary evil. Did they like what they had to do? Well, in Derrin's case she didn't think so – but she wasn't sure about the torturer himself, for there was a kind of gleam of delight in his eyes when he inflicted pain.

When the other interrogator finished, Nesbitt blacked out. Derrin threw a bucket of water over the man and began talking to him again as he came round. Within minutes he gave up the name of his accomplice and Derrin left the room.

Nesbitt was left bleeding and still tied to the chair for a few minutes, until the two soldiers who had tied him down came back in. They untied him and dragged him away.

The door to the observation room opened and Derrin came in. They looked at each other for a minute, and Mel saw Derrin take a deep breath as though he had to clear his lungs after the experience of the torture.

'There's a fine line that we have to tread sometimes to get the truth,' Derrin said. 'Are you okay? I know that wasn't pleasant to watch.'

'You got your answers,' Mel said. 'That was what mattered.'

'Did we?' Derrin said. 'Or did he just tell us anything so that we'd stop?'

'What do you mean?' Mel asked. 'You think he lied to you?'

'Do you?'

Mel understood, then, why she had been put in the room to watch. They wanted her opinion, though she was still confused as to why they believed in her so much. She looked back at the room, replaying in her mind Nesbitt's reactions to the interview and torture. He had been cool at first, cocky even. But that had all disappeared when they started on him. Now Mel saw the whole thing again behind her eyes, and it was all she could do not to flinch at her detailed recollection which was, in some ways, more than she had seen at the time.

'His fingernails will grow back,' Derrin explained, as though he knew what she was thinking.

'He told some truths but not all,' she said when her rerun ended.

'Meaning?'

'The man he named was possibly the one I saw, but he is probably not going to be where he told you. I suspect he has already fled, and Nesbitt would know that. Perhaps even played for time to help him get away. So, I think it's unlikely you'll find anything at the address he gave you.'

'Drive me there and we'll see,' Derrin said.

'All right,' Mel said.

By the time they reached the rendezvous Nesbitt had given them, General Bowman and his command were already coming out.

'Nothing there,' said Bowman.

Derrin looked at Mel and said, 'She knew that would be the case.'

'How did you know Private Greenway?' Bowman asked her.

'His eyes. The pupils dilated when he told you the location,' Mel explained.

There were other tells she had seen, too many to really list and to truly explain why they told her his story. A twitch of the lips that was almost a sneer, the trembling of his wounded fingers. So many ways to see a lie, and all these things would go unnoticed because they happened in the blink of an eye.

'You're a walking lie-detector, girl!' Bowman laughed. 'Get her to sign the Official Secrets Act, Lieutenant. She's on the team.'

## *South Yorkshire, 1946*

Mel pushed her memories aside as she went downstairs to Mrs Felman's office. She had believed a career was being forged that day. And for all the war years that was true. But after the army dropped her as soon as the war ended, she learnt the truth. She had been useful, but the forces were still male dominated and would remain so, and Mel's worth had disappeared along with the need for her quirky gift overnight. Mel learnt that no matter how talented or smart you were, being female was a disadvantage in the real world. Though times had changed during the war, Mel was nothing but a commodity to be married off now, or, when it was convenient, a semi-caretaker of her ancestral home because Jonathan was too lazy to oversee Avonby himself. The war days had permitted so many different opportunities. They had given her something special at the time, and Derrin had taken her under his wing to hone her natural talents, all the time not realising that afterwards they would mean nothing in civilian life. Yet here he was, still wanting her input, but without giving her any real credit. Mel wondered if, when this case was solved, she would even see him again.

The odd thing was, even though his stern questioning of Jonathan had triggered the memory of the first of many interrogations she'd seen, Mel was not traumatised by them. Perhaps, she thought now, the propaganda had worked on her as well. After all, wasn't everyone radicalised by the beliefs they were subjected to? Didn't each side believe that they were right and the other was wrong. *All is fair in love and war...*

Mel had been disassociated from it at the time; she knew their side had done their fair share of evil during the war. Even on their own territory, far away from the front, where such things were never talked about or shared with those back home. There was a lot of guilt to endure afterwards, when the world started to right itself, and the devastation around them reflected the damage each person had taken inside. They were all broken to some degree, and it would take years to recover – if, indeed, they ever could.

Mel pondered on this now, seeing herself as a reflection of the remnants of her old home, blown apart, with looters picking through the pieces, even while she tried to rebuild. The foundations of everything she held dear were still there, though, and Mel, despite everything, was reconstructing herself. Being at Avonby helped, because here she had history and a place to belong to, even though it wasn't hers. But she was a Greenway, and she belonged, no matter how much she was made to feel she was the outsider.

She pushed her dark thoughts away as she passed through the kitchen, turned right, and walked down the corridor to Mrs Felman's office. The door was open but the housekeeper wasn't there.

Mel stood at the doorway, wary of entering Mrs Felman's domain in her absence, but then she saw the 1945 diary on top of her desk. Mel went in and picked the hardback book up. She held it in her hand, before casting a glance around the room. Behind Mrs Felman's desk was a filing cabinet. The bottom drawer was open. Mrs Felman was usually very tidy, but Mel noticed a chaos in the room that wasn't usually there. Frowning, she looked back at the diary, and then she opened it, flicking to the first week in December.

The pages for the entire week were gone. Mel ran her fingers over the torn edges. Someone had removed them, and there was a motive for doing that. Evidence inside the diary might have proven Jonathan's guilt, but it also might have cleared him.

Taking the diary with her, Mel hurried out of the office and came face to face with Mrs Felman.

'I came to get you and this,' Mel said, holding up the diary. 'It was on your desk already.'

'Last year's diary?' Mrs Felman asked. 'That shouldn't have been out. I store all the old diaries in the cabinet behind my desk.'

'You didn't take this out?'

'No, I only need the current diary,' Mrs Felman said.

'Who's been in your office today?' Mel asked.

Mrs Felman looked confused. 'No one. But how did you get in? I locked the door when I went on my inspection rounds,' she said.

'The door was wide open,' Mel said.

Mrs Felman looked into her office, and saw the untidiness and the open drawer for herself.

'I don't understand,' she said.

'Someone has been in and searched. I believe it was for this,' Mel explained.

'But why? Who would do that?'

'Who else has a key?' Mel asked.

'Well, Mr Williams does. But he was upstairs just now, when I was checking the parlour had been cleaned properly. We do the rounds together.'

Mel thought for a moment. As she had passed through the kitchen she'd seen several of the staff working. Daisy, Toby and Mrs Weston had been present for sure. She also thought there was someone around the corner, in the nook she had hidden in only yesterday, but she hadn't seen who it was.

'Come with me,' Mel said to Mrs Felman.

They went into the kitchen, and there Mel saw again the few

servants she'd seen earlier, all still engaged in their work duties.

Mrs Weston looked startled as Mel hurried past her to the fireplace only to find the nook was empty.

'Mrs Weston,' she said. 'Was someone in here? Other than Toby and Daisy?'

'There? Why, no,' Mrs Weston said.

'I thought I saw someone,' Mel said. 'Who else has been in the kitchen this morning? Who might have been in the hallways near Mrs Felman's office?'

'Everyone is off working,' Mrs Weston said. 'I haven't seen anyone. But I've been making this stew for the last hour.'

Mel became aware that both Daisy and Toby had stopped what they were doing and were gaping at her.

'Did you two see anyone?' Mel asked.

Toby shook his head.

'Daisy?'

'I don't think so, Miss, er… Your… Ladyship…' Daisy said.

'You don't think so? Did you or didn't you see anyone?' Mel asked.

'Well… there was someone… a man… I just saw the back of him… I thought it was Mr Williams, so wasn't paying no mind,' Daisy said.

'Mr Williams was upstairs with Mrs Felman, so who else might it have been?' Mel asked.

But no one had an answer. There was no one that looked like Mr Williams but Mr Williams, they concluded.

'All right. Maybe Mr Williams was there,' Mel said. 'What time was this?'

'A few minutes before you came down, Miss,' said Daisy. 'You just missed him.'

'I was talking to Mr Williams around about then,' Mrs Felman said, looking very concerned. 'It can't have been him.'

'What's this all about?' Mrs Weston said.

Mel didn't answer. Instead, she went back down the hallway, checking the other doors along the way, followed by Mrs Felman. As they reached the housekeeper's quarters, Mel tried the door and found Mrs Felman's rooms unlocked.

'Did you lock this too earlier?'

Mrs Felman nodded, and a deep frown furrowed her brow.

Mel opened the door and stepped inside the small sitting room which the housekeeper had to herself. The room was sparsely furnished, with a small sofa, a coffee table, a threadbare rug and an armchair by the fire.

'The window is open,' Mel said.

The window overlooked the back lawn. 'I must have left it like that,' Mrs Felman said.

'Do you remember when you last opened it?'

Mrs Felman thought for a second. 'Last night, but I definitely closed it before retiring.'

'Someone left through it, but that doesn't explain how they got in,' said Mel.

Mel pulled the window closed and locked it.

'Let's go and see Inspector Bradley now,' she said, and still clutching the diary to her chest, she walked out of Mrs Felman's parlour with the housekeeper, now pale in the face, following after her.

# 13

Mel handed the diary straight to Derrin and filled him in on the intruder and the missing pages.

'Mr Williams was definitely with you, Mrs Felman?'

'Yes. I swear he was,' Mrs Felman answered.

'And you had your keys with you the whole time?' Mel asked.

'In my pocket.' She held up the keys. 'I never go anywhere without them.'

'Someone could have taken Williams's keys, I suppose,' Derrin said.

'Well, he used them when I was with him. The parlour is locked when not in use, so he locked it up after we inspected it.' Mrs Felman then explained that she had some local girls from the village that came in a few days a week to clean. 'Some of these girls try to get away with not cleaning properly. Mr Williams helps me keep an eye on that.'

'I see,' said Derrin.

Mrs Felman was flustered, and she fidgeted with her key chain.

'I'll get you some tea,' Mel said, reaching for the bell cord by the fire. 'Then you can talk to the inspector again.'

Mel told the housekeeper to sit down, and when Nancy answered the call, ordered a fresh pot of tea.

'We'll have to rely on your memory,' Derrin said to Mrs Felman when Nancy left. 'Do you remember any trips Lord Greenway took in December?'

'Trips?' Mrs Felman said.

'Times away from the estate?'

'He went to London at some point. I don't remember the dates now, though.'

'Did he travel more than once that month?' Derrin asked.

Mrs Felman shook her head and said she didn't know. Mel wasn't sure if this was because the housekeeper really couldn't remember, or whether she was scared to say the wrong thing. All she could tell was that Mrs Felman was really shaken by what had happened. Not least because of the invasion of her personal space.

She did confirm that there was 'at least one absence in December' that she remembered, and by the time Nancy returned with the tea tray and a few slices of cake, Mrs Felman was looking through the diary with Derrin, confirming what she knew of any of the times Jonathan was marked as away.

'As all entries are in your handwriting,' he said, 'can't you remember anything else?'

'It is six months ago,' said the housekeeper. 'But I do remember him coming back from visiting Lady Melinda and telling us she was coming to live here. We were all quite excited about meeting her.'

'When was that?' Derrin asked. 'The first or second trip to London?'

'Definitely the second time he went away,' Mrs Felman said.

She flushed to the roots of her hair when she realised she'd been tricked.

'So, you do remember another trip away?'

'No, I... I'm not sure. He did go away before that, but I don't remember when,' Mrs Felman dithered.

'Did you tear the pages out of the diary?' Derrin asked, his voice low and calm but no less intimidating.

'No! I swear I didn't!' Mrs Felman said. 'I'm as shocked as anyone. And my office – it looks like it has been looted.'

Mel put a hand on Mrs Felman's shoulder, and the woman began to cry.

'It's okay, Mrs Felman,' Mel said, looking at Derrin. 'I think that's enough now.'

'You can go,' Derrin said.

Wiping her eyes, Mrs Felman hurried away. As she closed the door behind her, Derrin gave a huge sigh and rubbed his hand over his forehead.

'Sorry. I hate intimidating women,' he said.

'I know,' said Mel. Being a bully really wasn't who he was, but he'd forgotten himself in the moment of trying to get to the truth.

'Have you any thoughts?' Derrin said.

'She was really shaken up that someone had been in her office and rooms. I don't think she ripped those pages out. Plus, as much as she was Williams's alibi, all we have to do is talk to him and I'm sure he'll confirm what she's said. Daisy saw someone, though, I'm sure of it, and Williams would have no reason to sneak out of the house via a window.'

'There's something going on here,' Derrin said. 'And one of them knows what it is. Someone covered for Lord Greenway today. Without that diary entry, we don't know his whereabouts. I'm going to have to take him into the station for questioning on a more formal level,' Derrin said.

'You mean, you're arresting him?' Mel said.

'No. I won't make it that official, not unless I get a confession… He was seen with our Jane Doe—'

'Or someone who looked like her…' Mel interrupted. 'We don't know for sure that it was her. Witnesses can be wrong. They can also lie.'

'Indeed.'

'Perhaps Laura can clear this up?' Mel suggested.

'Well, let's bring her in and have a talk to her, by all means,' Derrin said.

'This is preposterous!' Laura said when Derrin told her Jonathan had been seen in London with someone else. 'The only time he went there in December was with me. And we went to speak to Melinda. He never went before or after that trip.'

Mel could have predicted that Laura would give Jonathan an alibi, but despite Derrin grilling her, she stuck with her story. Laura was far more certain of dates and times than Mrs Felman had been, and Derrin couldn't trip her up, no matter how hard he tried. She spoke with utter conviction about Jonathan's whereabouts, making Mel think that she was either smarter than she had given her credit for, or she believed what she was saying.

Eventually, Derrin let Laura go and they were alone in the drawing room again.

Mel's head was hurting a little and the strain of the day was starting to tell on them both, but there were still some people left to interview.

'Who's next?' Derrin asked after they'd had words with Mr Williams – as expected, he'd confirmed everything Mrs Felman had said.

'Henry, the chauffeur,' Mel said.

'Ah. He would know if he'd driven His Lordship to the train station, wouldn't he?'

Mel nodded. 'He should.'

Henry was sent for and soon came in. Mel took her seat by the window to observe the interview again. But like Laura, Henry insisted there was only one trip to the train station in December.

'I'm still taking him in for questioning,' Derrin explained to Mel when Henry had gone. 'He might trip up if he is out of his comfort zone, and Mrs Felman did say two trips, even when she was trying not to. That gives me at least one person to corroborate that he wasn't on the estate at the time my witness says they saw him.'

'She was flustered. And Henry was very certain,' Mel said.

'Laura may have primed him,' Derrin said. 'I should have banished her to the study as well.'

That would mean Laura was more duplicitous than Mel knew her to be. In fact, Laura was stubbornly forthright in her opinions and Mel had always thought her an open book. Could she really be so clever?

'Without knowing more about this person who has come forward with this statement, I can't say more. But I'd need more to go on to prove Laura was lying,' Mel said. 'Derrin, please don't take Jonathan in. I'm sure he's not guilty.'

Derrin grew quiet, then he said, 'My instinct tells me that Lord Greenway is hiding something. But I trust your judgement and I value your opinion. Therefore, I am going to leave things as they are here for now. I will continue with my other avenues of enquiry nonetheless.'

'Thank you,' said Mel, feeling relieved. 'I really appreciate you doing this.'

'Now, I've involved you way too much in this business... leave any further investigation to me.'

Despite everything they had heard and discussed that day, Mel had been helping so much because she had hoped he would rule Jonathan out completely. Her loyalty was torn. Perhaps Laura's constant comments about the family honour were finally sticking, because the scandal of Jonathan being taken in for questioning would be bad for the family's reputation. Mel wanted to avoid that at all costs, and she wished she hadn't told Derrin anything about the conversation she'd overheard until she'd discovered more. She was sure it had played a part in Derrin's certainty that Jonathan was hiding something. Mel promised herself that she wouldn't overshare with Derrin again. Regardless of his wishes to keep her out of it, she was also going to do her own investigation. Something wasn't right at Avonby, and that meant she had to be involved, no matter where her enquiries led. It was important.

*Why did I tell him so much?* she wondered. But then her mind went to the many times they'd shared physical and emotional intimacy. They had a bond. Even now, when they hadn't been together for a couple of years. There was no getting away from that. And – she still trusted him.

Mel turned away and looked out over the gardens, because she didn't want Derrin to see the slight flush that was colouring her cheeks, in some part because of the memory of their lovemaking. He'd been her only lover, and she'd enjoyed their contact. Feeling alive in a time of disaffection. Sometimes, when she thought about it, she was a little ashamed at how eager she had been to be intimate with Derrin. She had needed that connection.

'You must be tired.'

Mel heard him approaching, and turned. She had been attracted to him from the day they met, and even now the allure was there. She fought with herself now because Derrin had shown little interest in resuming their relationship since he'd reappeared in her life.

'A little,' she said.

'I think we'll call an end to today,' Derrin said.

As he was so much taller than her, Mel had to tilt her head to look at him. Mel saw Derrin's eyes softening as he gazed at her. The atmosphere grew tense and something passed between them. Mel was sure he would kiss her, but she made no move to invite it, holding back for fear of losing herself in something that had once been dangerously close to obsession.

Derrin stepped back, pushing his hands into his pockets, and Mel recalled how every time they had been intimate it had been she who had made the first move.

'I'd better let Lord Greenway out of his study,' Derrin said.

Mel experienced a wave of disappointment as Derrin walked to the drawing-room door. As the physical distance between them widened she felt the tug of an emotional withdrawal on Derrin's part. He had never been that easy to read, which had been part of the mystique for her in the past, but now Mel wished she knew what he was thinking. She didn't want to be the one to put herself out there again. She didn't want to be vulnerable, only to be left behind when Derrin moved on to his next job, or next investigation.

She stared at the open door as Derrin disappeared down the corridor, and she used these moments to pull herself together. It was an effort not to call after him.

*What is wrong with me?* she thought.

'At last!' Jonathan said. 'Really, Inspector, I am not happy at all at spending the entire day virtually locked up in my study! And have you learnt anything at all?'

Derrin's voice was quieter than Jonathan's, and Mel couldn't hear his response. So, she walked to the door and looked out into the hallway. Seeing Derrin getting his hat and coat from Williams, with

Constable Jennings by his side, she grasped he was going to leave without even saying goodbye to her. The thought stung more than it should have, for 'goodbye' had such finality and she was sure she would be seeing more of Derrin until the case was solved.

Seeing her in the hallway, Derrin gave Mel a quick nod and, as Williams opened the door for him, left with Constable Jennings in tow. Only then did she make her way down the corridor to the study to talk to Jonathan.

# 14

'You better come in here and talk to me, Mel,' said Jonathan.

In the study, Jonathan offered her the chair opposite his desk as he sat down behind it. He wasn't his usual self; more guarded and shut down. Mel caught a glimpse of the army officer he would have been before they met. To distract herself, she glanced around the room. It was somewhat untidy, with stacks of books left on the table beside the fireplace where two armchairs were placed opposite each other. Here, Mel knew, Jonathan would sit and smoke, drinking his cognac and gazing up at the painting above the fire that he was so fond of. Mel's eyes ran over the picture: a ship in a storm at sea, by an artist called J M W Turner.

'What is Bradley's game?' Jonathan asked.

Mel looked back at him, bringing all her focus to her cousin.

'He's trying to follow up on any leads he gets. That's all.'

'He held me captive in my own home,' Jonathan said. 'You know that?'

'I'm sorry,' said Mel.

'I might have to complain to his superiors,' Jonathan said.

'If it's any help, I persuaded him not to take you down to the station for further questioning,' Mel said. 'He thinks you're hiding something.'

'You do have some sway over him, then?' Jonathan said.

'I wouldn't say that. But Derrin is very reasonable and if things are put to him calmly…'

She paused as she saw Jonathan's curious expression.

'What was your relationship with him in the army?' he asked.

'I can't say. I signed the Official Secrets Act,' she said, shutting down the Derrin conversation, which she wasn't about to get into. What had passed between them was their business and no one else's. Plus, it was true that she couldn't talk about most of what they had done together.

Jonathan's eyes widened at this piece of information and he changed the subject.

'Williams told me about the diary,' Jonathan said. 'I really didn't go anywhere else in December but to see you.'

Mel studied him. There appeared to be no guile or lie as he sat, calm and still, at his desk. He looked as if he was considering something, as though it were important.

'Someone ripped out those diary pages,' Mel said. 'Have you any idea who would do that, or why?'

Jonathan shook his head. 'The whole thing feels like a nightmare. There we were, sitting having lemonade, reflecting on the garden, and then a corpse is found. This has caused the household so much trouble. I feel cursed.'

*What an odd choice of word*, Mel thought.

'The body had been put there for a reason,' Mel pointed out. 'It wasn't a random act. It was deliberate. Avonby was intentionally put in the middle of something. A person or persons is behind this, not anything as abstract as a curse.'

She was tired and didn't want to talk any more, but Jonathan wasn't ready to let her go just yet.

'I know. It was a silly thing to say. But you see, ever since I inherited Avonby, I have felt like it has been a bad thing. It feels like this place shouldn't belong to me.'

Mel understood the guilt of surviving more than most, and she was sympathetic to Jonathan's emotions. So many Greenways had lost their lives during the war, and now Jonathan, so far down on the pecking order before it began, was the man on top, whether he wanted to be or not.

'In law it does, Jonathan,' Mel said. 'But I guess you weren't prepared for it.'

'Indeed,' Jonathan said. 'None of us were.'

A silence fell between them as they both thought of what they had lost, and perhaps gained. The responsibility of an estate like Avonby was a lot and for some that might be a burden. Mel, on the other hand, knew that she would have taken on such a task, which in some way, on Jonathan's behalf, she had. Though she had no access to the remaining wealth, of course, and no say about how it was spent unless it was within the budget Jonathan allowed her for maintenance.

'So... what has Bradley told you?' Jonathan asked, bringing the conversation full circle.

'Just what he told you,' Mel said.

'But you don't believe I could be unfaithful to Laura?'

'What does it matter what I believe?' Mel said. She was feeling agitated and so bone weary that her body ached.

'You're my cousin and I value your opinion. I care what you think.'

'Your story is being corroborated by Henry and Laura, and in the time I've known you, I haven't seen anything to suggest you would be disloyal. But I didn't know you six months ago. So, I'm still working everything out...' Mel said.

Jonathan's face flushed. 'But we are family! You should believe me! Blood is thicker than water. You need to remember where your loyalties lie!'

Jonathan had never once made such a comment to her, and now she wondered if this was a subtle reminder of her position at Avonby, which relied very much on his good graces.

'You asked for my honest opinion and I gave it. Please understand, I *am* on your side. But if there is something I should know, it would help if you told me now,' she said, showing no sign of the leap of fear his words had created.

Jonathan put his hand to his forehead and ran his soft, uncallused fingers across his brow. Even before his ascension to lord, he hadn't done a manual day's work in his life, and Mel didn't really respect that about him. Despite his comments about not having expected to inherit Avonby, he had still been privileged. More so, perhaps, than

Mel had been, and she recognised that pre-war she'd had a very good life with little worry.

'It's been a trying day,' Jonathan said. 'I think dinner and bed for all concerned.'

'If you'll excuse me, I might eat in my room tonight.'

Jonathan nodded, and Mel took this as permission to leave and be on her own at last. It didn't matter that he had given in easily to her request – as though he too needed to be alone, or would be glad not to see her any more that day. They all had to consider their position in this series of events, and no one would be exempt from scrutiny. Mel understood the strain that could cause.

Outside the study Mel took in a deep breath and let it out, releasing all the tension from her shoulders and limbs. Despite everything, she was sympathetic to Jonathan, who was as weary as she was with the whole process, but she was also upset and shaken by the possibility of his veiled threat. Maybe he hadn't meant what he said. He was upset himself, after all, and he'd wanted her to say she believed him. But blind belief, after all she'd seen and heard, wasn't something Mel could do.

Going back through the main hallway, Mel paused to look at the pictures of her ancestors. Seeing the portraits of the Greenways grounded her sometimes when she most needed it, for often she had insecurities that overwhelmed her. Looking at Anthony Greenway, the previous owner of Avonby, she was reminded again of how her father and Valentine should have also been up there.

*I belong here. Every bit as much as he does*, she thought.

But what was done couldn't be undone, the dead could not come back, and the codicil in the family will said she had no rights other than those given by the family in charge of the estate and fortunes. All of which were not a patch on what they once were and, justifiable or not, Jonathan could withdraw his support of her at any time. A matter that would no doubt please Laura. Mel would have to be careful in the future.

She heard someone traversing the landing above her and cast her eyes upstairs to see who was there, only to see the elongated shadow of the person. It was impossible to tell whether they were male or female. Mel wondered if it was Laura, but couldn't understand why she would be on that side of the house, as the wing to her bedroom was in the west and this was the east side.

Mel focused her attention on the movements of the person upstairs, aware now that the ever-so-silent tread had receded and was heading towards the servant's staircase that led all the way down to the back corridor, and the servants' quarters beyond the kitchen's. It was a staircase that Mel never used, and so she surmised that it might have been Mrs Felman doing her final rounds.

Mel left the portraits and made her way back to the servants' staircase that led up from the kitchen, and came out near the dining room with a plan to go down and ask for food in her room that night. Two whispering voices caught her off guard and stopped her in her tracks. The owners of the voices, not realising that the stairwell made a natural amplifier, continued to talk even as Mel approached.

There was a female giggle. An exchange of kisses that smacked loudly up the stairs, even as Mel suspected they probably thought themselves quiet. She smiled at the sweetness of it. Two of their staff had a relationship. She wondered who they were.

Another giggle floated upstairs, and Mel gave a sharp cough to alert them of her presence. Silence fell below, followed by the sound of feet scurrying away. She could have remained quiet and caught the lovebirds, but Mel didn't want to know who they were and believed they were entitled to their privacy. She hadn't observed anything between the young girls and footmen, but her suspicion was that it was either Daisy or Nancy, possibly with Toby since they all worked so closely together.

She waited a few more seconds before descending the stairs to give the couple time to be somewhere else, and then she walked down, making her tread heavy to alert anyone that might be there. The lights were off on the stairs and Mel, who often walked around the house in the dark, only noticed when she was halfway down and far from the light switch. The stairwell was in darkness ahead, she could see nothing. She paused for a second to steady herself and grab the handrail. As her foot reached down to find the next step, the front of her shoe caught on something. Mel almost went down and had she not been holding the railing she would have fallen. Not sure what was in front of her, she sat down on the step, feeling around in the dark. There was something across the stairs, right on that middle and darkest step.

Mel stood up and went back upstairs. At the top she turned on the light and looked down. She now saw a piece of wire, taut and held in place by a nail hammered into the wood on either side of the step.

'What on earth…?'

Mel thought of the many times she had used this very staircase in the dark. She had never seen anything like this before: it was a trap. But who was it for? Her or someone else?

At that moment Toby turned into the passage at the bottom and began to walk up the stairs with a tray in his hands.

'Stop!' shouted Mel.

A few of the other servants came running as they heard her, and they stood looking up at Toby, almost at the middle step, and Mel making her way back down the stairs.

'Blimey, what's going on?' Williams said from the top of the stairs.

'Mr Williams. I think we need to call the police again.'

'And say what, Lady Melinda?' asked Williams, baffled because he couldn't see the wire from where he was standing.

'I guess it's an attempted murder,' said Mel. 'Or at the very least intended injury?'

'Of you, Your Ladyship?' said Williams, his voice pitching higher than usual in shock.

Mel looked down at the wire.

'I don't know,' she said.

Mel and Jonathan were in the dining room, picking at the food on their dinner plates with very little appetite and no conversation, when the police car arrived bringing two constables in response to the call. Laura had retired, declaring she had a headache on hearing about the latest event.

Despite her wish to retire early too, Mel was forced to remain up to wait for the police, as she had found the tripwire. Feeling even more paranoid, she wondered if she had been the target, because she couldn't see who else would be. But that, perhaps, was going to be another line of questioning for the serving staff who used that staircase the most. The biggest question on her mind was: who had put it there, and how had they done it without being seen or heard? After all, hammering nails into wood was not a quiet business.

When Williams brought the constables into the dining room, Mel left her food and led them to the staircase, showing them the trap.

The constables took her statement, but Mel felt they weren't really equipped to investigate something like this.

'This *is* a possible murder attempt,' Mel said.

'Now, now, Miss,' one of the constables said. 'No one was hurt, so let's not get hysterical.'

Frustrated at being suspected of hysteria just because she was female, Mel became angry.

'I'm not "Miss", I'm Lady Melinda Greenway and you will show me some respect. I am not, and never have been, of a hysterical nature. You would do well to remember that when you deal with me.'

Williams, who was waiting at the top of the stairs, suppressed a chuckle. The constables were both inept and everyone knew it.

'I want Inspector Bradley back here tomorrow morning,' Mel said. 'This may be related to the...' She stopped short of saying 'thorn', '... body I found in the garden.'

'You think someone was trying to kill you, Miss... I mean, Your Ladyship?' said the constable, now taking her seriously. 'But this is the servants' staircase.'

'I use this staircase all the time,' said Mel. 'Everyone at Avonby knows that. But no, I'm not saying the target was me. I really don't know who it was intended for. Unless the perpetrator didn't care who was hurt. Now, go. And make sure to ask Inspector Bradley to come back tomorrow.'

The constables were shown the door by Williams and the staircase was shut off again.

'No one is to use it until Inspector Bradley sees it – though I'm certain he's very tired of being here by now,' Mel said to Williams. 'Make sure that all upstairs and downstairs staff are aware of the hazard.'

'Yes, Your Ladyship,' Williams said, with a gleam of respect in his eye, following his original mirth.

'One other thing. Do you know who might have been using the back stairs from the landing down to the staff quarters?' Mel asked. 'I thought maybe Mrs Felman, but she said it wasn't her.'

'No, I can't imagine who might be up there at that time. Everyone was having dinner in the kitchen as far as I know.'

Mel went to bed soon after, but the paranoia followed. She made a mental list of who might have been the intended victim of the tripwire. Her involvement in the interviews might well have made her a mark but there were other possibilities. Maybe it was aimed at Mrs Felman, who was the only witness to what might have been in the estate diary. Henry was also a possibility, though she wasn't sure how much the chauffeur used those stairs, if ever, as he often went into the kitchen via the back door. She ruled out Mrs Weston as the cook rarely came upstairs. But Daisy, Nancy, Toby and Williams were frequent users too. Thinking of it this way, Mel found herself further down on her list, as she didn't use the stairs half as much as anyone else, despite her immediate reaction that someone had targeted her for prying.

Her mind cast back to who might have been hiding on the stairs before she'd come down. She'd taken it as a lovers' meeting, but what if it wasn't? What if it was two people involved and not one? Perhaps covering their tracks with a pretend romance that everyone downstairs would know about and ignore, giving them the opportunity to put in the wire. Otherwise, the question of how this had happened without the culprit being seen still hung in the air. She now regretted letting them know she was present, and half wished she had sneaked down and caught them in the act. But then, she may well have caught her foot in the waiting trap. Things panned out in a certain way for a reason, and Mel couldn't regret not falling down the stairs and the possible injury that would have ensued.

It had been a long day, but Mel still remembered the lack of observation from Mrs Weston and Toby earlier, even though Daisy had spotted someone they suspected of raiding Mrs Felman's office. But why hadn't everyone been more alert after that had happened? They should have been paying attention, but the truth was most people didn't see things as they happened around them. She would have to give them all a talking-to tomorrow, for sure, because from now on, Avonby's usually lax security was going to have to be upped and Mel would see to it that it was.

Her thoughts stumbled. She was thinking of this as though it was some intruder from outside, when the most likely perpetrator was someone among them. The thought made Mel feel uneasy. They would be harder to catch as no one would want to believe it of their own.

Her mind ran over the occupants of the estate. She'd lived at Avonby for months and she couldn't imagine any one of the servants, who she'd trusted so much, being a murderer and then attempting to silence her or someone else they thought knew too much. The idea was unthinkable.

She cast her mind over the occupants of the estate again, just as she had on the night they discovered the body. The pieces on her mental chessboard were nowhere near in place to start this game, but Jonathan had entered the board, with at least some suspicion cast his way. Even so, there was no way he could have put the tripwire on the stairs: he'd been locked up all day in his study. Besides, he above everyone else knew that Mel didn't know anything much, and whatever anyone else knew wasn't worth killing them for. Even Mrs Felman was not a credible witness when put against Jonathan, Laura and Henry – that is, if Derrin would even be able to persuade the woman to speak out on what he thought she knew, which in the scheme of things was very little anyway.

Mel turned over in the bed, tucking her hand under the pillow.

'Ouch!' Something sharp was in the bed and she'd pricked her finger on the edge of it.

Mel switched on the bedside lamp. Lifting the pillow, she found a men's straight razor with an onyx handle lying under her pillow. Mel lifted the pillow away and picked the object up with the corner of her sheet. She saw the initials J G and the Greenway crest engraved on the handle. Was this Jonathan's? How had it got into her room, and who had put it there? Not only that, what did it mean?

She got up and placed the razor on her dressing table, careful not to touch the handle as she knew it could be useful if there were fingerprints on it. Then, pouring water into her washbowl from a porcelain jug, she washed the cut on her finger, wrapping a face cloth around it and holding it tight to stop it bleeding. It wasn't a deep wound, more a small scratch, but it stung. At least the blade had been clean, or at least she hoped it was.

When the bleeding stopped, Mel checked and locked her door before getting back to bed. Then, tired at last, she fell asleep, but the last thing that floated through her mind was the question of why the felon was showing their hand so blatantly. Did the razor mean she was the intended target all along, or was it a warning to stay out of the investigation? And, was it placed there by the mystery person she'd heard, and whose shadow she had seen briefly on the landing? A person that none of the servants were owning up to being…

After receiving a phone call from the police station the next morning, Mel learnt that Derrin couldn't call in until late afternoon. Mel had planned to have a normal morning before he arrived, but she was aware of the unrest on the estate and didn't want to get into any conversations before she had spoken to Derrin again and told him what had happened. She'd wrapped the razor in one of her towels, and buried it in the bottom of her belongings chest, locking both chest and her bedroom door before leaving that morning. All in all, she hoped the person who had left it for her wouldn't attempt to remove it. The possibility of this happening made her change her mind. She decided to take it to the police station instead, and leave it there. Going back to her room, she removed the wrapped razor and stowed it in a large handbag that she planned to take with her.

She hadn't been off the estate for so long. It was almost easy to believe that the world only existed here, and so she made an excuse that she was going out to do some personal shopping.

'Shall I get Henry to drive you, Lady Melinda?' Williams asked.

'Oh no, I think I'll take my motorbike today. It needs a run, and I'm sure His Lordship will need the car at some point.'

Before starting the bike, Mel had given it a once-over, in no small part due to some residual paranoia and because she hadn't ridden it for a while. Finding all well, she put on her crash helmet and goggles and drove off the estate.

The country lanes were quiet as Mel drove, and she was enjoying the ride so much that she decided to go farther than the local village police station and instead into York. Derrin was based at the station there, and perhaps it was better to see him and talk to him first anyway, before he came out to the house. As she reached the town, the roads got busier and she weaved in and out of ever-thickening traffic. The streets were bustling with pre-war normality as Mel parked her bike near the cathedral.

She got off the bike, removed her helmet, and put it in the box she had on the back for this purpose. Then she put the bag with the razor in it over her arm and headed off to find the police station, as she hadn't been there before.

A woman carrying a wicker basket who was heading towards the market pointed the way to the constabulary building, which was only a few streets away. This turned out to be a Gothic structure, not dissimilar to a small church with three rows of steps going up to an impressive oak double door that was studded with iron. One door was open and led into the main reception, and Mel went in and approached the desk, where a constable sat looking at a logbook as though it was the most interesting reading.

'I'm here to see Inspector Bradley,' Mel said.

'Who shall I say is here?' the constable said without looking up, and Mel found it rude and dismissive. Remembering her experience with the constable the night before, she knew what to do.

'Lady Melinda Greenway,' she said.

The constable looked up now and took in Mel's appearance. She was dressed appropriately for her motorbike, in slacks and a fitted jacket, but she didn't look much like a 'lady'.

'Ah! I've heard about you,' the constable said. 'Please take a seat, Lady Greenway, he's currently in a meeting with the Brigadier.'

'The Brigadier?' Mel said.

'Yes. Brigadier John Cheney. He's our new chief constable. Just arrived today and taking over from our previous one,' the constable said, and then in a whisper, as though sharing the biggest secret in the force, he added, 'we've never had a brigadier before.'

Understanding now why he had been so busy that day and couldn't come to Avonby first thing, Mel sat down on the bench near the door to wait for Derrin.

*He probably has his hands full*, Mel thought. *Maybe I should leave it today.*

Just as she was contemplating leaving, Derrin came out through a door beside the constable's desk.

'Lady Melinda, can you follow me?' he said.

Derrin took her through the same door he'd come out of, down a short corridor and into a small office at the back of the station.

'I've just seen your messages from last night and this morning. Tell me what's happened,' he said as soon as he closed the door.

'I've come at a bad time,' she said.

'New chief or not, policing comes first,' Derrin said.

She told him about the wire and the razor.

'What I don't understand is why put the razor under my pillow? I took it as a warning,' Mel said.

'It looks like that. But you were careful not to touch it, after discovery?'

'Yes. I have it with me. But Derrin, I think you'll only find Jonathan's fingerprints on it if you check. It was most likely his razor. I don't think it was him that put it there, though. He's not stupid, why implicate himself? Plus, I believe that whoever did this was upstairs when I was in the hallway, and Jonathan was in his study at that time. I know this because I had just left him.'

She took the towel and razor out of her bag and handed them to him.

'You did right to come here today to talk to me,' Derrin said. 'I think our communications should be away from Avonby for now. By being with me so much yesterday, you might have made yourself a target. I had feared that.'

'Maybe it's time to dust off my pistol,' Mel said.

Derrin was quiet for a moment, lost in thought.

'I hadn't thought you would still have that. Do you remember when I gave you that?' he said.

'How could I forget?'

Someone had been trying to kill them both that day.

# 15

*London, 1942*

As Derrin's private driver in the evenings, Mel had immersed herself in the darkness of London's war-torn underworld. Sometimes Derrin was working undercover, skulking in the seediest places, though he always made her wait for him, away from the danger, and she rarely knew what he was doing. For a few weeks, though, he had been spending time in an underground jazz club.

'Most of the intelligence leaks happened in these places,' he had told her, where local constabulary, politicians and aristocracy merged to break the rules and let their hair down.

With booze, loud music and sometimes drug abuse, they weren't always careful about what they let slip or who they mixed with. Although the clubs were breaking curfew rules, the army and the police had mostly ignored their operations because the powers-that-be told them to. London was on edge all the time, and any chance to feel something other than fear was a welcome break from the devastation in their daily lives.

The club they attended that night was just outside London, in Surbiton, and took place in a huge house, abandoned by country house owners who'd left until the troubles were over. Amidst other ruins the deserted house was still standing and had been taken over by a shiftless squatter, who had turned the basement into a club. Derrin had got wind of the location because of the careless gossip of a police chief who frequented the place with his mistress.

For once, Derrin hadn't been willing to leave Mel outside in the car in the middle of what was effectively a bombsite, and he had warned her to dress for the evening as he wanted her to come inside with him where he thought she would be safer. Mel had borrowed a dress from one of the girls at the barracks who frequently went out dancing and had plenty to wear. Mel's colleagues all thought that she and Derrin were an item, which gave her frequent excuses to be off base at night.

Mel had made an effort that day, and when she took off her coat inside the club, Derrin had bitten back a whistle. Up until then, he'd seen Mel as a young apprentice and colleague. Never just as a female. An assumption he now realised was foolish, considering he was so observant: Mel in a dress or in uniform was a very attractive woman. Once he'd looked at her this way, it was difficult not to see her natural beauty. He tried to be professional as he led her into the club and took her to a seat in the corner of the room.

'This is a great place to observe who is here,' he told her. Not adding that Mel could wait in relative safety for him if he had to go and talk to anyone.

Derrin paid the waiter to bring them water in cocktail glasses with olives – a rare commodity – so that it looked as though they were drinking bootlegged hooch like everyone else.

'Look like you're having a good time,' he said. 'Sip it like it's alcohol and never leave your glass unattended.'

Adrenaline rushed through Mel with the new adventure, and she looked around, excited at seeing so many dressed-up men and women, drinking, having fun, being wild at times. In between there was a band playing bebop with a mixture of older musicians, some white, some black, playing piano, saxophone and drums together. A female singer came out sometimes to change the mood. The woman sang some George Gershwin in a deep, rich voice, or other songs that were a more mellow jazz, and the dancers would grow closer together and sometimes kiss.

It was almost a year since she had lost her family, but Mel wasn't thinking about that or her impending twentieth birthday in a few weeks' time, as she would rather forget that date for the rest of her life. Mel was glad of the darkness inside the basement club, which was only lit with small lamps on the cabaret-style round tables and a spotlight pointing at the small stage, highlighting the singer and musicians. Down there in the semi-darkness, Derrin couldn't see the small flush of pleasure that rushed into Mel's face. The place was sexy, decadent and probably dangerous, but it all added to the excitement and despite drinking only water dressed as booze, Mel was intoxicated by the atmosphere.

Derrin was relaxed as he sat beside Mel. He was used to the environment and too self-aware to be taken in by self-indulgence. He watched the dancers too, but not as Mel did: he was making mental notes of who was with whom. Affairs of the heart were taking place in the room, but equally other deals were happening, and whether they were for the good of the country or not, Derrin saw all.

Mel was unaware of what Derrin was thinking as she reached out and touched his hand when a different singer came out: a beautiful black girl in a gold lamé dress. She started to sing with a lighter voice than the other singer and Mel was blown away by how she looked and sang.

Derrin folded her hand in his as he watched the stage, but he resisted looking at Mel, whose warm touch had sent an unexpected shiver up his spine. He watched her enthusiasm through the corner of his eye and it took his attention away from the room, as his focus was on her, not on what he was supposed to be doing.

Mel became aware that she was holding Derrin's hand and began to feel awkward, knowing she had been the one who reached out, but to pull away might send the wrong message to anyone observing them as they tried to fit in with the ongoing party atmosphere. Plus, she was enjoying how he held her fingers.

She had thought she would struggle to blend in, but being there was so much easier than it should be, and now Mel glanced at Derrin and found his eyes turned on her.

The music washed over them, and the voice of the slight girl on the stage drowned out the noise of the world which was carrying on around them regardless. Mel did not think of the potential air raids that might start up anytime, emptying the club as surely as they did any remaining houses. She was in the moment and only human, and her eyes fell on Derrin's lips as he leaned closer. She thought he was going to whisper some instruction to her, but instead their lips met.

'I'm sorry!' he said, pulling back after a few seconds. 'I shouldn't have done that!'

Mel only looked at him, eyes shining in the lamplight. Her only regret: the kiss was over quicker than she wanted.

Derrin gathered himself.

'We should leave,' he said. 'The person I wanted to see isn't here, and I doubt anything interesting will happen now.'

Derrin's words stung and Mel, having only kissed one boy when she was 15, began to wonder if it was her: perhaps she was bad at kissing and that was the reason he had pulled away so soon.

Derrin stood, and still holding her hand, pulled her to her feet. Anyone observing them would think they were two lovers, leaving to be alone.

They went back upstairs, and Derrin hurried her to the cloakroom, which was little more than a small closet on the ground floor and was unattended. As he helped her on with her coat, he saw someone come in who made him concerned because he grabbed Mel, pushed her back into the cloakroom and pulled the door shut behind them.

'Take this,' Derrin said, his voice barely a whisper. 'This is the safety. Remove it first and if anyone comes in here, shoot them point blank in the face. Don't wait to ask questions.'

'What's going on?' Mel said as he pushed the pistol into her hand.

'Something is going to go down and you can't be in the middle of it. Now hide!'

Mel slipped in between a rack of fine furs and fox stoles. The rack smelt musty, as though these items had been in the closet for years; maybe they had once belonged to the previous owner of the house and not to any of the occupants of the club. Her heart was pounding as she heard Derrin leave the room. A few seconds later she heard gunshots and screams. There was a stampede of feet as the club emptied. Mel shrank back as far as she could into the furs, whose bulk muffled some of the sound, but she was aware of chaos. It sounded like a police raid.

And then the door of the closet opened. Remembering what Derrin had said, Mel pulled back the safety and lifted the pistol upwards toward her chest, ready to aim and fire.

'Mel?' a voice said. 'Come on, I need to get you out of here.'

Mel peered through the furs, and seeing Derrin standing in the doorway, she came out. She was walking towards the door when she saw someone looming behind him. A familiar shape in a thick brown coat: a man she'd seen before. The man lifted his arm and Mel could see a pistol in his hand. She raised her arm, aimed the gun and fired.

The discharging of the weapon in such a small space left their ears ringing. Deafened and shocked, Derrin looked around. The bullet had flown past his ear, hitting his would-be attacker while narrowly avoiding him. He reacted in an instant, bending down to check the body. He found the man was wounded but not dead. He'd been hit in the shoulder, but the blast had knocked him off his feet and he'd hit his head as he went down, rendering him unconscious.

Derrin saw the gun he'd been holding, prised it from his fingers and stuffed it into his own belt.

Outside, chaos erupted as police sirens picked up in the distance. Derrin glanced back at Mel. The pistol she was holding was still smoking, but he knew then that she had just saved his life – again.

'Come on!' said Derrin, grabbing Mel's arm. 'We can't be involved in this.'

Outside, people were scattering to their various cars in panic. Mel and Derrin had parked farther away, down another street, but Derrin led Mel in the opposite direction, away from the fleeing cars and the incoming police.

'Where are we going?' asked Mel.

'We can't be caught; it will blow my cover.'

'What went on in there?' Mel asked.

'A gang war,' Derrin said. 'This way.'

Mel followed as Derrin appeared to know where he was going. They weaved in and out of the demolished streets until they came upon an area that had not been touched, and soon they were heading down full, undamaged suburban roads.

'We're here,' said Derrin, looking around to see if they were observed. Then he led her to a house at the end of a row of terraced houses and took out a key from his pocket. Unlocking the door, he stepped back to let Mel in first.

'You live here?' she asked.

'Yes.'

Closing the door behind him, Derrin threw a bolt across and drew a thick curtain over the door frame before switching on the hallway light.

After the dark outside, the sudden light hurt Mel's eyes, but she blinked a few times until she could see where she was. They were in a short hallway with a staircase on the left and three doors. Two right, and one at the end past the stairs. By the door was a small table with a black telephone on it.

'Come with me,' he said, taking her into the kitchen at the back of the house. Here he closed all the curtains again, then switched on a lamp that was on a small table near the door.

'I think we need a proper drink after that,' Derrin said. He opened a cupboard and retrieved a bottle of cognac and two glasses. He poured two generous measures, handing one of the glasses to her.

Mel took a careful sip, expecting the booze to catch in her throat, but it was smooth and slipped down easily, sending a warm rush down her throat to explode in her stomach. It settled the queasiness that had lurked there since she had shot the man in the club.

Her ears were still ringing but her hearing was back.

'That man I shot. I recognised him. He was the one with the limp,' she said, replaying the moment, seeing the shock on his face as the bullet hit him in the shoulder, throwing him back. Part of her was concerned about how close she had come to almost shooting Derrin.

'How could you? I thought you didn't see his face that night,' Derrin said.

'His coat. His shape and size. Plus, as he moved, one shoulder dipped slightly to accommodate that shorter leg.'

'You're an incredible girl,' Derrin said. 'And quick-thinking. You saved my life back there.'

'You're welcome.'

'I'll have to go and ring this in,' Derrin said.

He left her with the cognac and went back down the hallway. Mel heard him dialling and then speaking very low into the phone.

She looked around the kitchen, curious about how Derrin lived. It was small but neat and tidy. There was a stove by the back door, a sink beneath the window, a few cupboards and a fridge, as well as the table and chairs in the centre. Mel sat down at the table and found herself drinking more of the cognac. It was going to her head, but she needed it to calm her jangling nerves. She had saved Derrin and it had been an impulsive reaction, but she might have killed the man. She'd been aiming to do just that, she'd had to, otherwise Derrin would be dead now, and probably herself too.

'Bowman's men are on the way to the club,' Derrin said when he came back. 'We'll have to stay put until morning, but the general will make it right for you to be absent at roll call.'

He picked up his cognac and downed it in one.

'I've only one bedroom – but you take the bed and I'll have the sofa down here,' Derrin said.

'I can't put you out of your bed…'

'I insist.'

# 16

*South Yorkshire, 1946*

MEL WAS LOST IN THE PAST, RELIVING every detail of that night as Derrin took the razor away to be fingerprinted.

Everything had changed when they'd gone back to Derrin's house, and sometimes she wondered if he had planned it that way, but then she remembered how startled he'd been when she kissed him in the club in the first place. For now, she recalled how it was her that pushed forward and not him that day, even though he had taken the responsibility for it as he had responded.

*London, 1942*

He had shown her around upstairs to the small bathroom first – the room next to his bedroom. There had been another room, a box room, barely big enough for a study table, let alone a bed, and then they had gone into his room.

The place was clean, and his officer's uniform – not worn that night as he had been in civvies – was hung up on the back of the door, pressed and clean and ready for the next day. But even so, the room smelt of him, and Mel had been close enough many times to know that faint, fresh smell of musk that was his personal scent.

The cognac had made her warm and slightly feverish as Derrin showed her where she could find a shirt to sleep in. The idea of sleeping in his clothes had done something to her insides and an excitement rippled through her. Of course, she had known about desire and sex – the girls in the barracks talked of nothing else when they were together in the common room – but Mel hadn't been open to trying what they did with just anyone. It wasn't done in a family like hers, and the idea of promiscuity seemed to defile their memory. You married first, then you found out what things were like. Even so, she'd taken in what they'd said and learnt a lot about what men and women did behind closed doors. Married and unmarried, it happened a lot according to the female recruits.

There had been a feeling of powerlessness that night, followed by a sense of urgency, that at any time they could die and Mel would never know what it felt like.

Gladys, her roommate, said it was pleasurable 'mostly', and sometimes Mel had heard the girl making little noises in the dark, followed by a few deep sighs. She had felt embarrassed, knowing there was something Gladys was doing that was giving her a kind of release, but Mel had never dared to ask what it was. Nor had she explored herself for fear of being heard. There was no real privacy in the barracks and ultimately Mel was a very private person.

The short kiss had changed things for her that day. Derrin turned to leave the room, and Mel caught his arm. They looked at each other. Mel had seen some vulnerability in Derrin's face, yet he was, she believed, a man of the world. She moved in, pressing her lips against his, and opened her mouth, pushing her tongue into his mouth as Gladys, or maybe Alice, had described.

This time Derrin didn't tug away. He pulled Mel closer; his tongue searched her mouth – it was a glorious sensation as the emotions swept over her and a warmth rushed into her loins. The kiss deepened until they were both breathless, and then his hand slipped up from her waist and cupped her breast, fingers running over her nipple. Mel had felt the ripple, like music made by the hands of a pianist over keys. In her head she heard the sensuous notes of the night's jazz music and the light, beautiful voice of the singer in gold.

She gasped against his lips as the tension inside bubbled up, and knew what Gladys meant about that 'feeling you had to follow', and how 'sometimes you couldn't help yourself'. Mel felt all that, as she slipped off the borrowed dress for fear of spoiling it, while Derrin removed his suit.

In their underwear, they stood by the bed in a moment of sanity, but as Mel felt Derrin withdrawing again she had stepped closer, running her hands under his vest and over his chest. Her small fingers brought tiny gasps from his lips as they ran over his nipples, and Mel learnt something then she hadn't known: a man could like that too.

The kissing had started again, only this time it was more intimate as Derrin pressed against her semi-naked body. She had felt him, hard against her stomach, but he bent his knees so that the part of him she wanted, but most feared, pressed against her panties, and rubbed ever so slightly between her legs, making her groan.

Her bra and panties had come off and then they lay down, naked on his bed for the first time.

'Mel,' he whispered. 'Are you sure?'

Mel's lips had kissed him quiet. She had to see this through, she had never changed her mind once she had decided to do something, and she had no reason to do so now.

Derrin rolled on top of her, parting her legs with his, but he didn't 'go in straight away' as some of the girls had described, which was what Mel expected. Resting on his elbows so as not to crush her, he kissed her, drawing small gasps as his cock rubbed ever so slightly against her, with a gentle circling motion until a sensation built inside Mel and she thought she would explode. She rocked against him, gasping and crying as she came, overcome with the pure pleasure of it. And yes, it was a kind of release as her whole body seemed to melt and relax. Only then did Derrin lift her knees and push her legs further apart, before he plunged into her.

Mel's body jerked as a sharp stab of pain accompanied the first thrust, but she was still in the throes of orgasm, and the pain disappeared as Derrin's thrusts continued. The sensation of joining was so intimate that Mel had given into the sexual release once more, getting into the rhythm of his lunges as she moved her hips to meet him. It all came naturally to her, as if she'd already known what to do all along.

Driven to the edge, Derrin suddenly pulled out, his orgasm spilling on the bedsheets.

'Oh god, Mel. I almost didn't pull out in time. It was so good!' he said, still gasping. 'Sorry!'

He rolled away from her, taking a minute to recover, then reached for the lamp beside the bed. He turned to look at her as their eyes adjusted, a relaxed smile on his lips, but the smile dropped as his eyes swept her body and he saw the traces of blood on her thighs.

'I thought you knew what we were doing?' he said. 'Mel… I'm…'

'I live in a barracks. Girls talk.'

'You should have told me,' he said.

'Would it have made any difference?' she said.

*South Yorkshire, 1946*

'It'll take a few weeks for our experts to compare the prints. We'll have to get everyone at Avonby first to rule them out, or, if we're lucky, to find our culprit,' Derrin said when he returned to his office.

'All right,' she said, standing. 'I'd better get back. There is work to be done today. We'll see you later?'

'Are you okay?' Derrin asked.

His words echoed back to Mel's thoughts during his absence, she was shaken by the sudden onslaught of memory.

*'Did I hurt you?' he had asked.*

*'No,' she said. She had stretched and held out her hand, pulling him back into the bed. 'That was lovely. We both need some sleep now.'*

*'Well, at least the problem of who gets the bed is a moot point now,' he said.*

*Mel had felt like the cat who got the proverbial cream as he turned her away from him, pulling her back against him as, spooning, they curled up together and went to sleep.*

*Mel had slept soundly that night – waking up the next morning feeling refreshed and happy. The troubles of the war were still there, but as Derrin made her some tea and chatted with her while they dressed, there was no awkwardness or guilt. It was all so natural, and it had changed how she viewed what was happening in England and in the rest of the world. She knew they would survive and a new burst of hope about the future accompanied that surety.*

'I'm fine,' Mel said, even as she missed those heady days and nights, so long ago now, when them being together was good and right, and no one was around to judge – and if they had, Mel wouldn't have cared.

'You just seemed preoccupied, and that's not like you, you're always in the moment. Look, I know this is worrying, but we will get to the bottom of it. Maybe our felon has made a mistake leaving the razor to terrorise you and there will be a print,' Derrin said.

Mel came back to the present, keeping her face straight. Being reminded of what it felt like to have a resurgence of optimism, Mel now experienced the feeling again.

'I hope so,' she said. 'You'll catch this killer, won't you? I have no doubt. Well… I'll see you at Avonby?'

'I'll be there soon.'

# 17

Mel parked the motorbike back in the garage and made her way to the rear door out of habit. She'd taken a drive around the estate when she got back. After checking out the perimeters, she'd stopped by the hayfield and chatted to some of the workers to see if they had seen anyone unfamiliar on the estate. Particularly Ned Soames, who was a friendly young man and a hard-working farm hand. The answer was invariably 'no' from all of them, and disappointed that she had no leads, Mel had headed back to the house.

In the kitchen, Mrs Weston was taking an unusual break, and was sitting in the nook with a cup of tea and a piece of her homemade lemon drizzle cake. Daisy was peeling potatoes for the evening meal. She stood up and curtsied when she saw Mel come in.

'Oh Miss... Lady Mel, that inspector arrived and Mr Williams said I was to tell you when you got back in,' Daisy said.

'Thank you,' Mel said. 'Did anyone give the inspector a drink and some of that cake?'

Mrs Weston leaned forward and looked around the nook corner at Mel. 'The way to a man's heart, eh?' she said and winked.

Mel couldn't help but smile at the cook's cheeky comment and returned the wink. Mrs Weston was observant when she wanted to be, which made Mel question how she'd missed someone coming past the kitchen in order to ransack Mrs Felman's office.

'I'll get to it,' said Daisy.

'No need. I'll take it. I wouldn't mind some myself,' Mel said.

Carrying the tray up the main staircase, Mel was careful where she put her feet, for fear of missing another tripwire. She reached the hallway in time to see Henry walking outside, the tripwire in his hands, along with a hook claw hammer.

'What are you doing? I said not to touch it,' Mel said.

'The inspector...' Henry said.

'It's okay. I've checked for fingerprints around the stair skirtings, there won't be any on the wire. I thought it best to oversee it being removed so normal use of the stairs could resume,' Derrin said from down the hallway.

'Thank you. I have tea and cake. Let's talk in the drawing room,' she said.

Derrin followed her, and after he had consumed some of Mrs Weston's cake and finished the tea, he took his leave of Mel – but not before he'd made arrangements for some of his officers to come to Avonby to finish fingerprinting everyone.

'I don't know what more I can do until our culprit shows his hand again,' Derrin said. 'But if you need me, I'll come.'

'Okay,' Mel said, but all she could think was that this meant she wouldn't see Derrin unless there were further problems, or they had anything new to move the case along.

'Don't forget to start carrying your pistol,' he said.

She watched him leave with a sense of bereavement. Since her burst of memory, cursed as she was with such a good one, she was unsettled and couldn't stop thinking about the past.

*Much good it will do me!* Mel thought.

As she walked away from the front door, Jonathan called to her to come into the study.

'He's gone then?' Jonathan said as she came in. He was sat in an easy chair by the window, holding a book.

'Yes.'

'Close the door. I wish to talk to you,' he said.

Mel did as he asked and then walked into the room and stood by the window, looking out at the gardens, which were all looking so beautiful now they were in full summer bloom.

'I'm listening,' Mel said.

'I want to come clean about something. And this is in no way an admission of guilt.'

Mel's attention refocused; she turned her head to look at Jonathan.

'I did go to London the first week in December and I did meet up with someone,' he said.

'Oh Jonathan! You didn't! Why did you lie about it?'

'Now, before you get ahead of yourself, I wasn't having an affair. I met a woman on behalf of someone else. A close friend she was involved with. She was short of money and I took it to her. I don't know what the money was for, or where she went after that. But I haven't seen her since.'

'It's obvious what the money was for! It was a payoff. I suppose this friend of yours was married? Who was he?'

'It doesn't matter. She wasn't the girl they found, I'm sure of it because my friend recently told me he'd seen her. They are in regular contact, he says.'

'So, what was *her* name at least?' Mel asked.

'I haven't the faintest idea. I just went to the room I was told to go to in that wretched hotel. I gave her the money and that was it. No pleasantries. No conversation, in fact.'

'You should have told the inspector the truth. Now, if he gets more proof you were there, it looks worse for you. What would Laura think of a story like this?' Mel said. 'Does she know?'

'I told her what I was doing before I went. She doesn't know who I did it for, though, because I was sworn to secrecy. Other than that, there are no secrets between us,' Jonathan said.

'That is a blessing at least. So, did she or Henry rip out the diary pages for you?' Mel said.

'Neither of them did. There were no entries in the estate diary for the first week in December and I knew that. So we didn't need to do such a thing. It was partly because I didn't tell Mrs Felman I'd be away. I just got Henry to drop me in town, then I got the early train and came back later that day. I told everyone I was meeting friends for lunch. Then I met Henry outside a restaurant after I called Avonby and asked for him to come and collect me.'

'Why would someone tear out a page that had no entry in it?'

'I really couldn't say,' Jonathan said. 'I thought it didn't make sense at the time, and I hadn't been concerned about being accused until that happened.'

'That's it! Someone did it to cast doubt on you,' Mel said.

'But who? And why?' Jonathan said.

'If we find that out, then we may find our killer.'

'Mel, can we keep this between us for now? I don't want the inspector to know about my friend. Promises of confidentiality were made… There's a code here and I can't break his confidence unless there is no other way to clear my name,' Jonathan said.

'All right. I won't say anything for now, but if we need to protect you, your friend will have to be named, and so will this girl, to back up what you say. Whatever is between them, it can't be as bad as being accused of murder.'

Mel was a lot happier when she left Jonathan's study with the possibility of him having some kind of alibi after all, but the happiness was short lived when the full implication of what was happening at Avonby dawned on her. Someone might well be trying to frame Jonathan, or at least cast a bad light on his character. But why? And could this person be the real murderer? She still wondered who it was that had seen him in London with his friend's secret girlfriend, and why they would come forward now to point the finger and not six months ago when the incident occurred.

*It must be linked somehow*, she thought. And, if it was linked, that would confirm her theory that the body had been left with the intention of it being found.

Mel went upstairs. In her room, she opened her trunk and retrieved the handgun. It was wrapped in a velvet cloth and stored in a shoe box. She unwrapped it now, laying the weapon down on her bed. Since Derrin had given her the weapon she'd learnt not only how to use it properly, but about the gun itself. It was an Enfield 2 and was a top break revolver that took .38 calibre Smith and Wesson rounds. The bullets were commonly used in other sidearms that were army edition and 'easy to obtain', Derrin had said. Mel had a box of twenty of them stored under her bed, as you never kept a gun with its bullets: it made it too easy for the weapon to be used for the wrong reasons.

Mel lifted the gun, looking down the sight, and reminded herself of the slight recoil that threw this one off to the right: hence why she hadn't shot Derrin's mobster in the face, even though she'd aimed there the first time she'd used it.

As she cleaned the gun before loading, her mind flicked back to the many times she'd practised opening and loading the weapon with Derrin.

'I wasn't issued this,' Derrin told her when she questioned him about why he didn't need to keep it in his possession. 'You might say it is a spare. It's not registered so no one knows about it. Therefore, while we're working together and things might get dangerous, it's best you keep it in your custody.'

After the war, when she was demobbed, Mel should have handed it in, but she'd felt a sentimental attachment to the sidearm, which, to all intents and purposes, was the only physical reminder of her and Derrin's relationship. She had thought one day she would return it to him, but that day never came.

After making sure the safety was on, she put the weapon in the pocket of her slacks. Usually she wore a leather belt, which holstered the gun in the small of her spine, but Mel couldn't remember what had happened to that and such an item would be conspicuous over her casual clothing, whereas she had been able to hide the gun under her uniform jacket in the past.

Mel went downstairs, and, putting on her outdoor jacket, left the house and went for a walk. It had rained that afternoon, a heavy downpour that made the ground slippery and damp. Even so, Mel wanted to check that the house was secure, and she tried all the unused doors and French windows, finding them all locked as she had instructed Williams to do earlier. Up until that point, the occupants of Avonby weren't in the habit of locking up the house so tightly until late evening, to allow movement easily between the house and the land as needed. Mel was sad that they had lost this bit of innocence and their house rules now had to change, because they had lost enough through the war years as it was.

On her way back, Mel called at the greenhouse. She hadn't seen Joseph all day and thought she'd find him there, among his beloved saplings. But Joseph wasn't in his usual place, and Rosa said she hadn't seen him since that morning. Rosa wasn't concerned, as the old gardener was often seen wandering and tinkering until teatime, when he'd reappear in time to go back to the cottage with Rosa.

'Remember to lock the greenhouse after you tonight, Rosa,' Mel said. 'We have to get into new habits now.'

'Yes, M'lady,' Rosa said, and she shook the soil off her fingers as she began to pack up her planting tools for the night.

Mel didn't correct Rosa; she was starting to accept that there would always be a divide between her and the resident staff on the estate. She had tried to be one of them, because she wasn't the same as Laura and Jonathan, but she was learning there was no requirement to be like anyone else. She was different and sometimes that was a good thing. A revelation that was later going to bring her more peace of mind than trying to belong ever could.

# 18

When Mel came downstairs, dressed for dinner, she had made up her mind to try to get along better with Laura. Laura had never really wanted Mel at Avonby, and this had hurt so much that Mel had held onto her resentment for too long. With the new awareness and acceptance of her place *between* both worlds, Mel found she was coming to terms with Laura's dislike of her also. In fact, she now understood that it didn't matter to her at all and made no difference to what she did at Avonby. She had a pretty good relationship with Jonathan, and since the overseer, Paddy, had retired a month or two after Mel had arrived, she had stepped into those shoes so easily that a lot of the running of the estate had fallen naturally into her hands. Jonathan was aware of this and let it happen because he didn't want the bother of the day-to-day handling of disgruntled farmworkers, and he kept clear of the few tenants they had at the far reaches of the remaining acreage. Mel, on the other hand, often stopped in, and she solved problems before they ever came to the doors of Avonby. This didn't make her indispensable, no one was, but it made her so useful that Jonathan just left her to it and didn't question her decisions.

None of this was a big deal for Mel, who was naturally organised, and because she wasn't Jonathan or Laura, the workers were more receptive when she offered suggestions of change. Of course, anything she recommended came with an explanation of how it might improve things for the worker concerned, and not just for the sake of the landowners. Mel had a way with words that made everyone realise there were advantages to change, and it would be a win-win for all. As a result, a lot of the previous gripes and petty complaints dried up and those that didn't were dealt with on the spot, unlike when Paddy was taking care of everything, when he'd always blame 'His Lordship' for a negative answer, even when it came from the overseer who had been set in his ways and resistant to change.

Mel had learnt that respect was earned when problems were resolved head on, and because she was neither the owner nor a mere employee, but someone who did have a right to speak for the family and make decisions, her word was taken as final.

Now, as Mel made her way downstairs to eat with the family, she was aware of the advantages of her position. In fact, it was a unique situation. That didn't mean that she had *carte blanche* at Avonby, far from it. Where the house was concerned she had no say at all, as this was all Mrs Felman's and Laura's domain, but her ancestral land was another matter and Mel was determined to use her influence for the good of all.

She entered the drawing room on time for a change and found Laura nursing a cocktail glass alone.

'I'm glad you are here! Williams came to fetch Jonathan, but I think you need to go down to the kitchens to help him.'

'Jonathan's in the *kitchens*? What's wrong?'

'Someone is missing,' Laura said.

'Who?' asked Mel.

'I do not know who. One of the gardeners, I believe,' Laura said.

A sinking feeling hit Mel in the stomach. 'Not Joseph?' she said.

'That might have been the name used. But I really cannot say.'

Mel hid her disappointment at Laura's offhand comment. If it was Joseph, he had been with the family for years and the lord and lady of the house should know who he was. They should know the names of everyone that worked for them. Mel left the drawing room without pointing out this failing and hurried down the servants' stairs to the kitchens; a feeling of dread pursued her all the way. Despite knowing that the tripwire had been removed, she slowed her pace and took it carefully, just in case. But there were no new hazards.

Jonathan was with Williams and Mrs Felman in her office when Mel arrived in the kitchen, but the look on Mrs Weston's face told Mel that they were all worried.

'Joseph hasn't returned and no one has seen him all day,' Mrs Felman said.

'Where's Rosa?' Mel asked.

'She went out to search for him and hasn't come back either,' Williams said.

'Right. Jonathan, get your hunting rifle and meet me at the front of the house in a few minutes. Williams, get Toby and Henry to go to the farmworkers' cottages. We will have to put together a search party,' Mel said.

'What if we don't find him?' Jonathan said.

'We'll search first, then phone the police if we have no luck,' Mel said.

'What should we do in the meantime?' Mrs Felman asked.

'Make sure the house is locked up tight and all of you stay together in the kitchen. No one goes outside alone,' Mel said.

The woods were treacherous in the dark, but Mel led the small band of land workers and staff from the house as they swept the forest, armed with torches and whatever weaponry they could lay hands on. She had her handgun hidden in her pocket and Jonathan and Williams were both carrying rifles. They had already searched Joseph's usual haunts for over two hours but with no success, finding only Rosa as she looked for her missing husband. Mel had sent her back to the safety of the house, escorted by Toby, who returned soon after to help continue the search. On his return, he had sidled up to Mel as though he thought it his job to protect the only woman among the searchers, little knowing that she was more than capable of defending herself should the need arise.

'What do you think happened to him, Lady Mel?' Toby whispered as though he feared being overheard in the dark wet woods.

'He might have had a fall, that's the most likely scenario,' Mel said, trying to reassure him. 'Finding him in any case is crucial.'

But Mel was giving up hope as the evening grew longer and the damp air colder. They were subjected to another shower, which made the going tough as the ground grew wetter and mud slowed their progress as they slipped and slid in it. Mel feared an injury to one of them at any minute, and was about to call a halt to the search and get them all back inside to dry off and get warm as they were cold to the bone. Knowing they would have to ring the police if they didn't find Joseph soon, Mel struggled to make the decision to stop looking as she didn't want more controversy at the estate.

'Over here!' called a voice to Mel's left.

The other party members turned and drew together, heading in the direction of the caller – it was the young farm hand, Ned Soames, who was kneeling over a long shape that lay in the mud at the foot of an old oak tree.

Mel turned her torch on Ned and then she saw Joseph, unconscious and still. She hurried forward and pressed her fingers on his pulse, searching for a heartbeat.

'He's alive!' she said.

'Should we move him?' Williams said.

During the war she had become adept at assessing injuries. Mel now felt around Joseph's prone body, checking his arms and legs for breakages, and eventually found a wound on the back of his head, which explained why he was unconscious.

'Two of you go back to the house for the stretcher. We'll have to lift him carefully, he may have hurt his neck as well, I can't be sure, but it looks like he slipped and knocked himself out cold when he fell,' Mel said.

The relief at finding Joseph was vast, and Mel was also relieved that it appeared to be a mere accident and nothing more sinister. They were all feeling unsafe at the moment, and one more unpleasant incident could send them over the edge.

Toby and Ned returned with the stretcher. Mel supported Joseph's neck as they lifted him onto the taut canvas gurney and Toby and Ned took either side of his torso, while Williams lifted his legs. Once he was on the stretcher, Toby and Ned picked up one end each and lifted it off the ground before carrying Joseph back to the house.

The return with the injured man wasn't easy to do through the semi-treacherous terrain of raised roots, old moss and slippery mud, which was slowly getting worse the more the skies opened and the downpour grew heavier. Despite the torches it was difficult to see, but they made it back to the house, which was a welcome sight to them all.

'Where should we take him?' Toby said as they reached the back door.

'Onto the kitchen table. Williams, ring for the ambulance in the meantime.'

In the kitchen, the table was cleared and then covered with several thick blankets, on which they laid the stretcher until the ambulance arrived. Mel also put a wadded towel under Joseph's head to add extra pressure to the head wound and to help staunch the bleeding.

'Where was he?' Rosa asked as she held his hand.

'We found him in the woods,' Mel explained.

'The woods? What would he be out there for?' Rosa frowned. 'Will he be all right, Lady Melinda... Mel?'

Mel pressed her head against his torso; she heard a regular heartbeat, and felt the rise and fall of his chest. He wasn't okay, but he didn't seem to be in any immediate danger.

'I'm not a medic but he's breathing and his heart is steady. He's soaking, though. Perhaps we should get him out of these wet things?'

Mel hoped that the head injury wasn't too severe and that Joseph would wake soon and be able to explain what had happened himself. But there was a dark fear inside her still, and a suspicion that he hadn't just fallen, because she knew, like his wife Rosa, that Jospeh never went into the woods. Not for any reason.

Joseph started to come round as he was lifted into the ambulance. By then the nurse that came with the driver had bandaged his head and his clothes had been swapped out for some dry blue-striped cotton pyjamas. He was covered with a thick blanket, and because it was a head injury it was felt he would be better treated at the main infirmary in York.

Rosa got in the ambulance to go to the hospital with him, and Mel gave her the house telephone number, with a promise to send Henry to pick her up once Joseph was settled. But as Joseph groaned and started to wake, Mel got into the back of the ambulance and was the first face he saw as he opened his eyes.

'Joseph? Do you remember what happened?' she asked.

'Now, Your Ladyship. There will be time enough for questions after he's seen the doctor,' the nurse said. 'Leave him be.'

Mel left the ambulance. The doors were closed. The driver got in front and started the engine. Mel was left staring after it as the ambulance drove away.

'Come inside, Mel, you'll catch your death,' Jonathan said, taking her arm. 'I've had Nancy make a fire in the drawing room. Get that wet coat off and come and dry off. A stiff cognac is what is needed right now.'

Mel followed Jonathan back into the house, and without argument she dumped her boots and wet coat in the boot room and followed him, barefoot, up the stairs to the drawing room.

'Mrs Weston has left us a tray of beef sandwiches,' Jonathan said.

They huddled around the fire, shivering because, despite the time of year, the weather had turned cold as well as wet, and the damp had seeped into their bones throughout the search.

Mel took a sandwich off the small stack and bit into it, accepting a glass of brandy from Jonathan. The beef was tender and the bread had been smeared with butter. The combination was simple but delicious and still felt like a luxury.

'What a day!' she said.

'Indeed. Thank goodness he was found. I fear that a night out in this weather would have seen him off,' Jonathan said.

Mel found herself liking her cousin more for his compassion. She didn't ask where Laura was, because she knew already that she had taken herself off to bed after supping alone while the rest of them worried and searched. She wondered now if Jonathan saw Laura's flaws and lack of empathy as much as she did. Sometimes she wondered what had attracted him to Laura in the first place. Laura, on meeting Jonathan, wouldn't have had the expectations or any illusions that he would be more than a distant cousin of the Greenways. Even so, Mel knew she was the sort who would have married for money and not for love. Yet, they'd met before the previous lord and his family had died in the plane accident, and married during the war, not long before Mel and her family were caught in the Blitz. None of these tragedies could have been foreseen and so Mel knew that Laura must have had feelings for Jonathan. They did seem happy.

The cognac was good but it triggered thoughts of Mel's own former happiness with Derrin, and the fine French cognac he always seemed to have in his terraced house in Surbiton. Many a cold night they'd finished up there after the first time, and even now, Mel was grateful for the memories, which were the only good ones she had from the war.

'So, it looks like he slipped?' Jonathan said.

'Probably. I'll speak to him tomorrow and find out what happened,' Mel said.

Mel was ravenous and she finished off two sandwiches, barely noticing them going down, but they were tasty because the food was so needed. Although the sick feeling in the pit of her stomach had left now that Joseph had been found, the old adrenaline rush was pumping through her veins. She was wired. Excited. But also concerned. It was odd that Joseph had been in the woods when he never went there and had no business to be there. Going for a walk was one thing, but that wasn't the old man's style either. He loved his flower beds and plants, and they were all situated around the house where he could tend to them.

Mel sipped the cognac and the warming liquid sent the dampness from her bones. She poured herself a second one and topped up Jonathan, who was sitting in his armchair looking at the fire as it crackled in the hearth. He was deep in thought, but for the first time, Mel felt a kinship to him. He had rallied as any Greenway should in adversity, and her feelings towards his ownership of Avonby were now less torn as a result. Jonathan did belong here. He'd done what he should, and Laura, Mel thought, could be excused for not being the same as them. She was not a Greenway by birth, but by marriage. This meant that she and Jonathan weren't such worlds apart after all.

Having only just come to terms with their differences, Mel was now faced with their similarities, which were harder to accept because Mel had been holding onto her own form of snobbery. It was no longer a question of 'her versus them', and perhaps that feeling had only been in Mel, and not in Jonathan's and Laura's minds at all. Mel took another sip of her drink while contemplating what this would mean going forward.

'We should retire,' Jonathan said but he made no move to go.

Mel was too jittery for sleep and for once didn't want her own company. She took her newly filled glass and sat in the chair opposite Jonathan, bathing in the soothing heat of the fire. They sat in companionable silence, as if they were brother and sister, familiar, and not distant relatives as they had been before.

*That*, Mel thought, *is a step in the right direction.*

# 19

Mel arrived at the infirmary on her motorbike the next morning with a small basket of fruit and a slab of Mrs Weston's lemon drizzle cake. Rosa had been collected in the early hours by Henry, and both she and Henry had been told to get some sleep and not rush to do anything else that day.

Signing in at the nurses' station, Mel looked down the long ward and saw Joseph, head bandaged, sitting up in bed, a cup of tea in his hand. The relief was short lived as she saw him grimace with obvious discomfort as he bent his head to sip from the cup.

*Maybe he has injured his neck*, Mel thought.

As she approached, she noticed his hands were trembling, and fearing that he would spill the hot drink over himself, she took it from his shaky hands and placed the cup on the cupboard beside his bed.

'I'll help you when you need some more,' she said. 'How are you?'

'Head 'urts. But otherwise alive, Miss. I should be grateful for that. Rosa told me that you were all looking for me and wouldn't give up.'

The old gardener looked and sounded fragile.

'What happened?' she asked.

Joseph shook his head which resulted in another wince.

'I don't know. I was doing the gardens first thing. Pottering. Me usual. I don't remember anything from then,' he said.

She helped him take a few more sips of his tea and eat some of the cake she'd brought, after which Joseph looked a little brighter.

Mel wanted to question him further, but didn't see the point if he couldn't remember anything and held back. Instead, she reassured him that the garden wouldn't be neglected while he recovered and that the family would take care of him during that time.

The nurse on the desk called an end to the visiting hour and Mel said her goodbyes, promising that Rosa would be brought back to see him for the evening slot.

On her way out, she stopped at the reception desk.

'He seems to be recovering, but says he doesn't remember what happened, is that normal?' Mel asked the nurse.

The nurse looked at Joseph's notes, which she took from a filing cabinet behind the desk.

'Head injury.' The nurse shrugged. 'You'll have to speak to the doctor. I couldn't say really.'

'Is he available now?' Mel asked.

The nurse said she would go and see, and came back a short time later with one of the emergency doctors, a middle-aged, portly gentleman, who had treated Joseph when he'd arrived the night before.

'I'm Dr Hamilin,' he said, introducing himself. 'How can I help you, Lady Greenway?'

'Why has he no recollection of the accident?'

'He's very lucky to be alive, you should know. That was a bad injury. We've seen memory loss of this sort before, though. Shock because of the accident, or possibly because of the injury itself, can cause it. We just don't know at this point,' the doctor explained.

'Will his memory come back?' Mel asked.

'In most cases it does after a few days, but not always. It may take some time to know which it's going to be,' Dr Hamilin said.

Halfway home it occurred to Mel to go and investigate where Joseph fell in the light of day, to see if she could understand how it happened. Accidents on the estate were rare these days and it would be important to make sure nothing like this occurred again.

When she got home, she changed from her bike wear and put on her Wellingtons and a lighter jacket. She put the handgun and some spare rounds into her pocket for good measure, because she still had a nagging doubt that Joseph's fall had been an accident. There were too many discrepancies and that large hole in his memory of being in the garden and remembering nothing more could mean something.

The rain had stopped during the night, and it wasn't as wet and cold as it had been. Mel walked across the fields to the forest, hands tucked into her coat pockets, fingers grazing the gun in her right one. When she reached the woods, the air was heady with the smell of damp greenery, and the leaves were still dripping as captured rain struggled to find its way down to the ground.

Mel knew the woods as well as the rest of the land, and had passed through them many times on foot. She retraced their steps of the night before to find the oak tree, while keeping her eyes open for any clues. She scanned the ground on the way and saw signs of the search party's passing, with trampled bushes, broken twigs and the occasional cigarette butt. Nothing else appeared out of the ordinary considering the circumstances, and all could be explained by their presence last night.

As she approached the tree, Mel stopped. She examined the area while she worked out what was beyond the tree in each direction. South was the farmers' cottages. North – behind her – was back to Avonby. East was where the border met the main road which led to and passed the gated entrance to the estate. West was fields, unused and currently resting as the farming rotated, but they butted up against the stables and surrounding paddocks. All around her, Mel was enclosed by Avonby land. The only way anyone might enter unseen would be through these woods from the road. Mel stared beyond them, trying to work out a pathway that might have been taken. Her mind followed several patterns but came to only one viable conclusion.

Stowing the idea for later, she drew closer to the tree. She visualised Joseph's body on the ground, her mind's eye superimposing him where he'd been last night. It had been too dark to look around then, and more important to get Joseph to safety anyway, but now she saw the crushed foliage at the foot of the tree, the scramble of feet belonging to his rescuers, and a smear of blood from Joseph's head wound on a protruding root, near where his head had been. Was this the point at which he struck his head?

The positioning was odd, and so were some slight drag marks, as if his body had been pulled from somewhere else to be left in this spot.

Mel followed the scars in the ground. She saw another smear of blood farther away, in the direction of the house. Her mind explored the possible scenario of an assailant attacking Joseph in the garden and then bringing his body here, but the idea was improbable. Someone would have seen something with all the comings and goings that had happened yesterday. But then, maybe they wouldn't have. They were all distracted – herself included – by the tripwire.

Mel had been off the estate for most of the morning, taking the razor to Derrin and then dealing with him and examining the trap in the afternoon. They'd been busy.

She tried to think who might have spent any time outside other than Joseph and Rosa that day, and therefore who might have seen something. There were some of the causal gardeners that came in seasonally and worked, not only at Avonby when needed, but for other landowners in the area on a freelance, need for hire, basis. Mel knew none of them had been working there this week, having been drawn in to work longer hours prior to the garden party. No, it had been a quiet week on that score, but they would return in two weeks to help with lawn cutting and some weeding again that was too much for Joseph alone.

Who else might have seen something?

*What about Jonathan?* He and Laura often spent time sitting in the garden. But no. Yesterday was an awful day: Laura wouldn't have ventured out. It was unlikely Jonathan would have either without good reason. It was a perfect opportunity for someone watching the house to sneak about and take advantage of an old retainer doing his twilight-years job. Mel remained suspicious.

Mel heard a dull crack nearby as though a foot had stepped on a fallen twig. She put her hand in her pocket, feeling the comforting presence of the handgun. The metal warmed against her fingers as though eager to be used, but casting her eyes around her Mel couldn't see anything untoward. Even so, the idea of being watched by a silent assassin sent a sliver of suspicion through her limbs, galvanising her to start the brisk walk back to the house as she remembered Derrin's warning that no one should be alone at Avonby at any time.

She was wary all the way back, but no matter how often she looked over her shoulder, she didn't see anyone following or lurking. By the time she reached the house, Mel was convinced that she was being over dramatic and had probably imagined the whole thing, superimposing a natural sound onto something more suspicious. After all, nature made noises all the time that she had dismissed without thought until that day.

In the boot room, Mel pulled off her muddy boots then put them in the sink, washing them off for use again later. The kitchen next door was full of lively chatter, the panic of yesterday already forgotten. Mel observed how easy it was for all of them, post-war, to come back from any awful incident barely scathed. It worried her. As though they'd lost the ability to feel too deeply about anything, and life and death were events they took as normal; like waking and sleeping with little more impact than that.

She tried not to judge them now as little ripples of laughter and friendly banter echoed through the kitchen, and she waited until it subsided before going in. She was still wearing her jacket, and the gun weighed heavy in the pocket, while Mel thought about the woods and the drag marks. Could it be they were made from when the gurney was brought? Toby and Ned might have dragged their feet while carrying the heavy burden of Joseph back to the house. It was difficult to rule this out as a possibility, since there had been some back and forth to avoid obstacles on the way back.

She looked at the Wellingtons lined up on the floor in a neat row, trying to work out which Toby had worn, but like hers, all the boots had been washed clean for the next user.

Mel shrugged. Her head hurt from thinking so hard and very little sleep. She was trying to make round blocks fit into square holes and it wasn't possible. Not without more clues and information. Not without Joseph remembering what had happened.

She went into the kitchen and found Rosa sitting at the table.

'I saw Joseph,' Mel told her. 'He was sitting up and drinking tea.'

Rosa's mouth burst into a gummy smile. 'Oh thank you! Lord Jonathan said Henry will take me back there when I want to go.'

'Good!' said Mel. 'If he remembers anything later, I'd like to know.'

'You're so kind to care, Lady Melinda,' Rosa said. 'We don't deserve it.'

And then Rosa burst into tears as the strain of it all came tumbling down on her for the first time.

After giving the woman comfort, Mel left the kitchen and made her way back upstairs. It had been another long day, and a very trying few weeks since the body had been found in the rose bed. That incident, Mel realised, was a catalyst to most of what had happened since, and they were no closer to finding out who was behind it all.

As she came up into the hallway, Mel found herself face to face with Richard Stanley, who was standing looking down the servants' stairs as though he had been waiting for her.

'Lord Stanley,' Mel said. 'Is Jonathan expecting you?'

'Actually, Melinda, I came to see you,' Stanley said. 'And please, call me Richard. I thought we were beyond such formality.'

'What can I do for you... Richard?' Mel said.

'I wondered if you'd care to go for lunch with me tomorrow?' Stanley said.

'Oh. I'm working on the estate, I'm afraid. I'm not a lady of leisure...'

'Of course she will!' said Laura, coming out of the drawing room. 'Mel can take time off if she wants to. She is family and not an employee on the estate.'

'I really can't. There is so much to do and with Joseph...' Mel said.

'Nonsense. You work way too hard, and the garden will be fine for the sake of one day,' Laura said. 'It is so good to see you, Richard. You must stay for dinner.'

'Thank you, but I wouldn't want to impose,' Stanley said.

'You are not. It has been so dreadfully dull, the last few days. We need some cheery company. Now, come and have a drink with me while Melinda goes to change for dinner.'

Mel was blindsided and couldn't argue without appearing ungracious. As she went upstairs to change, she ran a new mantra through her mind. *I must be congenial. I must be friendly. I must try to like Laura.* All of which wasn't easy to adhere to, as she was annoyed that Laura would choose to answer for her and push Stanley her way again. Even so, she had promised herself she would try to make the relationship between them better. A challenge when her cousin's wife was such a tricky person to navigate. Laura was contrary: shallow one minute, then practical another, and now she appeared to be making an effort to treat Mel better also – which would be an improvement.

Mel wasn't interested in Richard Stanley, though; she found him too forward and stuffy. Mel stopped herself there. *That's my reverse snobbery again*, she thought. She had to stop doing that: Richard was hopefully a decent enough man, and she was sure she could like him if she got to know him better. The only problem being why he wanted to know her and spend time with her so much. Mel wasn't looking for a relationship. Certainly not now she had reconnected with Derrin again.

Mel's mind stalled. Derrin hadn't made any move at all to re-establish their wartime connection. Mel didn't know anything about his personal life, and the realisation of that stung. All they'd talked about was the events happening at Avonby, with barely a polite exchange about anything else.

But then, it had always been business between them, hadn't it? With some passion thrown into the mix that now, looking back on it, could have just been because they both knew at any minute they might die. Mel was anxious. Had she been holding onto the hope that Derrin may want to rekindle their relationship?

*I'm so foolish*, she thought, replaying the few times they had been alone in the last few days. All they had talked about was the case, and Derrin had been interested in her observations, while all along she hadn't noticed there was no attempt to touch or kiss her, only opportunities to do so, which he hadn't taken even when she'd hoped he would. Why those moments didn't pan out, Mel had blamed on interruptions by third parties, but the truth was, if Derrin had wanted more, they had been alone long enough in his office at the station.

It was obvious when she re-examined the evidence that he wasn't interested in anything other than her analytical skills.

*We're too distant now*, she thought. *Too much time has passed, and he hasn't missed me or he would have tried to find me before now, wouldn't he?*

Before he came to Avonby, Mel had given up on ever seeing him again anyway. Despite his explanation that he'd written to her, when he got no reply he could have come to find her, but he hadn't.

*Perhaps he knew it was time to end things*, Mel thought.

The war was almost over then, and Derrin must have known they couldn't continue as they had been. By then, any homeland espionage trips were no longer needed because all traitors had been caught.

*What did I expect?* Mel thought now. *He has never said he loved me.*

Nor was it likely he would, because Derrin had seen their relationship for what it was.

Mel had never put love in the equation at the time. Love was something you avoided in wartime, if she was being honest with herself. To love someone opened the possibility of more pain, because losses were a daily occurrence they all knew could happen. None of them wanted that. And yet, they had very deep emotions during those years: mostly hate and fear for the enemy. And passion, when it was known, was very intense. At least in Mel's experience it was.

Maybe in some way they had loved each other, but those days, those passions, those fears and anxieties were all receding and they were now in the normal world. At least, as normal as it could get.

Mel found herself wondering what normal should feel like. If she'd never been in the army and her parents and Valentine had lived, she would never have met Derrin.

And what of Richard Stanley? Would she have liked him enough to accept an offer to lunch? Or would she have just seen him as a potential husband because of his fortune? And what of Melinda, before the war? Was she Stanley's type? Or was post-war Mel more so because she was different from the usual girls he met in society? Mel wasn't sure, and she couldn't envision being any different from who she was now.

The reality was, she had met Derrin, and she was a different person by then anyway. Open to new experiences, embracing the life she'd chosen, because what other choice did she have?

With all these thoughts rattling around inside her head, Mel wasn't sure what she would do with her future. Derrin might never look her way again. He was certainly making no moves towards her, and Mel was curious about the flirty Richard Stanley, who had declared interest in her. What harm, therefore, would a lunch date do?

# 20

Mel was wearing one of her new outfits, a cream twinset which consisted of a dress with a short bolero jacket with bronze buttons. On her head she wore a bronze silk scarf to keep her hair from flicking around during the road trip, which she realised was a great idea once she saw Stanley's racing green MG TC Convertible with the top down. She felt like 'Lady Melinda' that day, dressed for the part, and not some mere poor relation of the family.

That day she was a master of her own destiny, willingly doing something out of character, in large part because of her understanding that she probably meant nothing to Derrin, and might never have been more than a curiosity and someone to warm his bed at night anyway. Even so, she looked back at those times with fondness; they made her who she was now, and there were no regrets.

The sun was out and it was a perfect day, with the last of the rain having dried up. Coupled with news that Joseph was recovering well, Mel's spirits were up. Though Joseph hadn't regained his memory, Mel was comfortable in the knowledge that he wasn't in danger and he would be back at Avonby soon.

'So where are we going?' Mel asked as she pushed the troubles of the estate away for a change. She wanted to relax and enjoy the day, and indeed learn more about Stanley, who had proven to be pleasant company the previous night at dinner, once she had decided to give him a chance.

'A lovely country club, near Rotherham,' Stanley said. 'The drive will be nice and the food is good there.'

Mel nodded.

'Thank you for saying yes,' Stanley said.

Mel was surprised at how humble he sounded, and it gave her the motive to be generous and more understanding of their previous meetings where she'd found him irritating.

'I haven't been to Rotherham,' she said. 'Though I passed through many towns on my journey from London. It was an interesting bike ride and took all day, with a few comfort breaks along the way.'

'Bike ride? You rode a bicycle from London?' Stanley said.

Mel laughed. 'No. A motorbike.'

Stanley glanced at her, his expression unreadable. 'So, you drive a motorbike as well as cars?'

'I thought you knew,' Mel said.

'No. Laura and Jonathan have withheld a lot of information about their mysterious cousin. I'm looking forward to finding out more about you along the way,' Stanley said. 'I've known all along you were different.'

Mel shrugged. 'There's not much to know. I was in the army, now I'm here.'

'I think that is an interesting discussion for the future, for sure. I don't know any "lady" that was in the army, though a few played Florence Nightingale and freelanced as nurses.'

Mel absorbed that thought, half imagining Laura in a nurse's uniform dealing with cleaning wounds and bedpans – she almost laughed out loud at the thought.

Stanley started the engine, and the MG roared down the driveway to the gates of the estate and out onto the main road heading for Rotherham, for the start of what turned into a very pleasant drive.

It was almost lunchtime when they reached Thrybergh Park, and Stanley drove them up towards Thrybergh Hall, which had been a golf club since 1906.

'You play golf?' Mel asked.

'I've dabbled, but I'm more involved in the club from a social point of view,' Stanley said. 'We have a table booked in the dining room. There will be some interesting comings and goings.'

The MG came to a halt by the door, and a valet opened Mel's door and helped her step out. Stanley gave the man his keys to go and park for him, and he and Mel went inside, passing through the reception and into the dining room.

'Lord Stanley,' said the *maître d'* as Mel and Richard approached. 'We have the table you requested.'

They were led through the restaurant to a table in the corner of the dining room, and Stanley offered her the choice of facing the room or having her back to it. Mel opted for facing and Stanley gave her an openly curious look. Her old habits from the war were still with her, whether they were conscious or subliminal: you always had your back to the wall if you could and then watched the room around you. That way, no one could approach that you hadn't seen first.

Stanley wasn't insecure, though, and it did beg the question as to what he'd done during the war days, so Mel asked him outright.

'Were you enlisted?' she asked.

'I was exempt,' Stanley said. 'My estate has several acres being used for essential farming during the war, and I was the only remaining member of the Stanley family trying to run it, with only older farmworkers because the fit and young were conscripted. They were challenging times and long, hard days.'

'So, you were essential to keep the farm running,' Mel said. 'I get that.'

'You don't judge?' he asked.

'Why should I?' Mel said. 'What you did was crucial too.'

'I didn't go into Sheffield all the time during the war. Uniformless, I was spat on, shouted at, sometimes attacked.'

'I'm sorry,' she said. 'That happened in London, too. People can show such ignorance. Not all reasons for being a civilian were obvious.'

'You didn't have to enlist, Melinda. So why did you?'

'My parents and brother were dead. Our home destroyed. I didn't feel I had any other choice at the time. But I don't regret it. I learnt a lot in the army,' Mel said.

'You could have come to Avonby and left London,' Stanley said. 'It was safer here.'

'I didn't know that at the time. I only found out that my Uncle Anthony and his wife and children were dead when I got in touch with them about my father's allowance after I was demobbed. That dried up during the early part of the war and my parents never told us why. But my father's solicitor said I had entitlements after he died. Tied to the estate.'

Mel met Stanley's eyes and flushed.

'I'm sorry. I shouldn't be talking about this. Money talk is vulgar, isn't it?'

Stanley didn't have an opportunity to reply before a waiter appeared at the table to take their order.

Mel regained her composure. She had been used to speaking her mind before she'd come to Avonby, and sometimes she slipped back into doing so at the worse times. This was why Laura found her so hard to deal with.

'We'll have the set menu,' Stanley said, 'with a glass of Sauvignon Blanc, followed by the Chateau Lafitte Rothschild, from my reserved bottles.'

'Oh no. Not for me!' Mel said. 'That's too much alcohol for the daytime.'

'It's only a glass of each, Melinda,' Stanley said. 'They'll keep the rest of the bottle for me for next time I'm here.'

'All right then,' Mel said, trying to be amenable.

'Going back to our earlier conversation, nothing is vulgar,' Stanley said as the waiter left. 'Not if you're adult and know your own mind.'

Mel smiled at this. 'Adult? Well, I'm 25, so I guess I qualify for that title.'

'I suspect you've been an adult for much longer than that,' Stanley said.

The starter course arrived along with the glass of white wine, and Mel picked at the expensive smoked salmon, drizzled with a delicious lemon and herb dressing, wondering how the restaurant could serve such extravagant food.

Mel *was* an adult, though, as Stanley had predicted, and she wondered now why he'd brought her here, and what the 'big show' was all about. She was a Greenway, and although not in control of the family fortune, she knew about extravagance and wasn't bothered by it. Yet Stanley was making every effort to impress her. Was he interested in her? Not just because she was different, but because he thought deep down she wasn't all that odd?

Laura would love it if they got together, Mel realised now that she wasn't attracted to Stanley that way, even though she had been curious about him. She'd been more than a little bulldozed into coming out with him today, and wondered if it had been a mistake, after all, to be amenable. He had never really lived in the 'real world', despite his claim of 'hard, long days' which she'd heard many self-entitled people claim they had known. The truth was, Stanley still had everything he could possibly want. His title, his estate, his family wealth. He didn't know what it was to own nothing. Just like now, he took a place like Thrybergh in his stride, expecting it to be there when he wanted it.

Mel took a final bite of the smoked salmon and looked up. Being seated at a table across the room was Derrin and a man in a brigadier's uniform, both men sitting in such a way as to view the room. As Mel's eyes fell on Derrin, he noticed her too. She gave him a small wave, then remembered who she was with and felt embarrassed about it. Derrin had already assumed she was seeing Lord Stanley, and seeing her out with him now would confirm he was right. But the truth was, although Stanley was a handsome man, Mel didn't really feel attracted to him.

Stanley looked around to see who she had seen, and saw Derrin and the brigadier.

'Good heavens! That inspector gets around, doesn't he?' he said. 'That must be the new chief constable, Brigadier John Cheney.'

'You know about him?' Mel asked.

'I knew the last chief constable well. Moved on to better climes now, I believe. But Cheney is hoping to fill his shoes, I'm sure. I should talk to him when dinner is done, if you don't mind?'

'No. Of course not,' Mel said.

The waiter came back and removed their starter plates, Mel excused herself and headed out of the restaurant to the ladies' room.

When she came out, she found Derrin outside.

'I didn't expect to see you here,' he said.

'No. It was a last-minute decision.' Mel said.

'Mmmm. It's quite a place.'

'Ostentatious. More than expected,' Mel said. 'Smoked salmon, steaks. Sugary desserts. I haven't seen anything like this in a restaurant since before the war.'

'The rich have never really suffered,' Derrin said. 'Look around you. This place hasn't changed for years. Even in the worst times, I bet most of the menu was available for the members who could afford it. Men like Stanley.'

Mel heard the dig about Stanley and tried not to read into what it meant. She had to keep her feet on the ground. Where Derrin was concerned, she was under no illusions.

'Or your new boss? The brigadier?' Mel asked, keeping the conversation light.

'Indeed. It wasn't my choice of place, but he wanted to talk to me away from the station,' Derrin said.

'More intrigue?' Mel asked with a slight smile on her lips. 'You're always in the thick of something.'

'Possibly... I'd better get back... Enjoy your lunch,' Derrin said.

Mel returned to the dining room in time for the service of the sirloin steak, which was rare and cooked to perfection.

Despite her objection to waste and excessive privilege, Mel enjoyed the food, but passed on the dessert because she was full and not used to eating so much during the day. If war had taught her anything it was how little food she needed to survive, and overeating was never going to be a thing she would do.

After dinner, Stanley went to talk to the brigadier and introduce himself. Mel remained at the table and drank some coffee, but she watched the interaction between Stanley, the brigadier and Derrin.

When Stanley came back, he suggested a stroll around the gardens before the journey back to Avonby.

Mel agreed as she felt the need to walk off some of the lunch, but as the afternoon grew late she broached the subject of returning.

'I really ought to get back,' Mel said.

'I'll get the valet to bring my car around,' Stanley said, then he went back into the hotel to speak to them.

Stanley was a while inside and Mel watched the comings and goings of the golf members. She recognised some faces from the garden party – a judge and a few lords and baronets. It was then that she became aware how few women were present at the place.

She saw their valet walking up to the reception as Stanley came out.

'I'm afraid the car won't start, Lord Stanley,' said the valet. 'I can get a mechanic out, but not until morning.'

Stanley glanced at Mel and then began a debate with the man, insisting on having a mechanic there sooner as he had to return Lady Greenway to her home.

Mel listened to the argument for a few seconds before intervening.

'Where's the car?' she said.

'I… it's in the parking area,' said the valet.

'What's the problem?' she asked.

'It won't start,' said the valet.

'Take me to it,' Mel said.

'I'm sorry, Melinda,' said Stanley. 'I don't know what the issue is. The damn thing only came out of the showroom a month ago.'

'I'll look at it. Sounds like the alternator might be stuck.'

'But how would you…?' Stanley asked.

Mel followed the valet round to the parking area with Stanley close by. When she reached the car, she took the keys from the valet's hands, got in and tried to start the engine. There was a whirring sound, but the car didn't start. She turned the ignition off and got out.

'That's not the alternator,' she said. 'Let's get the bonnet open.'

The engine was, as Stanley had said, new and clean. She soon discovered that the alternator was fine.

'Fanbelt,' she said. 'That's odd for it to tear like that. Considering it is brand new.'

From the corner of her eye, she noticed Stanley exchange a look with the valet.

'I didn't know you knew mechanics,' Stanley said.

'Army training,' she said.

'So can it be fixed?' he asked.

'Yes, but not without another fanbelt,' she said.

'Oh dear,' said Stanley. 'What should we do?'

'I had heard a women's nylon might be used...' said the valet and Stanley gave him a cautionary glare.

'Not without setting fire to your engine in the attempt...' Mel said.

Back at the reception, Stanley said, 'We could always stay here. They have rooms when needed.'

Mel sighed. She'd never been in this awkward position before, but had heard of instances of fake breakdowns from the other girls. She wasn't sure how else to explain a torn fanbelt – other than deliberate sabotage.

'I'm going home. But stay here by all means, Lord Stanley,' Mel said, and then she turned to the receptionist and asked if she could use the telephone.

She dialled Avonby. The phone rang a few times before Williams picked up.

'Mr Williams, it's Mel. Can Henry come and collect me from Thrybergh Hall, Rotherham?' she asked.

'I'm afraid he is out with His Lordship this evening,' Williams explained. 'I'm not expecting them back until late tonight.'

Mel gritted her teeth, thanking Williams as she hung up. It would have to be a taxi, but it was a long way back to Avonby and not many of them would be willing to go that far out of their way.

She turned from the desk to think. Lord Stanley was loitering by the door and then she saw Derrin.

'You're still here?' he said.

'Lord Stanley has car trouble,' she said. 'And Henry has gone out with Jonathan for the evening.'

Derrin eyed up Stanley, his eyes narrowing. 'Has he indeed. I'll take you home. My car is outside.'

Mel almost sighed with relief. 'Thank you. If you're sure?'

'Of course. I'm heading back that way anyway, as I just bought a house in Avonby village,' he explained. 'Should I tell him, or you?'

Mel gave a small smirk at the devilment in Derrin's voice. 'I will.'

She walked to the door with Derrin, and Stanley looked more than a little surprised to see how comfortable they were together.

'Thank you for lunch. I hope you get your car fixed. Inspector Bradley has offered to take me home.'

Stanley looked even more shocked by this turn of events, and he didn't say a word as Mel walked past him with Derrin and then headed off to the car park.

The black Jowett Javelin was parked near the hall and Derrin had his keys with him.

'I never use valet parking,' he said. 'You just don't know what can happen to your car.'

As they left the car park, Mel saw Lord Stanley at the door smoking a cigarette. He was furious, and he watched them go, thunder in his eyes.

'Oldest trick in the book,' Derrin said, without looking at her. 'I take it you aren't an item, then?'

'No,' said Mel.

Derrin's expression was unreadable as he kept his eyes on the road and his full concentration on the drive.

# 21

'I THOUGHT I'D BETTER COME ALONG AS WELL,' said Derrin the next day, when he arrived with Constable Jennings to take fingerprints from Avonby's staff.

'What's this all about?' Jonathan asked.

'Someone left what I thought was your razor under my pillow to find,' explained Mel. 'I think it was a warning. I took it to Inspector Bradley for fingerprinting.'

'My razor? That's impossible. I still have mine,' he said.

'I brought it back, now that we've done what we need to,' Derrin said.

He held out the razor, wrapped in the towel that Mel had brought it in.

Jonathan opened it, saw the onyx handle and gasped.

'Why, this went missing when we moved in a few years ago. I had forgotten all about it,' he said. 'It wasn't mine, though, it was my father's, Julian Greenway. The same initials as mine.'

Derrin wanted to know where Jonathan had kept this family memento, and he took him upstairs to show him the box that contained the rest of the matching set of razor, comb and brush.

'What I don't understand is where it has been all this time,' Jonathan said. 'And who had it?'

'Well, whoever that was must have placed it in my room,' Mel said. 'It has to be someone who works here, and I don't really like the thought of that.'

'We did find a print,' Derrin said to Jonathan. 'I'm hoping it belongs to our culprit.'

The main house staff were brought into the drawing room after that, and Mel watched as each of them was fingerprinted. There was general bemusement among them as to why this was necessary, and some were worried because sometimes things had gone missing in the house and they didn't want to be accused.

Once he was done, Derrin stored the prints and, putting away the kit, left with Jennings to take the test farther afield and out to those working the land.

'I'll come with you,' Mel said, returning from washing the fingerprint ink off her hands. 'They know me and it will be less awkward for you.'

Outside, they got into Derrin's car and Mel directed them to the cottages and fields until they had found most, but not all, of the people who worked at Avonby.

'Who's missing?' Derrin asked.

'Ned. He's one of the farm hands who moves around, working wherever is needed on the estate,' Mel said. 'I wonder where he is today?'

'Isn't he the man who found Joseph?' Derrin asked.

'That's right.'

They asked a few of the farmworkers where Ned might be, but they all claimed they hadn't seen him that day.

As they got back into the car, Mel said, 'I can take you to his cottage. Perhaps he's there.'

Mel gave directions to Ned's cottage and Derrin followed the perimeter of the estate, round and back towards the woods. As they approached the cottage, they saw smoke coming from his chimney.

'Looks like he is home,' Mel said.

'Good. We can wrap this all up today and get on with the job of finding our perpetrator,' Derrin said.

'I hope so,' Mel said.

They pulled the car in front of the cottage and Mel got out and went straight to the door. Knocking hard, she waited outside for an answer, but none was forthcoming.

'Jennings, go and check around the back,' said Derrin as he peered through the window into the small living room.

Mel knocked again. 'He may be in bed,' she said.

'Not with a fire blazing in the hearth downstairs, what's the point?'

Mel tried the door. It was unlocked, so she opened it, looking inside but not crossing the threshold.

'Ned? It's Mel here. Can we come in?'

There was no response and so Mel and Derrin went in.

The cottage was small, with one tiny sitting room and an even smaller kitchen divided by a steep and narrow staircase that went upstairs. There was no one in either of the downstairs rooms, so they went upstairs.

'Ned, it's me, Mel,' she said again. 'I'm coming upstairs to make sure you're okay.'

There were two doors at the top of the stairs, one left and one right, and Mel opened the left one, discovering a dressing room which also had a tin bath stored in there. On top of the chest of drawers was a bowl and jug for washing, along with a small mirror and a razor. There were signs of its recent use, with a hand towel left drying on the side of the bath. Unlike the main house, there was no proper plumbing upstairs and so no toilet. Ned would have to get his water from downstairs and bring it up. A lot to do after a hard day out in the fields, Mel observed, and thought that she must speak to Jonathan about getting the cottages fully plumbed at some point in the future. Mel looked over her shoulder and shook her head to indicate that Ned wasn't there.

Derrin opened the other door and found Ned's bedroom, which contained a single bed, a wardrobe, a small chest of drawers and a chair by the tiny window. There was everything there that a single man would need and nothing more, Mel observed.

But Ned was nowhere to be seen, and Mel began to worry about him for the first time.

'If he's not out working, he should be here,' she said.

'Inspector?' called Jennings from downstairs.

Mel and Derrin came downstairs to find Jennings standing by the back door with a man who was slightly obscured by the low back door frame, as he was quite tall.

'You looking for Ned?' the man asked.

'Yes,' said Mel. 'Do you know where he is?'

'I'm his uncle. His ma was taken sick,' the man said.

'I'm sorry,' Mel said. 'Is she in hospital?'

'No. Bit worse than that,' said Ned's uncle, 'she passed away this morning. I'm just back to pick up some of his things for a night or two.'

'I'm so sorry,' Mel said. 'Was she your sister?'

'That's right. Anyway, I'd better get what Ned needs,' Ned's uncle said. 'If you don't mind?'

'We'll leave you to it,' Derrin said. 'Come on, Jennings.'

They left Ned's uncle by the back door, exiting by the front. Mel, Derrin and Jennings got back into the car.

'You might find the culprit in the prints you have,' Mel said. 'I'd hate to think Ned was involved, anyway. In fact, I'd struggle to put the blame on anyone at Avonby. I just can't imagine one of them doing that, or killing that woman. And you know I'm not naïve.'

'No one wants to believe people they spend time with every day are capable of murder,' Derrin said.

Derrin put the car in reverse and backed up, turning it around to head in the direction of the main house. They traversed the driveway that circled the estate back to Avonby Hall.

They didn't speak again until Derrin pulled the car to a halt at the front of the house.

'We need to get these prints back to be processed,' Derrin said.

'I understand. Thanks for dropping me off, I'm not exactly in the right shoes today for a trek across the fields,' she said, opening her door before Derrin or Jennings could get out.

'No problem,' Derrin said. 'I'll be in touch.'

Mel closed the car door, and only then did she notice one of the farm hands running across the paddock towards them.

'Inspector! Wait!'

Seeing the man approaching, Derrin got out of the car. The man reached them, chest heaving from the exertion. He drew in a lungful of air to try to catch his breath.

'We found... Ned!' he gasped. 'He was in the field out back.'

'But we just saw his uncle...?'

'*Uncle?* Ned dunt have an uncle. He's an orphan. Grew up in the orphanage over in Sheffield,' the man said.

'Where is Ned now?' Derrin said.

'In t'field. I told you! He... in't breevin'!'

'Get in the car and take me there,' Derrin said. 'Jennings, call an ambulance and the station, but don't leave Lady Melinda's side. Is that clear?'

'Yes, Inspector,' Jennings said.

'I'll come with you,' Mel said.

'No,' Derrin said.

Derrin bundled the still-huffing farm hand into his car and drove away, leaving Mel and Jennings behind. Mel stood for a moment, watching the car go, deciding whether to stay or to follow anyway.

'Can I use your phone?' Jennings said beside her.

'Come on,' she said. 'Let's get that ambulance here as soon as possible.'

Mel was irritated with Derrin for not letting her go with him, because she could have used her first aid skills at the scene. She was worried about what had happened to Ned, but also concerned about the stranger who had come to his cottage, as bold as brass, pretending to be a relative. Was he just some random thief who had the cheek to rob one of the cottages? Or was he someone more sinister?

After a short time, they heard an ambulance siren, followed by police sirens, one of which came up to the house to confer with Jennings. Mel told them about the stranger, and sent them to check out Ned's cottage, hoping they would find him still there, but she had a suspicion that he wouldn't be anywhere near Avonby by now.

'I can't stand it!' Mel said eventually. 'I have to go and see what's happening.'

'The inspector said...' Jennings began.

'He said you weren't to leave my side, so you can come with me,' Mel said. 'Or not. But I'm going to see what's happening.'

Jennings didn't want to argue with the lady as she wasn't equipped to win such a battle, and he knew it when he saw the determination on her face.

'We'll go on my bike,' Mel said.

Jennings clung on to Mel's waist, terrified of falling off, but more afraid of the inspector seeing him with his arms around the lady. They arrived at the back field just as a stretcher was loaded into the ambulance. Mel pulled off her goggles and jumped off the bike, leaving Jennings floundering before he took off after her, barely able to keep up.

Mel saw Derrin talking to the farmer and farm hands, but made her way towards the ambulance first to see Ned. What she saw when she got there was the thing she most dreaded: the body was covered with a blanket which had been pulled up to cover his face and head.

'Oh Ned!' Mel said. 'What happened?'

One of the ambulance men looked back at her as they strapped the body into place.

'Dead, Miss,' he said.

'I can see that! But *how*?' she asked.

'Best speak to the police inspector,' he said. 'We have to get him back to the mortuary now. Please excuse us.'

Mel turned away from the ambulance. Her heart was heavy with the thought of never seeing Ned again. She set off across the field to speak to Derrin, reaching him just as he finished talking to the farmworkers.

A dark scowl appeared on his face as Derrin saw Mel. She wasn't sure if he was mad at her for coming to the field against his wishes or with Jennings for letting her.

'She insisted,' Jennings said as they reached him. 'I couldn't stop her.'

'This way,' Derrin said.

Jennings began to follow him back over the field.

'Not you! Mel,' Derrin said, his voice heavy with annoyance.

Mel walked along the field, focusing her full attention on the scene in the hope that she would observe something that Derrin and his constables hadn't.

'They found him here,' Derrin said, stopping.

Mel saw the blood. 'What happened?'

'Shot.'

'Are we saying accident? Or murder?' Mel asked.

'Execution,' said Derrin.

Mel glanced around and noticed that they were now far enough away to be unheard. 'Back of the head?'

Derrin nodded.

Mel had a vision of Ned being forced to his knees at gunpoint. She felt sick at the thought, and the idea that another person had been injured or killed on Avonby land was horrifying. Things were getting out of hand and she didn't know what to do.

'The man at the cottage?' she asked.

'Already gone,' Derrin said. 'Mel, you must keep your head down and don't go anywhere without an escort until we catch him. I'm going to leave a constable here at all times.'

'So, we have to be prisoners in our own home? I can help you,' Mel said.

'And you have. But this is too dangerous. If I'm right, this man has shown himself to us today. Blatantly. He feels untouchable.'

'You think he killed Ned?' Mel asked.

'Don't you?' Derrin said.

Mel nodded. It was very likely.

'Derrin, we could get an artist's impression. Even though we didn't get a clear look at him, I can still describe him,' Mel said.

'I know you can, but… I don't exactly trust that to remain a secret at the yard. If your skills become common knowledge, this man may want to make sure you can't identify him,' Derrin said. 'He's dangerous. You can see that now, can't you?'

'But you saw him too,' Mel said. 'By the same vein he should also want to silence you and Jennings – who was stood next to him and saw him better than either of us.'

'He won't see us as an easy target, but you, Mel…'

Mel laughed, 'I'm not easy either.'

'No. But I'd rather he didn't try. He might get lucky. Go back to the house with Jennings and stay there, please?'

'I should at least tell Jonathan what's happened. Will you come back to the house when you're done here?' Mel asked.

'Yes,' he said.

# 22

Back inside Avonby, Mel discovered that Jonathan and Laura had gone out soon after she had left with Derrin to do the farmworkers' fingerprinting. She left Jennings in the hallway on a chair with strict instructions not to divulge what had happened to anyone in the house, while she went into Jonathan's study for some peace and quiet. She had to think and just couldn't with Jennings hovering over her all the time.

She sat down by the unlit fire and wrapped her arms around herself, sinking down into her thoughts. The day had yielded yet another shocking turn of events and she was struggling to accept that Ned would no longer be on the farm with his cheery smile. If that fake uncle was also Ned's killer, Mel couldn't understand the motive. What had an ordinary man like Ned done to deserve such a fate? The only link that might possibly exist was that Ned was the one to find Joseph, but how would that bring him to the attention of his executioner? Unless Joseph's accident wasn't an accident at all but another attempted murder? In which case, his attacker might think Ned had known something. At this point, that was the only possible explanation she could find, and she had suspected all along that Joseph was attacked and hadn't fallen.

Even so, Mel couldn't believe what had happened. She had a strong stomach, but was a little nauseous at the thought of someone shooting Ned point blank in the back of the head – execution style – in the middle of one of Avonby's most-used fields. It was risky at the very least, as they could have been seen, heard or caught. It showed a complete lack of fear on the killer's part, and someone with that much confidence was a very dangerous person indeed.

Mel let her mind go back to Ned's cottage. The fire was lit, which meant Ned had not long since been there and might still have been alive at that point. They may have just missed him heading out to the main crop field. Had the man come looking for him there first, only to find her with the police instead? Had their presence spurred the action that followed? Or, was Ned already dead by then, and the man came to the cottage for another reason? The latter was the likely scenario, because the timeline between Ned being found and their return to the house was so tight.

Mel replayed the appearance of the man. She hadn't seen him that well, if the truth be known, and Mel cursed herself for not paying more attention as her mind had been focused elsewhere. She had lost some of her edge since being demobbed, and not having to always be alert of her surroundings. But he had stood at the back door with Jennings as they'd come downstairs, and taken a small step back out as they reached the bottom step. All she knew was he had grey hair, and was around six feet tall. Not overweight, but not athletic. A man she'd taken as being in his forties: an acceptable age for an uncle for a man of Ned's years. In fact, they'd all taken him at face value, and that was because his voice was so calm and moderated, with no guilt making him speak just a touch too high or too fast. Otherwise, both she and Derrin would have picked up on it.

Mel had wanted there to be a valid explanation for Ned's absence and not some sinister one, which was a major factor in her acceptance of the stranger and his story of where Ned was: a total lie that she hadn't picked up on.

*His hands...* Mel thought. Yes, she'd seen one of his hands. He'd put it briefly on the back door as she, Jennings and Derrin turned to leave by the front. Perhaps they'd find a fingerprint? *But his hand?* There was something about it that was at odds with the accent and the voice, which was very local but somehow wasn't quite right – had she seen his lips moving, she may have noticed that sooner. His hands were clean, with neat fingernails. Not a farmworker's hands at all.

*Ah! But why should they be?* Mel thought. He hadn't said he was a farm hand. He could be doing any job, none of them had thought to ask. Perhaps that wasn't a clue at all and meant nothing, but Mel still stored it for further consideration. Because they knew the man had lied about being related to Ned, it wasn't too far a stretch to see that his appearance at the cottage and Ned's death were connected. And might his soft hands be those of a killer?

A range of emotions was playing over her as Mel thought about the finality of never seeing Ned again. She was sad that she hadn't known he was an orphan, but then she had never had those kinds of conversations with the farm hands at Avonby. It was always about the work, and she was irritated with herself for even feeling guilty about that, because that was life. Why should she ask about anything that wasn't related to the job he was doing? Such questions were intrusive and she had no right to ask them. And why would he volunteer this information to her when their relationship was just business? They hadn't been friends, after all, even though she'd liked him and thought he was hardworking.

Yet, his co-workers knew, and it had been important to Ned or it wouldn't have been discussed with them. He was a loner, and on some level Mel had recognised that, and liked him for it, as it made him somewhat like herself in that regard. Ned had friends among his peers. She was glad now that this had been the case, even though those friends would now be hurting far more than Mel was over his loss.

Mel thought of the many people who had died over the last five or six years. A daily and unavoidable occurrence if you lived in London during the war. Mel had felt all those deaths in one way or another, and Ned's passing affected her in the same way. She felt unsafe, afraid, shocked, and experienced an overwhelming sense of loss.

Mel held onto her hands to stop the shaking as the tremors began. She couldn't give in to her emotions, not now! There was still too much to sort out and she saw her tremors as a pathetic weakness that left her useless to everyone around her.

She sighed, drawing in slow, steady breaths as she forced herself to be calm, and for once it worked without her having to disappear for a while to her room. Her hands steadied as she breathed, and pushed back at the memories that weakened her the most, refusing to let them consume her.

Perhaps the study was private enough to deal with her fragility, she thought. *Now to the job in hand.*

Jonathan would return soon, and she would have to tell him what had happened before it became common knowledge on the estate. Ned's death affected them all, and would no doubt send some of their employees into a spin. They had to be prepared for that and how it would impact their daily lives.

She heard movement in the hallway and got up, going to the door, hoping it was her cousin. The heavy burden of the news she would impart weighed on her, and the sooner she told him, the sooner she could relieve herself of some of it.

As she opened the door she saw Derrin, not Jonathan, being let in by Williams. He let the butler take his hat and coat.

On seeing the inspector arrive, Jennings had stood up and left his chair by the study to go to talk to him.

'Constable Perkins is going to give you a lift back to the station and then he'll come back here,' Derrin said to Jennings. 'You're relieved until tomorrow, when I want you to come here first thing and take over from Perkins.'

'Yes, Inspector,' said Jennings.

Jennings left the house and Mel found herself alone with Derrin in the hallway, as Williams had gone off to hang up his coat in the cloakroom.

'Any luck finding the stranger?' she asked.

'No,' Derrin said. 'We've searched extensively. I have also had Ned's cottage locked up for further investigations.'

'Good. We might find something that can help,' Mel said.

'We might, but you're not,' Derrin said.

'Derrin…'

'I'm not discussing this further,' Derrin said. 'You're out of this investigation as of now.'

Williams came back, preventing Mel from arguing with Derrin.

'I think His Lordship's car is coming up the driveway,' Williams said.

He opened the door, and Mel saw the Rolls-Royce pull up outside the house, proving the instinct, or good hearing, of the butler.

Henry opened the back door, Jonathan and then Laura got out.

'Williams!' Laura called, seeing the butler waiting for them. 'We have some packages. Can you get someone to help Henry and have them taken to my room.'

Williams rang for Toby and the two of them helped Henry bring in hat boxes, bags and packages. Laura and Jonathan had been on a shopping spree.

Mel and Derrin stayed out of the way while the Lord and Lady of Avonby came in with a great deal of fuss; but as Jonathan entered, he saw them standing outside the study.

'Inspector, you're still here?' Jonathan said. 'I thought the fingerprinting would have been over by now.'

'Unfortunately, I have some more bad news,' Derrin said.

'I should tell him,' Mel said.

Derrin shook his head. 'May we go into your study?'

Mel was a little cross when Derrin closed the study door behind them, leaving her outside, but instead of eavesdropping, she went downstairs to the kitchens to make herself useful.

In the kitchen, Mel found Mrs Felman with Mrs Weston.

'We have something to tell you all,' Mel said. 'Can you gather all house and garden staff and bring them up into the hallway, please?'

'Are you all right?' asked Mrs Weston.

Mel caught sight of herself in the glass of the kitchen window, which the darkness outside had turned into a mirror. She looked pale and drawn, but also sad. Not surprising.

'I'll see you all upstairs,' she said.

By the time Derrin came out of the study, and Laura had gone in to hear the bad news from Jonathan, Mel had the entire staff ready to be briefed.

Derrin came out and saw them all waiting, and took point again on telling the employees of Avonby about the tragedy.

'Ned Soames was killed today,' Derrin told them. 'We are investigating how and why that happened, but I want to tell you all, it was not an accident. Ned was murdered.'

A ripple of shocked murmurs took up among the servants. Both Daisy and Nancy began to cry and consoled each other. Mel glanced at them both, noting how Nancy was more upset than Daisy, and knowing she was a sensitive girl after how she reacted when the body was found, understood why she fell apart now.

'I'll be leaving a constable here on rotation night and day for a while.'

'Do you have a suspect, Inspector?' asked Mrs Felman.

'I'm not in a position to discuss that right now, but we are still making enquiries,' Derrin said. 'But I recommend that no one is ever alone outside on the estate and that from now on you go out in pairs only.'

When the servants had dispersed, and Perkins returned to take up his post in the house for the night, Derrin said his goodbyes and left without another word.

Mel was a little aggrieved that she hadn't had a chance to have a final discussion with him. She had wanted to mention the need to fingerprint Ned's back door but didn't have the opportunity. As she watched Derrin drive away, she realised that he had intentionally avoided further conversation by never being alone with her.

'Mel, can we talk?' said Jonathan from his study door.

Mel wondered how long he had been watching her as she'd gazed out of the hallway window, watching the Jowett Javelin lights disappear down the driveway. She turned and went into the study with a feeling of *déjà vu*, as this was becoming quite a common occurrence.

'What's going on with you and Bradley?' Jonathan asked bluntly.

'I've been helping to facilitate his investigation.'

Jonathan shook his head. 'It's more than that. You do have *history*.'

'During the war we were an item,' Mel admitted. 'But I'd appreciate you not telling Laura.'

'I knew it!' Jonathan said. 'Was it… serious?'

Mel shrugged. 'Does it matter?'

'Okay, I guess it is none of my business. I won't tell Laura, she's hysterical enough. She has gone to bed with a headache tonight. Terrible news about Ned.'

'He was a good man,' Mel said.

'But this Bradley thing… It's not on the cards again, is it?'

'My dealings with Derrin are purely professional and he's told me he doesn't want me involved in the investigation any more, as he believes it might put me in danger. So, I don't suppose I'll be seeing that much of him now.'

'Good grief! Then you must listen to him,' Jonathan said. 'Focus on the estate and nothing else from now on.'

Mel found herself paying close attention to Jonathan as he spoke, and she began to wonder if Derrin had already answered the question of their relationship and previous association, or maybe refused to when asked. Mel hadn't wanted to lie to Jonathan when he had been so direct; she didn't fill in all the details, though, as it wasn't his business.

'That's a little hard to do when there's a murderer on the loose,' Mel said. 'But I will, of course, keep my eye on the estate as a priority.'

'Good. On another note, how was your lunch with Richard?'

'Fine,' Mel said.

'You seeing him again?' Jonathan asked.

'No.'

Jonathan looked surprised. 'I thought you two were hitting it off.'

Mel shook her head but kept her own counsel on her real opinion of Richard Stanley, because she knew that he and Jonathan were friends.

'Oh well,' Jonathan said and the mood changed, becoming somewhat awkward. 'I'll stop Laura pushing him your way.'

'I'd be grateful if she did,' Mel said.

# 23

ALTHOUGH HE WAS STILL A LITTLE FRAIL, on returning home, Joseph's only wish was to take a walk around the garden. To make sure he didn't start doing things, since he was on strict instructions to rest, Mel went with him. They took a leisurely stroll from the back of the house, called in at the greenhouse to see Rosa, and then went on to the main landscaped gardens and Joseph's beloved rose bushes.

'You see, everything is in order, you don't need to worry,' Mel told him. 'You'll still be paid, and all you need to do is take this opportunity to recuperate.'

'Thank you,' Joseph said.

'And how is… your memory?' Mel asked.

'Still don't know how I came to be in the woods,' Joseph said. 'Can we check the flower beds at the front of the house?'

'Yes, if you feel up to it and aren't tired walking that far,' Mel said.

'Oh no, it's nice to get some fresh air.'

Mel took Joseph's arm and they walked around the house, coming up to the front entrance, where Joseph had planted some summer blooms to make the frontage more colourful and welcoming.

'Well, they are looking good,' Joseph said.

'They make me happy every time I see them. Let's get you back to the kitchen and some tea and cake.' She didn't add how much they all needed to be cheered up with what was going on around them.

Just then Derrin's car turned into the driveway. Mel and Joseph paused to watch his progress.

'If you don't mind,' she said to Joseph, 'I'd like to speak to the inspector.'

Derrin parked the car between Jonathan's Rolls and the police car that Jennings had come in that morning.

'You're looking better,' Derrin said to Joseph as he got out and walked towards them.

'Will be even more so if I get some of this fine country air every day again,' Joseph said. 'And thanks to Lady Mel's company.'

'I have news,' Derrin said to Mel.

'Please tell,' she said.

Derrin hesitated, glancing at Joseph, and then said, 'We fingerprinted Ned.'

'Joseph, let's get you back inside for the tea and cake I promised. I won't be a moment, Inspector.'

Once Joseph was safe and back inside the kitchen, Mel hurried back to the front of the house to find Derrin leaning on his car.

'What did you find out?' Mel asked.

'Ned's fingerprints were on the razor,' Derrin said. 'So, I think it's a safe bet he put it under your pillow, and probably stole it three years ago when it first went missing.'

'*Ned?* I can't believe it! I don't remember ever seeing him at the house,' Mel said.

'Well, the evidence is there,' Derrin said.

'But why? Why steal the razor and why leave it in my room? We know he couldn't be the killer because he was killed by them,' Mel said.

'Honestly Mel, I don't think we know anything,' Derrin said. 'Every time I think we are getting somewhere, something happens to throw us in a different direction.'

Mel grew quiet and thoughtful for a moment.

'Come into the kitchen with me,' she said. 'Let's ask some questions about Ned's movements. Maybe someone will know more about it than I do.'

'Okay. But I'll ask the questions, I don't want you to be seen to be involved.'

Mel shrugged.

'I am already involved, Derrin. This affects everyone at Avonby. There's no getting away from that.'

In the kitchen, they found Joseph nursing a hot drink and nibbling on some of Mrs Weston's delicious fruit cake. Daisy, Nancy and Toby were all busy doing chores, but Mrs Weston wasn't in the kitchen. Mel was just going to ask where she was when the cook came in from the downstairs hallway, holding a bunch of parsley, newly collected from the herb garden.

'Inspector Bradley has some questions,' Mel said.

'We'll carry on working while you ask, if you don't mind,' said Mrs Weston.

Derrin said he didn't and then went straight into his questions without any preamble. Mel could sense a growing frustration in the inspector, obvious from his previous words about curveballs. It did seem as though they were walking in circles, on the periphery of an answer that never quite materialised.

'Can any of you tell me anything about Ned? Did he ever come up to the house? Or have any of you seen him loitering around the building?' Derrin asked.

Daisy shook her head. 'Didn't know him.'

'I used to see him out on the fields and sometimes shared a few words if we met at church on Sunday,' Toby said.

'Same here,' Mrs Weston said. 'He was a quiet one. Not like Toby here, who can talk the hind legs off a donkey when he gets started.'

Mel glanced at Nancy, who was making no comment as she kept her head down while she was peeling carrots.

'Nancy?' Mel asked.

The girl's shoulders were shaking and silent tears slid down her cheeks.

Mel sat down next to the girl, then put her hand on her arm. Nancy looked up, then fell into Mel's arms, weeping into her shoulder.

'We was getting engaged,' she said through sobs.

When the tears subsided, Mel took Nancy outside with Derrin to talk to her in private. This reveal hadn't taken her by surprise as much as it should have, because she'd noted how much Nancy had cried when they'd announced the murder; unlike Daisy, who had only shed a few shocked tears. Things were starting to add up.

'So, Ned was here the night we found the tripwire?' Mel said. 'You were both on the stairs in the dark.'

'Oh yes, Miss! But he didn't do nothing wrong. Just sneaked in to see me,' Nancy said.

'Did anyone else know about you two?' Derrin asked.

'No. He wanted to keep it secret, until he'd earned enough for our wedding,' Nancy explained.

'How often did he come to the house?' Mel asked.

'Not much. Only a few times a week,' Nancy said. 'We didn't want to get caught.'

She revealed that she would sneak him in through the herb garden, which backed out onto the corridor at the end of the downstairs hallway.

'There's a doorway out to the gardens there, see?' Nancy said. 'But it's hidden behind a trellis wall.'

'How did you know about it being there?' Mel said.

'Ned told me,' Nancy cried again. 'Oh, it's so awful, him being killed and so young and lovely.'

'Nancy, did Ned ever say anything to you about the family? Or about the woman that was in the rose bushes?' Derrin asked.

'He didn't know anything about that, I swear he didn't. But… he didn't like His Lordship much. Said he wasn't a nice man. He wasn't happy when Mr Peters got the sack, you see, on account of things going missing in the house.'

'Mr Peters? I don't know about him. When did this happen?' Mel asked.

'More'n six or seven months back now. He was the butler, before Mr Williams. Ned and he were friendly, and he said the man was innocent of it all,' Nancy said. 'But… I didn't care for Mr Peters much and I did wonder at their friendship.'

'Is it possible that Ned was still in touch with Mr Peters?' Derrin asked.

'I don't think so. Ned said he left and that was the last they heard from him,' Nancy said.

'That's enough for now,' Derrin said, after he had clarified the days and times that she could remember when Ned was in the house with her. 'But I will want to speak to you again.'

Still tearful, Nancy went back into the house, leaving Mel and Derrin outside and alone.

'You don't know this Peters?' Derrin asked.

'No. But I didn't live here then. Jonathan will remember, of course,' Mel said. 'I wonder why no one has mentioned him before now?'

'He was a thief,' Jonathan said. 'I caught him taking one of Laura's rings from her jewellery case. She'd already lost another one, which we never got back.'

Jonathan explained that Aidan Peters had been working as the butler for the late Lord Greenway and his unfortunate family. When he and Laura took up residence, it wasn't long before several personal items went missing.

They had decided to keep the thefts secret, not making any comment about them at first in the hope the thief would show his hand.

'Peters got sloppy because he thought we didn't notice,' Jonathan said. 'Even caught red-handed he denied it. He claimed he saw the ring out and was putting it back. I knew he was lying.'

'But what was he doing in your rooms? I thought only Toby went up there when you needed a valet,' Mel asked.

'Peters doubled up for me in those days, as he had always been the previous lord's valet before his promotion to butler,' Jonathan said.

'Nancy says that Ned claimed Peters was innocent,' Derrin said.

'The thefts stopped as soon as he was gone. It proved to me we got the right man,' Jonathan said.

'You're certain nothing went after he left?' Derrin said.

'Yes,' Jonathan answered. 'It stopped immediately. Then we found Mr Williams, and the house has run so much smoother with him and

Mrs Felman working together. I gather there were some conflicts between the housekeeper and Peters as well.'

'Did you ever ask what they were?' Mel said.

'No. It didn't matter once the fellow had gone. But I did notice an improvement in the general atmosphere,' Jonathan said. 'The staff were somewhat happier.'

Mel left Derrin with Jonathan, as she had the urge to talk to the other employees who would have known Mr Peters. She wondered if any of them had seen or heard from the man since his dismissal.

'We should have mentioned Mr Peters sooner,' Mrs Felman said. 'That awful man.'

'And lose our jobs?' Mrs Weston said. 'His Lordship banned us from speaking the man's name ever again!'

Mel reached the bottom of the servants' stairs and came face to face with the startled women.

'Why did he bar you from talking about Peters?' Mel asked.

Mrs Felman was red in the face and shook her head, as though afraid to speak out even now.

'There was a fearful row,' Mrs Weston said, brave as always. 'We were coming back from church and there was His Lordship, beating the man all the way down the driveway.'

'Beating him?' Mel said.

'He was so angry. Calling him a thief, demanding to know where this ring was that had belonged to his mother. He'd given it to Lady Laura, then it went missing. I've never seen such rage before,' Mrs Weston continued.

'We sent Nancy running to the house to get Toby. Then he helped us take His Lordship back,' Mrs Felman said. 'But he was shouting and yelling that he'd kill Peters if he saw him again. I had Toby pack all of Mr Peters' things, and I was about to send him with his severance pay, but His Lordship said, "No." He could have his possessions but no remaining salary because he'd been stealing from them, and he reckoned he had been paid enough with what he took. I said we should call the police and have him arrested if that was the case, but His Lordship just wanted him gone.'

'And did Toby find any of the stolen items in Peters' possessions?' Mel asked.

'No. I asked him to search his room, and His Lordship was stood over him as he packed Peters' bags,' Mrs Felman said. 'We think he had sold all he had stolen already.'

'Who saw the man last?' Mel asked.

Mrs Felman and Mrs Weston exchanged a look.

'That'd be Ned,' Mrs Weston said.

Mel found Henry around the back of the house, smoking a cigarette as he sat on a stool outside the garage.

'I've just heard about Peters,' she said.

Henry took a long drag of the cigarette, then dropped it on the floor and ground it out with his foot.

'Oh yes?'

'What can you tell me about the last time you saw him?'

'I took his bags to Ned's cottage. Peters was there then. That was the last I saw him,' Henry said.

'Did you see him leave the estate?' Mel asked.

'No. But, I heard that Ned borrowed the farmer's truck and drove Peters to the train station,' Henry said.

'And you definitely haven't seen or heard from Peters since he left?' Mel asked.

'No, Lady Melinda. And if I had, I would have told His Lordship and got the police to him,' Henry said, and the vehemence in his voice made Mel ask a further question.

'You didn't like Peters then, before this?'

Henry shook his head. 'No one liked him. He had a darkness in him. He was mean to the staff. Never "asked" for anything but "demanded", and never gave no one any respect. He was also a little too friendly with the young girls on the estate. There was this one he just wouldn't leave alone: Ruby.'

Henry spat on the ground as if talking about Peters had left a bad taste in his mouth.

'Sorry, Your Ladyship!' he said, regaining his normally formal composure. 'I don't befriend men of his sort. He liked girls young, and little Ruby, well, she looked younger than her years, if you know what I mean?'

'I do,' Mel said, feeling slightly sick herself at the awful creature Peters appeared to be. She was glad he no longer worked at the estate for she was sure she wouldn't have liked him either. 'Thank you for your honesty.'

As Mel walked back to the house, she was beginning to see where the occupants of Avonby fell on her imagined chessboard. She had at last a starting point to this mystery and she believed that Peters might be an important piece. But for the fact that Peters had an axe to grind, it didn't quite add up, because why would Ned be friends with someone that nearly everyone didn't like or trust?

# 24

Joseph was making a slow return to the gardens and Mel thought it best to let him do so in his own time. He had been overseeing the freelance gardeners that came in to mow the lawns and to help with some of the bigger weeding jobs, and Mel had agreed he could continue to do this, as long as he remained seated on a chair and didn't start doing any physical work himself.

'Pardon me, Your Ladyship. May I have a word?' Joseph said when he saw Mel approach on her rounds with Constable Jennings in tow.

'Is everything all right?' Mel asked, but she was thrown by Joseph's formal address when for months now he'd called her 'Lady Mel' or just 'Mel' when he forgot and they were working side by side.

Joseph nodded. 'I've had a memory,' he said. 'Sparked, I think, by the inspector coming here the other day, and by other things… things the house staff have told me went on.'

'You've remembered something?'

'Yes, Your Ladyship.'

'Jennings, you had better write all this down for the inspector,' Mel said.

*One week earlier*

Joseph was pruning his prized rose bushes, still trying to nurse them back to health after the police had dug around, removing the body. He had his back to the house but had a weird feeling and glanced over his shoulder. Ned was behind him, pulling open the old gate behind the herb garden, which only Joseph used when he went in there to weed and it was one of those doors, hidden inside by a trellis, that very few people on the estate knew about. He was amazed that Ned did, but even more surprised that he was near the house when it wasn't his place to be.

It was an hour or so later when Ned emerged, and Joseph saw Nancy giving the man a kiss before he ran off back across the fields and towards the woods. But, as he did so, something fell from his pocket.

Joseph went to look at what Ned had dropped. He found a ring, tied to a piece of blue gingham hair ribbon which he recognised as like the one Nancy wore in her hair on Sundays. The ring was gold with a red jewel, and looked expensive. Thinking he'd discovered their budding romance, and not wanting Ned to have lost the engagement ring, which must have cost the man's savings, he followed, hoping to catch up with him.

Joseph wasn't as fast as Ned, who was much younger than him, so he called to him to stop.

'Ned lad!'

Ned stopped by the old oak and turned to look at Joseph.

'You dropped this.'

Ned looked shocked as Joseph handed him the ribbon and ring.

'Where did you find this?' he asked.

'You dropped it, after you came out from t'herb garden,' Joseph said.

'You saw me?' Ned said.

'Yep and your girl, but don't worry lad, we've all been in love before,' Joseph said. 'Maybe one day you and she will be wed and happy like me and Rosa.'

Ned took the ring and looked at it. His face was very serious and he was thoughtful.

'Pretty. Must have cost you a small fortune,' Joseph said.

'It was an heirloom,' Ned said.

'Really? Nice,' Joseph said.

He wished Ned good evening and then turned back towards the house.

\*

'Then, something struck me hard from behind,' Joseph said. 'That was the last I remembered.'

'Do you think it was Ned?' Mel asked.

'I don't want to think that, but who else?' Joseph said.

'It's not a nice thought,' Mel said. 'But I see your point.'

When they finished asking questions, Mel and Jennings went back to the house, leaving Joseph with Rosa and his team of gardeners. Another conversation with Nancy was warranted. She'd said she and Ned planned to marry, and Mel wondered if he had proposed, and whether she now had the ring in her possession; because if she did, she hadn't mentioned it. Mel wanted to see this heirloom, because Ned had no family to have inherited it from. It had to be a lie.

'Will the inspector be calling in today?' Mel asked Jennings.

'I'm not sure, Lady Melinda,' Jennings said.

'I think you ought to let him know about Joseph,' Mel said. 'You can use the phone in the hallway, of course.'

'Thank you,' Jennings said.

Back at the house, Jennings went off to call Derrin and tell him about the conversation with Joseph. Mel was left to her own devices, and she went into the drawing room and looked out on the lawns, watching the gardeners work.

She had a nagging doubt about the ring Ned dropped and what it would mean if her suspicions were right. What if Ned had been the thief at Avonby all along? That would explain his ownership of an expensive ring, for where else had he got it from?

After making comparisons with Nancy's list of the times he'd been in the house, Mel had found a correlation with the razor being left under her pillow and the tripwire being set. Ned had been in the house and had the opportunity to do both of those things while Nancy was working and he was hiding in the house waiting for her. After the vague description Daisy had given after she spotted someone in the corridor, he might well have been the person who stole the pages from the diary, too. The only thing she couldn't put together was motive. Why would Ned do all of this? If he was the thief, Peters had taken the fall for him, which meant Ned had got away scot-free. Could he truly hate Jonathan for accusing the wrong man under the circumstances?

*If he was the thief, at least he had the sense to stop once Peters was accused and fired*, Mel thought.

It was easy to make assumptions about someone based on a few details, she thought. If any of it proved to be correct, then her view on Ned would be changed forever.

But there was one major and glaring problem with believing the worst of someone she had found to be kind and caring in person: who had killed Ned, and why? What had he been involved in? She wondered now about the conversations Derrin must have had with the farmworkers and what he might have learnt, and was frustrated that she hadn't been included. The pieces of this puzzle were still so fragmented, and it hurt Mel's brain to have such empty spaces, with no new information to bridge the gaps because maybe, just maybe, one of them might have given something away that would fill in all those missing pieces.

She had once considered that Ned could be the knight, moving in an L-shape around the board. Somehow, he had ended up next to a rook: one swipe and Ned's story was over. But now she couldn't see him as any kind of hero if the evidence stacking up against him was true.

But why would he attack Joseph? There had to be a motive.

*Joseph had seen the ring.*

If Ned had stolen it, Joseph was the one person who could link him to the theft. But there was a major hole. *Nancy.* She must have seen the ring; he'd dangled it before her to prove his intentions. But Nancy was too close to Ned to be suspicious. She had been in love with him and thought he was going to marry her, therefore he had no fear she would betray him by mentioning it to anyone. He had manipulated her into secrecy, no easy feat when all a young girl would want to do was tell her friends if she was engaged. It showed Ned was very clever, smarter perhaps than any of them gave him credit for.

There were so many questions running through Mel's mind that she found herself in a quandary.

None of it explained why Ned was killed and who the man was that they found in his cottage. If they found that man again, they might have some answers. Mel couldn't imagine that happening.

An hour passed and Mel heard the doorbell chime. She came out of the library, and without waiting for Williams, opened the front door to see Derrin standing there.

'I'm glad you're here,' she said. 'I need to talk to you.'

'I thought you might,' said Derrin.

Mel looked around the hallway and decided they would be better outside, where their conversation was less likely to be overheard.

'Let's go for a drive,' she said.

Outside, they climbed into Derrin's car and she directed him back to Ned's cottage.

'What are we doing here?' he asked as he parked in front of the house.

'Did you search this place yet?' Mel said.

'A brief search, yes, but we're dusting for prints tomorrow and a more thorough examination will happen then. Why?' Derrin said.

'Jennings told you about the ring Joseph saw?'

'Yes, but I'd like to hear your thoughts on it,' Derrin said.

Mel ran through everything she had been thinking. Ending with the final stumbling block of motive for all of it.

'I think we can both agree the ring is likely to be Laura's ring, based on what we know about Ned's circumstances,' Derrin said.

'More than likely, I'd say,' Mel agreed.

'Then we have a motive for the attack on Joseph,' Derrin said.

'I thought that too at first, but no. It doesn't add up,' Mel said. 'Ned *found* Joseph. He was relieved when he was alive. I saw it on his face.'

'Maybe he thought he wouldn't remember who hit him.'

'Ned wouldn't have had any way of knowing that the blow would mess with Joseph's memory,' Mel said. 'Not even the doctor knew how or why that happened. Ned may have witnessed Joseph being hit, though, and deliberately helped us find him in time because he didn't want him to die. This shows he was not a bad person, and makes me think he wasn't capable of such a violent attack anyway.'

'He may have panicked when he saw the ring,' Derrin pointed out. 'Many a man has been guilty of attack out of fear.'

'I know. It's what I thought at first… but I don't believe he did it.'

'What if he witnessed the assault…?'

'That would mean he wasn't working alone,' Mel said. 'His accomplice hit Joseph.'

Mel looked back at the cottage.

'No, Mel,' said Derrin, reading her intention. 'It's locked up. If we go inside, we'll be tampering with evidence.'

'I think the ring is in there,' Mel said.

'I doubt it will be. But supposing you're right about all of this, what if the stranger we saw was Ned's collaborator? He's probably taken the ring along with any other items Ned may have stolen from the house, and all the proof of that will already be gone. Damn it! Why didn't I question that man more? Why did we take it all on face value?'

'He was very calm. He sounded authentic. I was taken in too, so you can't blame yourself for any of that. We're not infallible.'

'We used to be,' Derrin said.

Mel felt his eyes on her, but she kept her gaze on the cottage. She didn't feel strong enough right then to meet his gaze, as too many memories of their work together imposed themselves. They had thought themselves invincible. Mel now knew they weren't.

'We won't know if the ring is gone unless we search. After all, you weren't looking for anything in particular last time,' Mel said, changing the subject.

'That's true, but I can't allow you to go in there.'

Derrin put the car in reverse and drove back to the house.

'Are you going to talk to Joseph?' Mel asked.

'Yes. And Nancy. I'd like to see if she has the ring,' Derrin said.

'Can I come with you?' Mel said. 'Nancy is likely to be tearful, you can excuse my presence on saving you the embarrassment of a woman's tears.'

Derrin laughed. 'Have you ever known tears to upset me?'

'Not in the old days, but things are different now, aren't they?'

She didn't add that she wasn't sure where his heart lay these days, nor if she wanted to find out. They looked at each other as things unsaid hung between them like a thick smog. But then the moment was gone.

Back to the business at hand, Derrin got out of the car and came round to open her door for her. For once, Mel let him, as she was still too deep in her own thoughts to object.

# 25

SINCE THE REVELATION OF HER ROMANCE WITH Ned, the occupants of Avonby had left Nancy alone to wallow in her misery. Once the dam of grief had opened, the girl was in tears at the drop of a hat. After a few days it had begun to grate on Mrs Weston's nerves, whose staunch attitude to work was what kept her own memories of lost loved ones at bay. And as Mel and Derrin came into the kitchen looking for the tearful housemaid, they found Mrs Weston in the throes of tearing Nancy off a strip.

'Good grief, Nancy!' she snapped. 'If you thought more about your work, you'd think less about unhappy things. Stop your whimpering, girl, and do something for a change.'

Mrs Weston's harsh words snapped the girl to attention, and she wiped her eyes and set to chopping up the vegetables for dinner with only the occasional sniff.

'If we may, Mrs Weston,' Derrin said. 'We'd like to talk to Nancy again now.'

'Well, if you must, Inspector, but we have people to feed around here and dinnertime waits for no man. She'll have to talk to you while she works. Lord knows she's been dawdling enough today.'

Derrin gave a small smile, in no small part because he respected brutal honesty and hard work above anything else, and the brusque cook reminded him of many stoic people he'd come across during the war. Sometimes there was no room for indulgence when work had to be done.

'We can do that,' said Mel. 'I'm here as support, Nancy.'

Nancy began to snivel again with the welcome sympathy, which drew a loud tut from Mrs Weston.

'Now stop that, girl,' Mrs Weston said. 'The inspector doesn't want to talk to a wet blanket.'

Mel covered her mouth with her hand, to hide the mirth that rippled up at Mrs Weston's words. A humour that disappeared as soon as Derrin started to grill Nancy about her engagement to Ned.

'So you did see a ring?' Derrin said.

'Yes. I wore it when we were alone,' Nancy said.

'But he always took it away with him afterwards?'

Nancy nodded.

'And you don't have it now?' Derrin asked.

'No, Inspector. I'd be wearing it in Ned's honour if I did. But he told me it was mine, and we tied my ribbon on it, so he could wear it round his neck when we weren't together.'

Nancy's mention of the ribbon confirmed that Joseph's story was not a false memory, which was something Derrin had feared.

'What did the ring look like?' Derrin asked and Nancy described it much the same as Joseph had, a gold band with a ruby.

'Where did he keep it in the cottage?' Mel asked.

'The cottage? I dunno. I never went there. Ned always came to see me,' Nancy said. Then Nancy began to sob again at the memory.

'That's enough,' Mrs Weston said. 'She's got to get some water on to boil these potatoes.'

Derrin nodded. 'I'm done for now. Thank you, Mrs Weston.'

'Get a spurt on now, Nancy,' Mrs Weston said.

Mel gave her a nod, because she knew what the cook was trying to do. Nancy had wallowed enough. Ned wasn't coming back and life had to go on. It was how the world moved since the war, there was no time for self-pity, and the sooner you got on with living the better.

It had been a hard day, full of revelations, and although Mel had been used to many varied and sometimes dangerous events during wartime, her months spent at Avonby had dulled her senses. She wasn't as adept at dealing with such dramatic twists and turns any more and she didn't always have the energy for it.

After Derrin left, despite being tired, Mel wanted to go to Ned's cottage and poke around. She had a feeling that the ring and anything else of any value would be well hidden, but would be there. The challenge of finding them first appealed to her: she was competing with Derrin again, and it was something they had drifted into back in the day when they were lovers. It was partly Derrin's fault, of course: he had told her she couldn't disturb the cottage until the police had been in, and being told 'no' only made her want to do it more.

She floundered in the hallway, frustrated, wondering whether to go to her room to be alone, or to seek Jonathan and Laura's company, which would take her mind off things. If she had dinner with them this evening, though, they would want an account of what had happened during the day. Mel had no doubt, despite being out all day, that Jonathan would know Derrin had been there again, talking to her and their staff. Williams would have told him, even if one of the others hadn't.

The phone rang and Mel, being nearby, went to pick it up.

'Avonby Hall, can I help you?' she said.

'Ah, Melinda! Just who I wanted to speak to,' Lord Stanley said. 'Are you free for dinner this evening?'

Mel was shocked by the front of the man, but never short of words, and trying to deal with him politely, she told him she was busy.

'I heard about your farm hand's death. Must be stressful being there right now. Are you sure you can't excuse yourself?'

Some choice language sat on the tip of her tongue, and had Mel still been in the barracks she would have used it, but she forced herself to remain civil, while making sure that Stanley was put in his place once and for all.

'Look, I'll be honest – I'm not interested in continuing a friendship with you, Lord Stanley.'

'Oh come on! You can't blame a man for trying? It's not like I forced myself on you.'

'Good evening, Lord Stanley,' she said. 'Please don't call me again.'

Mel hung up the phone only to find Laura staring at her from the bottom of the stairs.

'Oh really, Melinda. Have you no sense at all? Stanley is a good catch!' Laura said. 'He was really interested in you and is on the market as his bachelor days have to come to an end now he needs an heir.'

Mel bit back the response she wanted to give, something along the lines of how she wasn't a brood mare and didn't want to be married off anyway.

'Stanley is a creep. And I will say no more than that out of respect for your friendship with him,' Mel said.

Laura flushed with anger and appeared to be about to have a tantrum until Williams came into the hallway to see if they were ready for dinner.

'I'll eat upstairs tonight,' Mel said. 'Laura, please excuse me, I'm very tired.'

Laura walked away, her small heels clacking on the wooden floor as she headed towards Jonathan's study, leaving Mel with Williams.

'If Lord Stanley calls in or telephones to speak to me, no matter what he says, I'm unavailable,' Mel told Williams. 'As for dinner, Lord Jonathan and Lady Laura will ring for it soon.'

'Has he been bothering you?' Williams said.

'I think I've dealt with it, but just in case he is persistent,' Mel said.

'He won't get past me,' Williams said.

'I know. Thank you.'

Men like Stanley didn't take rejection well, and Mel had met his sort before. He might react in any number of ways to how she had cut him off at the knees. He could accept it and move on – that's what a real gentleman would do – or he might see it as a challenge and pursue her harder. She hoped that Lord Stanley would just take her disinterest and leave her alone. Especially as it was obvious she hadn't been attracted to him from the start.

In her room, Mel's thoughts turned back to the occupants of Avonby, still moving in all directions on her imaginary chessboard. She worried that at any moment another one of them would be wiped from the game. A scenario she didn't relish, but after all they had discovered that day, she wouldn't be surprised at anything that happened.

Mel's mind fell to Nancy – she saw her now as a poor expendable pawn, being pushed around by Ned. But what shocked her most were her new thoughts regarding Ned. She had lost all respect for him without any real proof. All she knew was that he may be a thief, was possibly involved with Joseph's attack, and that he had the opportunity to create a tripwire on the staircase, which might have killed or injured someone if she hadn't found it. An act that, if he was guilty, made him far from innocent, and certainly no protector. Mel could only wonder how she had been so taken in by him. How they all had been. Ned was the last person she had suspected of any of these things, until the evidence started to pile up.

She lined up the pieces now. Laura and Jonathan were the king and queen, Ned – no longer a white knight – but what was he instead? Was Ned's fake uncle the rook?

A knock on her door brought her from her reverie and Mel found Nancy there, holding a plate of food for her. The girl's eyes were red-rimmed and her nose shiny from being blown. For a minute she considered questioning her again, but then thought better of it. Nancy was not in a good place, and she didn't want her to get any more upset than she already was.

'Your dinner, Lady Melinda,' Nancy said, but she didn't look Mel in the eyes and Mel knew it was because the girl was still so close to tears.

Mel took the plate, thanked her, and didn't bother to correct her from using the formal title. All she wanted was food and sleep because she had some plans that would see her up very early in the morning.

# 26

THE NEXT MORNING MEL WOKE FEELING STRONGER. Pulling on a pair of slacks and a loose-fitting blouse, Mel slipped the handgun into the waistband of her trousers under the blouse, and some extra rounds in her pocket. It was early, but Mel left her room, knowing there would be few people around to see her. She was determined to be at the cottage before the police arrived, and she planned to look around with or without permission. After all, the Avonby estate owned the cottage, and she argued to herself that she had every right to look inside on Jonathan's behalf.

Constable Perkins was at his post in the hallway when Mel went downstairs. Jennings would be arriving soon to relieve the constable and take over the day shift, and Mel knew she had to get away before then because Jennings wouldn't let her out of his sight thereafter. Mel gave Perkins a wave and walked past him, heading down the stairs to the kitchens. She slipped quietly by the closed kitchen door and went unnoticed into the boot room.

The night before, Mel had come downstairs on the pretext of getting some hot milk and she'd put a lock-picking kit (another left-over tool from her army days) into the pocket of her tweed jacket. She checked the pocket now, making sure the kit was still there along with her gloves. Then she pulled on some outdoor shoes before sliding back the bolt on the door and letting herself out of the house. For the first time in days, she was alone and unattended, and the sudden freedom felt good.

She hurried past the stables and across the paddocks, then skirted the woods as she took a round trip towards Ned's cottage, to avoid being seen by the farmworkers who would be out already. Arriving in the back garden of the cottage, Mel looked around, aware that this was probably the route the stranger had taken to appear at the back door when they had called and were looking for Ned.

In a field nearby, she could hear one of the tractors running and a few calls and shouts as the farm hands, who were always up at the crack of dawn, worked and chatted. Mel pulled on the gloves, then took out the lock pick and began to work on the back door. It wasn't long before she was inside the house, but a wave of nostalgia for where she had learnt how to do this came over her and she paused. Derrin featured again in the memory and guilt soon followed as she knew she shouldn't be here against his instructions. She pushed the thought away with new determination. He should know better than banning her from doing something anyway, knowing that in the old days she would always take it as a challenge.

There was an eerie quiet inside the cottage, and although it was only late June, the interior was cold. Mel looked around the small kitchen and began opening cupboards. Ned had an excess of tin cans inside his cupboards, hoarded perhaps, because of the lack of certain foods over the years. He liked beans, tinned carrots and tinned potatoes, with a few cans of soup. There was a bag of porridge oats, which Mel examined and poured out into a large bowl she found in another cupboard. She was trying to make sure that nothing was hidden inside the food where a normal searcher wouldn't look. But the cans were genuine and all sealed and the oats were just as they appeared to be. She poured them back into the packet and continued her search, systematically and carefully rifling through drawers and the remaining cupboards but coming up with nothing. After each search she straightened whatever she'd moved so that it wouldn't be obvious she had been there.

Once she had swept the kitchen, Mel looked at the living room. She tipped over the two-seater sofa and checked in the lining underneath. From the lock pick set, she took out a penknife and slit the lining at one side, searching inside. There was nothing there. She found a rucksack in the corner and searched it to no avail.

Aware that she was running out of time, Mel hurried up the stairs and into Ned's bedroom. It was slightly warmer upstairs, but there was a chill inside the building that didn't reflect the temperature outside. Mel looked in Ned's chest of drawers, the wardrobe, searched pockets of clothing, but there was no sign of the ring or anything unusual. Ned looked to be innocent, but she wasn't convinced yet that there was nothing to hide.

She pulled off the bed linen and looked under the mattress, finding a few pounds that Ned was obviously saving. Afterwards, she placed the money back: it wasn't what she was looking for and hardly enough to show for any sales of stolen items. Then she dragged the bedding back into place. But not before she bent down and looked under the bed. She could see right through to the other side and there was nothing underneath.

Disappointed, Mel was about to give up when she thought about the dressing room. She opened the door and went inside. She went straight to the dresser and searched the drawers, finding only bits of clothing, men's undergarments and socks.

Frustrated now, Mel looked around the tiny room, then she saw a small square of blue gingham ribbon trapped under the tin bath. She got down on her knees and lifted the bath off the floor on that side, thinking that perhaps there might be a loose panel on the floor, but there wasn't one. What she did find, though, was a wad of newspaper, taped up against the bath, from which the ribbon protruded. Mel pulled it off, ripping open the paper. Inside she found the ring with the ribbon tied around it, and a further surprise: a locket necklace.

Mel opened the locket and saw a faded sepia photograph of a young woman about Nancy's age, holding a newborn baby. Mel realised that what she'd possibly found was a picture of Ned's mother, and maybe himself as a baby. She could just make out a ring on the woman's finger, a ring that could be the one Mel now held.

*Maybe this* was *a family heirloom*, Mel thought.

Completely thrown by this turn of events, Mel pushed the items and the newspaper into her pocket, and then she hurried downstairs and out the back of the cottage, being careful to relock the door. She glanced over at the small shed that was Ned's outhouse, containing the toilet, and considered again how conditions needed to be improved for the workers on the estate; even the servants' quarters at Avonby had plumbing now. Granted, it had all been modernised when the army had taking residence, and hadn't been from the Greenway coffers. As she plunged into the woods behind, she heard cars arriving at the cottage and knew she had made it out in time, because the police team had arrived to search and fingerprint it.

She was in less of a hurry as she made her way back to Avonby, knowing she'd have to come clean to Derrin. She'd explain how she'd searched, careful not to leave prints that might confuse the police's fingerprinting experts, but not before she learnt what it all meant.

Ned had told both Joseph and Nancy that the ring had been his mother's, but he'd also told his fellow farmworkers that he was an orphan and had never known his parents. One or the other tale was the truth, unless the ring and locket had been kept for him by another family member. A member who might really be his uncle after all. If that were the case, then Ned was probably not a thief, and the stranger was probably not Ned's killer as they had first thought. A fact that might mean they were all back to square one when it came to tracking down who was.

Mel rubbed her forehead as her head ached a little with the intensity of her thoughts. She had no idea what Derrin would make of her findings but knew he wouldn't be pleased with her for disobeying him.

Mel stopped by the oak tree, thinking about how they'd found Joseph. She had struggled to see Ned as guilty, and she might now have found the proof that he wasn't. She took the ring from her pocket and examined it. It was pretty but not nearly as expensive as Joseph had described it to be: the ruby, though genuine, was far from perfect, and the item would not have been something Jonathan's mother would have left, nor would he have given Laura such a ring. Laura was a snob and would have turned her nose up at it. Not everything in life had to be expensive to be loved, though, and Mel knew Nancy had loved the ring because of its meaning to Ned.

But if it was Ned's mother's, why had Ned not let Nancy keep it? That behaviour was one of the reasons she and Derrin believed it to be stolen in the first place.

Mel returned the ring back to her pocket and walked back towards the house, her mind no less confused, as she couldn't come to any conclusion that would give her a definitive answer as to who killed Ned and who killed the woman whose body started this whole thing in the first place. She was still no closer to knowing, and it wasn't a situation she was happy about.

As Mel emerged from the woods, she came face to face with Derrin.

'When I heard you had given Perkins the slip, I knew I'd find you out here,' Derrin said. 'I have some news. Ned really does have an uncle. He came into the station yesterday after finding out he was dead.'

'I wasn't expecting that,' Mel said. She slipped her hand into her pocket and felt the ring and locket. 'Ned lied about being an orphan?'

'It's rather a sad tale, I'm afraid. His mother had a breakdown after he was born. She had spent all this time in an asylum. Ned's uncle, Jimmy Soames, didn't know she'd had a child out of wedlock until last year, when he found Ned's birth certificate among his sister's possessions.'

'So, he came to find Ned?'

'Yes. And Ned had been visiting his mother regularly ever since. But she did pass recently,' Derrin said. 'Apparently, that day we met Soames at Ned's cottage, Ned had gone off to let Farmer Johnson know he'd be away a few days while his uncle went to collect some things for him. He then took what Ned had asked him to collect and left, because Ned had said he'd meet him later.'

Mel took the ring and locket out of her pocket. 'So he was telling the truth? I suppose these belong to the uncle now? Unless he wants Nancy to have them.'

'Oh Mel! You're incorrigible.'

'I had to know if Ned was a bad person, it didn't correlate with what I knew of him,' Mel said.

'I suppose I'm to blame, I should have known you'd do something. I just *hoped* you wouldn't.' Derrin sighed, but there was a small twinkle in his eye that also showed he was at some level a little pleased because she'd found the ring. 'You'd better give me those.'

'This does mean, I suppose, that Ned was not in cahoots with our lady-killer,' Mel said.

'I don't know,' Derrin said. 'Someone killed Ned for a reason that we haven't discovered yet. And Ned did have the opportunity to take the diary pages and to leave the tripwire. And let's not forget the razor with his print on it. Maybe there is still a link to the missing trinkets and Lady Laura's ring?'

Mel fell quiet.

'The fact is, we still have a killer on the loose and you shouldn't be wandering around alone until we find them,' Derrin said.

'Maybe that's exactly what I should do,' Mel said. 'Try and draw him out. Have you had any luck finding the girl, Ruby Lewis?'

Derrin shook his head.

'And we still don't have a clue who Jane Doe is, either?' Mel asked.

'No,' Derrin said.

'Perhaps they are connected after all.'

'How so?'

'I've been thinking. Ruby went missing at the same time as our Jane Doe's body was dumped…'

'Yes, but we know she can't be her…' Derrin said.

'That's right. But what if she saw who did it? Maybe she was so scared, she is making sure she won't be found by us, or whoever killed Jane Doe.'

'She'd have to have help and a false identity,' Derrin said.

Mel glanced back through the woods. Ned was appearing to her as a knight again: this time on a shiny white horse. Maybe he had helped the girl escape from whoever was pursuing her, which would mean that he too had known who the mystery woman's killer was. Reason enough to get him a bullet in the back of the head, but why didn't he tell them what he knew?

Mel's mind went into overdrive, but she didn't share her thoughts with Derrin for now. She wanted to reflect more, and watch the behaviour of the occupants of Avonby – this time with a new stage of enquiry going through her mind. Perhaps a slight slip of the tongue would reveal the motive and the killer.

# 27

Despite the latest revelation throwing a spanner in the engine, Mel was relieved that Ned wasn't so bad after all. There were still so many unanswered questions, things that Ned may well have been able to clear up for them. Derrin had confirmed that Ned's mother and uncle existed, and now she believed that Ned kept his mother a secret from everyone because of the stigma attached to her condition. Most people were uncomfortable with the idea of any form of mental malady, and one so bad that the woman had spent her entire life locked up must have weighed heavily on the young man and his future with Nancy. In some ways, it explained a lot about why he might hide the ring and locket from his co-workers, avoiding explanations for fear that some might think her disease had passed on to Ned. An ignorant attitude that Mel knew many people entertained.

Ned's body was released to the uncle and a funeral was arranged, but in another town, where Ned's mother was buried. Mel exchanged a letter with Jimmy Soames, confirming that she would attend on behalf of the family. She also offered to take Nancy with her, but the girl said she couldn't face it.

Mel wanted to talk more to Soames about Ned, and she had so many questions that she was sure he could answer. So, when the funeral day came, Mel went alone, driving her motorbike through country lanes until she reached the small village and tiny church.

There were very few people at the funeral, none of whom were friends of Ned. Mel sat in one of the back rows of the church, listening to Soames, who she saw now was quite a distinguished figure, as he said a few words for the nephew he was only just starting to know and had so suddenly lost.

After the service, when Ned's coffin was in the ground, Mel introduced herself properly to the uncle. He shook her hand, and she remembered again that she'd noticed his callous-free soft hands at Ned's cottage.

'I had planned to bring Ned's fiancée, Nancy,' Mel said. 'But she wouldn't have coped well. The poor girl has obviously taken his death very hard.'

Soames nodded. 'The inspector mentioned her.'

He reached into his suit pocket and took out the ring, still attached to the ribbon.

'I'd like you to give this to her,' Soames said. 'I think Ned would have wanted that.'

Soames, whose measured tones held only a trace of the local accent, revealed he had lived in Europe for many years and planned now to go back there.

'I came back to find my sister only to learn about Ned, and I then lost them both,' he said.

'I'm sorry for your loss,' Mel said. 'But can I ask you, did Ned ever say anything to you about being scared of someone, or did he ever mention a girl called Ruby Lewis?'

Soames looked surprised by the questions.

'I know someone killed Ned,' Soames said. 'The inspector said it was murder. But I don't know why. He never gave me any impression he was worried about anything. But he was very pleased that I had found him and introduced him to his mother. Even though, sadly, she had no idea who he or I was. But sorry, no, that name means nothing to me. I wish I could help more.'

Mel gave her sympathy again, before leaving Soames by the graveside and heading home.

'I'll wear it always!' said Nancy when Mel gave her the ring on her return. 'What a nice man Mr Soames must be.'

Mel agreed he was, but there was still something nagging her about Ned's death. His few possessions had been packed, and Soames hadn't wanted them, asking if they could be sent to the orphanage where Ned grew up. She had offered Nancy the chance to look through his things first, and the girl had gone to the cottage with her, but all she kept was a scarf that she'd knitted for Ned for Christmas because she said it still smelt like him. The rest of Ned's meagre possessions had been taken to the orphanage in Sheffield by the farmer in his truck, in the hope that they could be useful there.

After that, life at Avonby returned to a semblance of normality, as Derrin deemed the occupants safe enough to remove his constables.

'I think Ned was the link between our Jane Doe and the killer,' Mel said, reviewing what she had been thinking. 'He may have helped Ruby Lewis and therefore knew why she left. It doesn't explain why he didn't tell anyone else, though, or why he didn't encourage Ruby to come forward and tell the police what she had seen.'

'I wondered when we'd discuss this,' Derrin said. 'I had been thinking the same. His silence doesn't add up, but with him dead, I suspect the killer has moved on.'

'Do you think the killer found out where Ruby Lewis went?' Mel asked. 'Do you think Ned gave her up in those final moments?'

'We may never know, but I'm keeping the case open. And our search for the girl will continue,' Derrin said. 'She is the only possible lead we have.'

After Derrin removed the police protection, Henry drove Mel into the town a day or two later as she wanted to follow up with him. She wasn't expecting anything to come of this trip, because the case was growing colder by the day, but Mel wasn't happy with the lack of conclusion, and every day she watched the occupants of Avonby for any small sign that one of them knew something. In the background she suspected that Derrin was still following what leads he had, but as time passed it seemed even more unlikely that the killer would be caught. Even so, she wanted to check in with him, and remind Derrin that she was still alert and hopeful.

There was a tentative confidence returning to the occupants of Avonby, with no further 'accidents', and Mel had noted that even Nancy had some cheery days, though she suspected it would be a long time before the girl's eye would wander in the direction of another possible suitor.

Henry dropped Mel off at the station door and she told him to wait for her.

'Hopefully I won't be too long, but I may have to wait to see him if he's busy,' Mel said.

Mel went in and, after asking to see Derrin, she was escorted into the small office she'd been in before. Derrin wasn't there, but the constable who took her in told her he wouldn't be long.

There was a file on the desk and Mel saw that it was their case. Glancing at the door, she waited to see if Derrin was about to come in. But when, after a few minutes, he didn't arrive, she pulled the folder to her. Opening the bulky file, she began to flick through the statements and notes Derrin had made on the case, speed-reading the information and committing as much of it to memory as she could. There were several photographs of the body and the rose patch, and Mel was lost for a time in the full exposure of the grave as she absorbed the images of the girl. There was a clear six months of decay on the body, but she was thrown into her makeshift grave with no respect or grace, as if she were some garbage to be disposed of. Her soil-caked hair looked as though it may have been possibly brunette, but it was difficult to tell with the black-and-white images.

She turned the page eventually, having seen enough of the body, and then she saw a letter inside the file from a person claiming to have seen Lord Greenway with a woman in London. The letter was loaded with intimation, inferring that Jonathan was having an affair with the woman. The handwriting was neat and Mel thought it familiar, but the name on the bottom was not one she recognised.

Even so, she made a mental note of the name, Peter Sandi, and the Sheffield address at the top of the paper where he lived, and decided she'd make her own enquiries to find this man.

Mel heard someone outside the office and she closed the file, pushing it back into place, exactly where it had been when she arrived.

'I'm sorry, Lady Greenway,' the constable said, coming back. 'I think the inspector is going to be some time.'

'Never mind,' Mel said. 'I'll come back later. I have some errands to run.'

The constable led her out and Mel reached the doorway only to see Henry in deep conversation with a young woman she'd never seen before. There was something about the way the girl looked around that made Mel hang back and watch. She saw Henry slip something into her hands and the girl thanked him, giving him an impulsive hug, before she turned and hurried away.

'Ah, Your Ladyship,' Henry said when he noticed her coming down the station steps. 'I didn't think you'd be out so soon.'

Henry opened the car door and Mel got into the back seat. 'Who was that?' she asked.

'Who?'

'The girl that hugged you,' Mel said.

'Oh, just some girl I know,' Henry said.

Mel studied Henry through the rear-view mirror but said nothing more. It didn't matter who Henry was seeing, that was none of her business, and her mind was on the name and address she had seen and memorised in the file right then and nothing else. She considered asking Henry to drive her straight there, but thought better of it as she wanted what she knew to remain a secret for now.

'Henry?'

'Yes, Lady Melinda?'

'Drop me at the train station, please,' Mel said.

'The station?'

'Yes. I'm going into Sheffield.'

'Wouldn't you like me to take you?' he said.

'No. Just drop me and I'll call you when I get back,' Mel said. 'You could go and spend time with your lady friend, if you wish.'

Henry blushed but didn't answer.

\*

At Sheffield station, Mel had to wait to get one of the few taxis working the area, and gave the driver the address of Peter Sandi that she had taken from the file on Derrin's desk.

'I just want to know where this is,' she said, not knowing the city very well.

The driver took her away from the station and out of the town, and before she knew it she was back on country lanes, heading, it seemed, to a location that was in the middle of nowhere.

'There it is, ahead of us, milady, 'bout half a mile,' said the driver.

'That cottage?' she asked. 'Can you pull over *here*, please?'

'That's the address you asked for. The Drover's Cottage, Bellamy Lane,' the taxi driver said.

Looking through the taxi window, Mel checked over the cottage at a distance as she didn't want anyone to notice them at this point. Today wasn't the day to find out more, just the location. From her vantage point the garden looked a little overgrown and unkempt, but she couldn't tell more as she was too far away.

'Do you know who lives here, by any chance?' she asked.

'No. Sorry,' he said.

'Okay. Take me back to the station, please,' Mel said.

'That's it?' said the driver.

'I've seen what I wanted to,' Mel said.

She paid attention to her surroundings as they drove back. Bellamy Lane joined Sheffield Road and went on into the city, going from rural landscape to a built-up area, with houses, shops and pubs.

When they reached the train station, Mel paid the driver and got out. She went into the station through one of its impressive arches and made her way to the ticket booth.

While she waited for the next train back to York, she went outside the station to a telephone box she'd spotted earlier. She dialled the number for Avonby Hall, and after a few rings, Williams answered.

'Mr Williams, will you ask Henry to collect me from the police station at five o'clock this afternoon?' she asked.

'Certainly, Lady Mel. I'll go and tell him now,' Williams said.

Once her collection was arranged, Mel went back into the station. She took a seat in the main concourse to wait for her train platform to be announced. Knowing she would be back by four, she hoped that the collection time would allow her the opportunity to speak with Derrin first.

While she waited, Mel cast her eyes around the large concourse. The station was busy, with plenty of trains coming and going, particularly the Sheffield-to-London route that Mel knew ran daily. Shorter trips to York and back were more frequent, with a few round trips taking place throughout the day. Mel saw a woman in a brown raincoat pulling two children – a girl of around eight years old, and a boy of about three or four, wearing short trousers and carrying a miniature car clasped in his hand – towards the ticket booth. Mel's eyes followed them as the mother struggled with the young boy, but then she noted a man, standing by the timetable board. He was wearing a brown suit, holding a folded newspaper in one hand and an umbrella in the other. He kept his face averted, and because of the brown fedora he was wearing she couldn't see his face or hair. There was something off about the man, even though he appeared to be reading the board. Mel thought he was watching her from the corner of his eye.

A commotion started at the ticket booth as the little boy in short trousers dropped to the floor and screamed in a temper tantrum. Mel's attention switched to take in what was happening. She saw the start, and rapid end, of a tantrum as the little boy's mother pulled him up off the floor and delivered a resounding slap across his legs. Mel winced as she saw a red mark beginning to flare up on the child's skin, but the slap had stopped the bad behaviour and he let his mother take his hand again. Tickets now in her grasp, she pulled him and his sister off towards one of the platforms.

Distraction over, Mel's eyes sought the man with the newspaper again, only to find he'd gone. She scanned the concourse with her eyes, but he appeared to have either left the station or gone to whatever platform his train was on. Either way, he was nowhere to be seen.

A prickling sensation brought the hairs up on the back of Mel's neck. She looked around again. She knew she was being watched, though she couldn't pinpoint who and from where.

An announcement came over the Tannoy and Mel's train and platform were finally called. With a final glance around, she stood and hurried off to Platform One to get her train.

The journey back to Sheffield was uneventful but Mel was left with a residual feeling of being under scrutiny, even though it was impossible. She was in one of the first-class carriages with only a couple of men sitting opposite her. Both men were engrossed in the financial pages of their newspapers and barely looked up when she came in.

The train was on time, and as soon as it arrived back at York station, Mel opened the door to her carriage and stepped onto the platform. She hurried from the train station, making her way on foot to the constabulary buildings. All the way there, she had that same sensation of being watched or followed, but several glances over her shoulder revealed nothing unusual. She was either imagining it, or her shadow was very adept at not being seen. She was relieved when she finally reached the station and went inside.

This time, when she asked to see Derrin, she wasn't escorted into his office but asked to wait. She took a seat once more on the bench by the door.

'I'm so sorry I wasn't free when you called earlier,' Derrin said, coming out of the door by the reception desk.

'It's okay. I just wanted to see if you had any developments?'

'Let's go somewhere else to talk,' Derrin said.

'All right, but can I leave a message for my driver? He should be here looking for me within the hour.'

Mel left a note with the constable on duty, and then Derrin led her straight from the station to a small tearoom a few doors down.

Derrin ordered a pot of tea and some cake, and once the waitress had gone, he turned to Mel and said, 'I have just got back from looking into an anonymous tip that Ruby Lewis was staying at a local boarding house under a different name.'

'You found her?'

'Not quite. A girl fitting her description had lived there, but she left a week ago. It was sudden, and she paid extra to give her notice early.'

'A week ago? That's around the time of Ned's death,' Mel said.

'It's not only around, but coincided perfectly. When we were over at Avonby interviewing the farmworkers and collecting Ned's body, this girl was moving out.'

'I take it she wasn't using her real name?' Mel asked.

'No. Lis Burey,' Derrin said, then he spelt the name in letters.

'That's almost an anagram of Ruby Lewis,' Mel observed.

'Pretty obvious one, too.'

'Hmmm. Why would she make it so easy to be found?' Mel said. 'It doesn't make sense. Unless… she wasn't Ruby at all.'

'You think it was a coincidence?' Derrin said. 'A girl with a name that has exactly the same letters as our missing girl starts living in a boarder right under our noses?'

'I don't think anything is a coincidence, Derrin,' Mel said. 'But I also don't think this woman was Ruby Lewis.'

The tea came and Mel realised how much she was ready for a drink, having spent most of the day travelling to and from Sheffield. She didn't tell Derrin any of this, though, as she didn't want him to know she'd read some of his case file.

'Can you share anything else?' she asked, to see if he would.

'No. And I shouldn't have told you this, except I knew you'd pick up on the name and might have some ideas,' he said.

'At this point I can only draw the same conclusion you have already.'

'Which is?'

'Someone paid this lookalike girl to check into the boarding house and then they pointed you at her. Otherwise, why be anonymous? They may know where the real Ruby is, and if so, they also know why she disappeared.'

'You're right,' Derrin said. 'That's exactly the conclusion I came to.'

Mel picked up her teacup and sipped the warming tea again, relishing it.

'But what is most concerning is that this person seems to have first-hand knowledge of what is happening at Avonby.'

'It would appear so, if the timing of the girl moving out wasn't a coincidence,' Derrin said.

'The thing is, what are we going to do about it?' she said.

'We?' Derrin said.

'Well, it's obvious that you need my help to draw this person out,' Mel said.

'Mel, I told you, I can't put you at risk,' Derrin said. 'That's definitely not why I'm talking to you.'

'Then why are you?'

Derrin didn't answer right away, as though he was contemplating the best answer.

'I want you to be vigilant, and remain safe, if I'm honest. You see, I don't know if this person is still at Avonby and if they are dangerous.'

'How so? If they are helping Ruby to hide...?'

'But that's the thing. They may not be. This may all be to throw us off the scent. Ruby Lewis could be dead for all we know. And if she is, then this fake Ruby has been paid by her killer to make it appear as if she's alive.'

'If that is true, then you need to find the fake Ruby just as much as you do the real one. She is probably the only person who knows who our killer is. She may even be in grave danger because of it,' Mel said.

'I hadn't thought of that, and you're right. I'll get my men on it and we'll try to track her down,' Derrin said.

'Maybe look for another anagram of the name?' Mel said, and then she backtracked, reasoning that this was probably a one-time distraction. 'I think whoever is behind this isn't stupid enough to do a stunt like this again.'

Mel and Derrin walked back to the police station just after five, and Mel saw Henry waiting nearby in the Rolls.

'Please keep me in the loop,' Mel said.

'If I can,' he said.

Mel got into the car and the moment of saying her goodbyes to Derrin was not lost on her. She had said those words many times over the last few weeks, and even though it was polite and formal, it reminded her of how their relationship had been cut short and ended without any words spoken at all.

Henry reversed the car out of its parking spot, turning around in the road to set them back on the way to Avonby.

'Productive day?' he asked, glancing at her in the rear-view mirror.

Mel tried to meet his eyes, but Henry returned his gaze to the road. There was something in the way he'd asked that subtle question that set Mel's intuition tingling. After all the discussions with Derrin about someone possibly spying on them at Avonby, Mel was very aware of how well placed to do just that Henry was.

She toyed with the idea of telling him the police had almost found Ruby Lewis, to see his reaction, but then kept her own counsel. If Henry was involved, then he may give himself away without her showing her hand. But then Mel remembered how disgusted Henry had been when Avonby's former butler had been over-friendly with the girls on the estate, especially Ruby. His reaction had been so genuine that Mel was sure he wasn't someone who could hurt a young girl, and therefore not who they were looking for.

'Not really,' was her benign answer to his question, even though she was not obliged to reply at all. But despite her belief that he wasn't a killer, Mel didn't fully rule him out of knowing something. Walls, and chauffeurs, had very big ears sometimes.

# 28

THE NEXT DAY, MEL TOOK HER MOTORBIKE out for a ride to Sheffield to the Drover's Cottage. She wanted to get a surreptitious look at the man who had reported Jonathan to Derrin. Who was this Peter Sandi anyway?

Her mind was full of the latest information that Derrin had given her, and she couldn't help but test the two theories with the pieces she'd gathered already. It was clear the killer was no mere thug, but an intelligent foe and one that she had to be wary of. Who they were and what their ultimate game was were questions that remained unanswered, though Mel hoped they would show their hand soon. The more the perpetrator did, the more leads they would have that could ultimately help to catch them.

Sometimes, the obvious was not all it appeared. Mel knew that, but talking it through with Derrin had helped to clarify that Avonby was not the safe space she had thought it to be, and it was a possibility that someone there was involved because there were too many events that couldn't be explained.

'So why, then, did you remove the constables from the estate?' Mel had asked.

'To give our killer a false sense of security. You see, if they believe themselves safe from discovery, then it makes everyone safer on the estate.'

'How so?' Mel had wanted to know.

'Because the killer thinks they have already removed anyone who could unmask them,' Derrin had explained. 'What would be bad now is if we continue to poke around too conspicuously. We can't reveal that we know anything about Ruby. I'm actually still hoping to find her alive and I don't want to put her in any jeopardy.'

Mel understood this logic. It would only take the culprit to *feel* they were still being searched for or suspected for them to act – probably with fatal results – against whomever they thought was on to them. Like Derrin, she hoped Ruby Lewis was alive and that if she was, she knew something that could help. But more importantly, that they could find her long before the killer did.

If the danger was over now that any potential witnesses to the crime were gone, it didn't help them solve the case, which frustrated Mel for many reasons. She had a very strong sense of justice and wanted the killer to be caught, but she also wanted answers as to why they had done what they had. Motive was always something that was good to learn if you wanted a satisfying conclusion to a mystery. Motive, as she'd known at the beginning, was the key to everything.

The question was, how could she continue to make enquiries without drawing any attention to herself? But Derrin had given her an idea on that score. She could tell Jonathan that Derrin had a lead on Ruby, which told them the girl was alive. As she knew, walls at Avonby had ears, and if the culprit was still around, and had killed the girl and was behind the fake Ruby, then he might be relieved that the police had fallen for his bluff. Conversely, if the villain didn't know where Ruby was, and was still looking, she may well be putting the girl at risk in order to draw the killer out. It was a problem she wasn't sure how to solve. Not without knowing if Ruby was alive or not.

As she drove down the country lanes towards Sheffield, Mel was still working her way through those motives. There was a cause and effect in play for everything in life, she had learned, and although not all murders had such logic and some were opportunist, Mel felt this one wasn't. It was planned. In fact, it was more than that: it was staged, and the poor Jane Doe at the centre of it was collateral damage for something else. That 'something else' was what Mel couldn't put her finger on.

In her mind's eye, Mel saw the photographs again in Derrin's folder. The victim had been left to be found, she'd always known that. Maybe the killer had thought that would happen sooner than it had because the grave had not been deep. Even so, if Mel hadn't been so vigorously weeding and turning the soil, perhaps the 'thorn' would still be hiding in the roses? It was difficult to know.

But the Jane Doe was dead, and because she was pregnant, Mel believed this had been the motive. The father was someone who didn't want to have anything to do with his handiwork, therefore, not a good person or a trustworthy one. Of course, that didn't make him a killer, but still the most likely suspect even so.

Mel summarised what had happened since the body was found. The investigation was common knowledge to anyone on the estate or living in the area. Soon after it became public, the man living in the Drover's Cottage had pointed the finger in Jonathan's direction, in an attempt to get him arrested. An effort that failed, because Derrin was not a knee-jerk detective, but a man with sound and strong investigation skills.

However, because Jonathan had refused to tell them who the woman was that he met in London, or who he'd done it for, this left Derrin with a problem. Mel wasn't satisfied with Jonathan's argument that the woman was alive and happy. She recalled that this information had merely come from the mystery friend and not because Jonathan had seen her again himself. Mel had filed this point away but unpacked it now, knowing that information was only reliable if it could be backed up with proof. She knew she would have to force him to reveal the identity of the 'friend', and that might explain a lot anyway.

Then there was Ned's death. The execution of a seemingly innocent farm hand appeared to be unconnected to the body in the roses. But it was, Mel thought, still connected to the attack on Joseph. They had at first believed that Ned had either seen the assault, or aided it, but now they had learned that the ring Joseph had seen had belonged to Ned's mother, the motive for his involvement had disappeared. It still left the huge question of why someone would attack Joseph, though.

There was too… the razor. Ned had opportunity, but him putting it there didn't make sense. She believed that he and Nancy were kissing on the stairs at the same time Mel noticed someone was upstairs – the same someone she now believed had placed the razor in her room, and possibly had put the tripwire in before that. All of which she could see now as someone leaving a warning to stop her and others investigating further.

But these incidents had no link at all to each other once you removed the possible motives that appeared to connect them.

And then… there was Ruby Lewis. How did she really come into this? If indeed she did. Was she just a red herring that the killer had thrown in for good measure? Mel really didn't know, and her head hurt a little as she tried to pull the fragmented pieces together again.

They weren't linked – but they *were*. She knew it deep down, that gut feeling, female intuition, call it what you may. She just couldn't figure out how. There were still more questions than answers, and that was the main problem. It was so frustrating.

She reached Bellamy Lane before she realised, and she slowed the motorcycle down, hoping to pass and get a glimpse of Peter Sandi to see if she recognised him. The cottage, however, looked deserted. As she passed, she noted there was a broken window at the side and the garden was overgrown. There was, in fact, no sign that anyone lived here.

Pulling the bike over into the next lane, Mel wheeled if off the road and around the back of a bush. She came back round to check if the bike was well hidden and couldn't be seen from the road. Satisfied, she went back behind the bush, climbed over the fence into the next field, and made her way around to the back of the cottage.

Crouching down, Mel traversed the field, while looking around her to make sure she wasn't observed. There were no signs of any farmworkers and the field was devoid of livestock, so she hoped it was merely one left in rotation that probably had very little traffic to or from it.

From the field she could see the back of the cottage. The back garden was in an even worse state of repair than the front, with several broken windows in the cottage, and the grass so tall and neglected that Mel could barely see a way through it. She climbed over the wall separating the cottage from the field and entered the garden. Now was her chance to see what was inside the building, while remaining unseen from the main road.

She made her way through the grass and narrowly avoided falling over an old bicycle that had been abandoned and left rotting and rusting. When she reached the back door, Mel was cautious even though the house looked deserted. She peered through the broken windows and saw that the inside was a complete wreck, with broken furniture scattered around the rooms. Old newspapers were left in a pile, and a tea chest had been tipped upside down as though it had once been used as a table. There was a thick layer of undisturbed dust, leaves and cobwebs over the wooden floors that Mel felt sure would have shown the footprints of any occupiers if there had been any.

The back door of the cottage was unlocked, and for good measure, Mel went inside and did a quick walk around.

As expected, she found no clues inside. The place hadn't been disturbed for years. Therefore, the address Peter Sandi had given the police was a fake: a fact that somehow proved to her that the statement he'd given was too. He had, however, gone to great lengths to make it look authentic. The name Peter Sandi was more than likely false too, and wouldn't be much help. But there was one clue in there: whoever he was, he'd known that Jonathan had met with a woman alone in a hotel room. And although she doubted that Peter Sandi witnessed this first hand, she did think that he had heard about it happening. Either directly from Jonathan or from the person he was covering for. All of which meant that Mel really had to learn who that was, and the sooner the better.

Mel noticed a broom in the corridor and retraced her steps, sweeping the dust and rubbish to obscure her footprints. No need to leave more evidence should the police decide to come and visit Mr Sandi themselves.

Mel left the cottage via the front door and walked down Bellamy Lane, as she now realised it didn't matter. No one important was going to see her; although Sandi had known about the cottage, he wasn't and never had been there. The trip had been pointless and she was no closer to solving the mystery. She had to admit defeat, even when she didn't want to.

Mel reached the lane and retrieved her motorbike. She put her helmet and goggles back on, switched on the engine and drove to the end of the lane. At that moment she saw a black Rolls coming down the lane with a uniformed driver at the wheel. As it passed, Mel saw Lord Stanley in the back. Although he didn't glance her way, Mel was grateful for her helmet and goggles, as they were a disguise of sorts. She wondered what he was doing in the area, then realised the Stanley estate must be nearby.

Turning in the direction his car had come from, Mel drove back down Bellamy Lane, past the cottage and beyond. About a mile down the road, she found the gates leading to the Stanley estate, whose field she must have walked through to get to the cottage in the first place because the Drover's Cottage backed onto the estate.

*I have to speak to Jonathan,* she thought.

Mel's mind was all over the place as she drove back to Avonby. It could be a coincidence that a cottage so close to the Stanley estate had been used by the person who had tried to set Jonathan up, but Mel had a strong suspicion that it wasn't.

As she reached the gates of the Avonby estate, Mel noticed a farmer's truck at Ned's cottage and saw that the final remaining items were being cleared out. It made her feel sad that the place would soon go to a new farm hand when the role was filled. It was a sign that the world kept moving even when someone died, a hard fact she had learnt over the past few years. But death was not something you got used to, and seeing this small thing happening made her more determined to find out who had killed Ned, the woman, and possibly Ruby Lewis too, before they did any more harm.

Mel left her motorbike at the front of the house and hurried inside, throwing off her boots at the front door.

Williams was there to help remove her coat, helmet and goggles, even though it was unusual for her to enter like this at the front of the house.

'Is His Lordship home?' she asked.

'Yes. In his study,' Williams said.

Without knocking, Mel barged into the study. Jonathan looked up from his desk, surprised by her appearance and the suddenness of her entry.

'Was it Lord Stanley?' Mel asked.

'What do you mean?'

'Was Stanley the friend you covered for, the one whose girlfriend you paid off?'

Jonathan flushed and became agitated. 'Mel, I told you I couldn't betray a confidence. And I never said I paid a girl off.'

'Then what did you take her the money for?' Mel asked.

'What's got into you?' Jonathan said.

Mel flopped down into the chair in front of Jonathan's desk. She was wound up and her nerves were on edge after her discovery.

'You need to tell me who it was you are covering for. Was it Lord Stanley?'

Jonathan leaned forward. 'Mel there's a code between—'

'Fuck codes and male bollocks, Jonathan!' she said, resorting to her barracks vocabulary in frustration.

Jonathan was shocked by her language, and Mel knew she had to get him on side or he would never tell her the truth. She straightened up and looked him square in the eye.

'Forgive me. I'm very frustrated. A girl died and was dumped in our rose patch,' she said, making her voice as gentle as possible. 'Joseph attacked and Ned murdered. I need to know who you are covering for and… I'm not going to let you off this time.'

Jonathan got out of his seat, came round his desk, and went to the open door. He closed it, then calmly came back and retook his seat.

'My *friend* came to me with a problem. He'd been seeing a girl who claimed to be carrying his child. She wasn't the sort of girl a chap marries, if you get my drift, and so he didn't know if she was telling the truth. Even so, he asked me to take the money and see her right.'

'And this friend's name was?'

'Let it go, Mel!' he said.

'I can't!'

'Why are you doing this? Why now?' Jonathan asked.

Mel told him about the letter in the police file. How the accuser had used the Drover's Cottage that butted onto the Stanley estate.

'I think Lord Stanley may have set you up,' Mel said. 'I think he sent you to see that girl so you could be accused: you were the adulterer, you killed her... it all adds up. And it got rid of his problem.'

'But she's not the same girl. I told you... he saw her a few weeks ago.'

'He *told* you he saw her. Maybe he thought you were suspicious?' Mel said. 'And he had to clear that doubt away in case you were.'

Jonathan's usual pink colour blanched to white.

'It *was* Lord Stanley,' he admitted. 'They'd had a few evenings together, a "bit of a fling" he said. A few months later, she told him she was pregnant.'

'He's a cad, Jonathan. He rigged his own car when he took me for lunch to get me to spend the night at the club with him.' Mel rubbed her hand across her forehead. 'He's not a good man.'

'That is out of order, and I suspected something had happened when the inspector brought you back instead of him. But Stanley is no killer. He paid her off. She was happy. I told you... she wasn't the sort you marry. She was probably after money all along.'

'Why? Because she wasn't "one of us"?' Mel said, and she couldn't keep the bitterness from her voice.

'I'm sorry,' he said. 'Laura should hold her tongue more than she does. I do think you're one of us, Mel. You prove your worth every day at Avonby.'

'Thank you for that,' Mel said. 'Are you open to a discussion of what I think has happened?'

Jonathan nodded but he looked tired.

'Stanley killed that girl and dumped her here. Then he penned a letter to the police. False name, false address, pointing the finger your way once she was found. It wouldn't surprise me if he was the man who slipped inside and stole the pages from the diary. He's been here often enough to know the entrances and passages of the house.'

'But it doesn't make sense, we have always been the best of friends since our school days. He has no motive for framing me.'

'Jealousy maybe?'

Jonathan shook his head. 'No Mel, Stanley is stinking rich. He has had none of the struggles we've had. And even though the estate is recovering now and things are righting themselves, he has nothing to be jealous of. Plus, he's a really handsome chap and has always had women falling over themselves to be with him. It's why I didn't mind Laura pushing him at you. I knew you'd be financially safe if you and he got together.'

Mel gave a deep sigh. The thought of 'getting together' with Richard Stanley made her feel queasy. Even though, as Jonathan had pointed out, he was an attractive man. But his looks weren't the problem: there was something off about him and she had sensed it from the start.

'Stanley has been overly interested in the crime since the beginning,' Mel pointed out. 'I thought it just morbid curiosity at first, but now I wonder if it is because I'm right and he's involved. He's frequently asked about it, or mentioned you'd told him details.'

'Mmmm. I discussed the murder with him when the body was discovered, but not since. Even so, curiosity isn't a crime,' Jonathan said. 'And I have to come back to the fact that the girl was satisfied with the payment.'

Mel grew thoughtful.

'I still think, despite what you say, we need to tell Inspector Bradley. He can't solve a case without all the information. He needs to check out that cottage. And Stanley's story about seeing this girl again. Perhaps if he gives Derrin her name, he can check her out and clear him from the investigation,' Mel said.

Jonathan couldn't argue with her logic and so he agreed to let her bring the inspector in to talk to him again.

\*

When Derrin arrived, Mel locked them all in the study until she had told him everything they knew and suspected.

'I think Mel is onto something here,' Derrin agreed. 'But the only thing I'm unsure of is the tripwire and Ned's death. None of that adds up in this scenario.'

'That's been the problem all along. Too many things that don't make sense. But you'll speak to Stanley?' Mel said.

'Oh yes. He's got secrets and I intend to find out what they are,' Derrin said. 'Especially who the girl is and where I can find her. An answer he can give if he told the truth about seeing her recently. But if he can't, then we might learn she is our Jane Doe after all.'

'And if he's innocent?' Jonathan said.

'I hardly think a man not taking proper responsibility for his actions is innocent,' Derrin said.

Jonathan didn't reply.

'But I'll get to the bottom of everything,' Derrin continued.

Derrin took his leave with the aim of going straight to the Stanley estate, after first ringing the station to send over some constables as support. A precaution that Mel thought wise under the circumstances. After all, Stanley was now a suspect and had a very obvious motive for the murder.

When Derrin had gone, Jonathan poured himself a large glass of cognac.

'What have we done?' he said. 'I hope it was the right thing. Richard's never going to speak to me again.'

'If he is innocent, and a true friend, then he will,' Mel said.

# 29

Mel didn't hear anything from Derrin over the next few days, and was left wondering what had happened with Lord Stanley and how the interview had gone. But as no rumours of any scuffle on the Stanley estate reached them, Mel knew that at least nothing bad had happened.

'Let's not tell Laura anything right now,' Jonathan said. 'Not until the inspector speaks to Richard. I don't want her to think badly of him if he can prove he hasn't done anything wrong.'

Mel didn't reply, but Stanley, in her opinion, was far from innocent. He was a product of his privilege, which Jonathan and Laura were too. Though she couldn't fault Jonathan on that score, since the war had shaved off so many of those selfish edges and he was always a decent person in any given situation.

Though he was concerned, Mel was left in no doubt that she and Jonathan had done the right thing in talking to Derrin. Whatever he discovered, be it innocence or guilt, she knew there was a lead somewhere, even if it was down to who might have used the cottage as an address. He had to know something about that, at least.

As the days passed, and the silence from Derrin continued, Mel began to feel frustrated. He knew she would want to know what was happening and yet there was no contact. Not even a call to say they hadn't or had spoken to Richard Stanley. What was worse was Jonathan continually asking if she'd had any news whenever Laura was out of earshot.

The much-awaited news came mid-morning on the fourth day.

Mel heard the phone ring and hurried to the hallway just as Williams answered. She hovered while Williams spoke, then listened, and then he looked up at her as he held the receiver. Mel hurried forward and took it from his hands.

'Hello?' she said.

'Mel?'

It was Derrin.

'Inspector Bradley,' she said, keeping formal while Williams was still in earshot, but she was fighting the urge to tell him off for his lack of contact.

'I'm sorry I haven't been in touch. It took a few days to catch up with Stanley as he's been giving us the runaround.'

'Why? What happened?'

'I called in and was told he was away for a few days. Anyway, I eventually saw him. You'll be pleased to know our Jane Doe has now been identified,' Derrin said.

'Oh my god. Who is she?' Mel asked.

'I'll call in and talk to you soon and tell you what happened. Is Lord Jonathan home? I'll need to speak to him, too.'

'He and Laura are out right now, but due home around four,' Mel said.

'I'll be there when they arrive,' Derrin said.

He hung up without another word.

Mel was left with a feeling of apprehension mixed with excitement. Finding the identity of the dead woman was a huge leap forward and Mel couldn't wait to hear more.

'Lady Mel,' said Williams. 'I've just had a message from the farmer asking if you could drop by, as he wants to discuss something with you.'

'Did he say what the problem was?' Mel asked.

'I'm afraid not,' Williams said. 'But he said to meet him at Ned's cottage.'

Wearing her outdoor shoes and a lightweight jacket over her slacks and sweater, Mel hurried through the woods towards Ned's cottage.

Her mind was on Derrin and his news, and she was aware of the time galloping on and didn't want to miss his arrival. She glanced at her watch and saw that she had less than an hour before he was expected. She sped up, passing the old oak tree and onto the back field that led to Ned's cottage.

She reached the cottage in time to see farmer Davy Johnson arriving at the back door.

'Lady Melinda!' Davy called. 'Thanks for coming.'

He unlocked the door and then stepped back to allow Mel to enter the cottage.

Mel crossed the threshold and saw the now empty kitchen. A wave of sadness for Ned and for poor Nancy washed over her: a life gone too soon and with no apparent reason. She wondered now that if they had married, would they have lived here together, perhaps raised some children?

'It's all so sad,' she said. 'I wish I knew what happened. But what can I do for you, Davy?'

'Well, me and the lads cleared the place out as you asked us to, but when we were taking down the bed, Harry tripped a bit and we saw this on the stairs.'

Davy pointed to the staircase and Mel could see a protruding panel in the wood of the top step.

'Some kinda hidey-hole,' Davy said.

'Did you find anything in it?'

Davy nodded. 'I left it in the sitting room.'

Mel followed the farmer through to the now bare front room and saw the small wooden box on the window ledge. 'Thought you'd like to give it to Ned's uncle. Seems to have documents in it. Might be important.'

Davy said his goodbyes and excused himself to go back to work.

Mel saw an engraved plaque on the top of the box. It was somewhat worn but the name BERYL SOAMES could still be read, which meant the box had to have belonged to Ned's mother. But why had Ned hidden a box of paperwork – and now she thought of it, why had he concealed the locket and ring, too? It was almost as if he were afraid someone would find them and take them away from him.

As the farmer had deduced from a brief glance inside, the box held some folded documents. Mel took some of them out and laid them on the ledge, opening the papers up one by one.

She found Ned's birth certificate and discovered for the first time his full name – Edward John Soames junior. The next document was a marriage certificate for Beryl Agnus Ledger marrying Edward John Soames – it was Ned's parents! Ned wasn't born out of wedlock as Ned's uncle had claimed. They had been legally married well before his conception. But why lie, when he must have been the person to bring Ned the documents in the first place?

Plus, if Soames wasn't Beryl's maiden name, then Jimmy Soames was not *her* brother as he had claimed to be. No, Edward Soames, Ned's father, was his brother. Another lie! Subtle, and hardly necessary, but now they appeared so blatant that Mel had to question why he'd lied at all.

Mel found another two documents at the bottom of the box. She opened the first. It was a few pages long and full of formal language, with a solicitor's logo on the top. Mel read some of the details of a will. Not only was Ned's mother married, she had also been a woman of means. The will was dated soon after Ned's birth, and was legal and binding in Ned's favour as far as Mel could see.

She looked at the final piece of paper and discovered a death certificate for Edward Soames. He'd been struck by a car and killed a few days before the will had been made. Mel glanced back at the will and discovered that James Soames – Jimmy? – was executor and would be legal guardian of Edward junior, known as Ned, should anything happen to Beryl, and therefore caretaker of Ned's inheritance!

Mel's mind flew to Soames and his smooth, unworked hands. His fashionable and smart clothing. Soames had been overseeing Beryl's estate all this time. Which meant that, even as Ned had been dumped in an orphanage as a baby, believing he had no family, his uncle lived well on his money.

'Oh my god,' Mel said aloud. 'Jimmy Soames knew all along that Ned would inherit his mother's wealth.'

Ned had been over 25 so he no longer needed a guardian. Soames would have lost access to the money as soon as Ned learned the truth. It was motive for murder! Was it also a motive to have Beryl institutionalised?

But it didn't make sense. Soames had his hands on everything already. Why did he have to befriend Ned? Why did he then tell him about his mother being in the asylum? He could have just kept quiet and left Ned to be the orphaned farm hand, knowing nothing of his family or his mother's money. There was still a huge piece of this puzzle missing.

*I have to get this to Derrin!*

Mel folded the documents back up. But she put the large wedge of paper into her inside jacket pocket, as the box looked cumbersome.

She turned and left the cottage, closing the back door behind her, totally forgetting to lock it, even though Davy had left the key on the kitchen worktop by the door.

The sun was high in the sky when she began her trek back to the house. Mel glanced at her watch; she had lost track of time while reading the documents and she was sure that Derrin would already be at Avonby. She picked up speed and began to hurry across the field.

As Mel reached the border of the woods, a prickle of unease sent the hair scurrying up on the back of her neck. She looked back over her shoulder, seeing Ned's cottage in the distance, but the open field was empty. All was quiet but for the birds, and she could hear the odd bleating of one of the sheep somewhere on the farm to the right. All was as it should be at that time of day, yet Mel entered the forest with a feeling of disquiet which she put down to having seen Ned's cottage stripped bare, and the unsettling contents of the box that had sent her imagination into overdrive.

All she wanted to do now was reach the main house and check in with Derrin. She would give him Ned's documents, along with her thoughts on what they meant, and hope that he'd pull in Jimmy Soames for a conversation. Though, she reasoned, it might mean nothing. Maybe Soames came looking for Ned after he discovered Beryl's plight, giving him the papers and letting him know about his inheritance. He could be innocent of any wrongdoing.

*That might be so if Ned had not been brutally murdered*, Mel thought, her suspicions on that score now fully aroused.

She reached the oak tree, glanced its way as she always did since Joseph had been found under it. The pieces on her chessboard were moving again. She saw Ned now, back as the white knight, moving around blindly until he came face to face with his killer. That killer could be Jimmy Soames, but what if it wasn't? Who else might be responsible? Mel could see no replacement face in the slot of killer. Even so, Mel questioned her instincts as she continued through the woods. Soames had been so plausible. So calm. Had he spent all his time perfecting the lie that gave him access to Ned's fortune? Had he been so good he could fool Derrin, let alone herself?

Mel heard a crunch of twigs and glanced to her left. A deer bounded through the trees as though startled. Mel paused. She did a 360-degree turn, looking all around, but saw nothing untoward.

*And why should anyone be following me?* she thought. *No one knows I have these documents. No one knows I've even been to the cottage.*

Unless there was someone watching the cottage and they saw her go inside?

There was a sudden noise behind her and Mel spun just in time to see a thick log being swung through the air. She ducked to avoid being hit full in the face but received a glancing blow on her shoulder. She yelped in pain.

She found herself face to face with a man she didn't recognise; not Soames. A tall man with greying hair, not dissimilar in build to Williams, but he had a meanness about him that the Avonby butler didn't have. Through the sneer on his face, Mel recognised the type of man who not only had no qualms about inflicting pain, but might find some kind of perverse pleasure in it, too.

As he was already raising the log again, Mel tried to defend herself, but her shoulder was dislocated and her right arm hung useless at her side. Knowing she was disadvantaged, she turned and ran, feet pounding through the very familiar woods; she knew where all the protruding roots were, and despite the pain as it jarred her arm, she leapt over anything that might otherwise have tripped her up and left her at the mercy of her pursuer.

The heavy log tumbled to the ground behind her, and she heard her attacker's feet pounding the ground as he took off after her. Mel pushed herself as hard as she could, knowing that any cry for help would be swallowed by the trees. If she reached the open fields she would have more chance of being heard.

With her damaged arm and shoulder, she couldn't even reach into her pocket for the handgun, and she recalled how Derrin had said the killer might come after her, and might get lucky – a thought she had completely dismissed because she had been secure carrying the gun. The irony was not lost on her.

Mel had almost reached the border of the woods and the horse paddock when her pursuer threw himself at her from behind, catching her around the waist and hurling her to the ground.

She gasped in pain as her shoulder was forced back into its socket, at the same time as the wind was knocked from her lungs. Agony in her arm, as well as trying to gasp the air back in, left her vulnerable. She found herself flipped over onto her back, and even as her lungs reinflated, the man had the advantage, and his big hands grasped her throat and began to squeeze.

*Mel heard the screeching of the doodlebug followed by an eerie silence – she knew the moment had come and silence always accompanied an explosion nearby. She tensed, waiting for the blast, and as the bomb went off she pulled the covers up over her head.*

*Derrin was there as the trembling took over, and she felt his arms around her, stroking her back. He turned her to face him and then his fingers slipped up and around her throat.*

*Mel felt the air cut off and slipped into a deep dark oblivion…*

Air pulled into her lungs. Mel coughed and spluttered as the man was dragged from her. Her neck felt bruised, but she pulled herself up, wincing when she used her injured arm, even though it was now, at least, back in its socket and functioning. She put her hands to her throat, then turned her head and threw up.

As she came back to herself, she became aware of the scuffle that was happening nearby. She saw Derrin holding down the man, his arm yanked behind his back, face crushed down into the soil and tree roots. Yes, he was a big man compared to her, but no match for a former soldier like Derrin, who was fitter and younger to boot. Mel pulled the pistol from her pocket and staggered to her feet. She was shaking, not least from the half-distorted thoughts her oxygen-starved brain had unleashed. She may well have gone to her grave believing Derrin was her killer! She pointed her gun now at her real attacker, ready to fire should he get free. Anger flared inside her as she continued to breathe hard, and part of her wanted to shoot him in the face even if he didn't!

Derrin managed to get one of the handcuffs onto the man's right wrist. He was still struggling but the fight in him was growing less, and then Derrin caught his second hand and snapped the handcuff onto his left wrist. He was now more under control. At this point Mel started to feel she had seen the man before, and a vague memory of seeing someone of this height and build in the train station at Sheffield came back to her. Mel knew then that he must have followed her, perhaps had been on her tail all along. But how and where from, she wasn't certain.

Just then, Constable Jennings came running into the woods with Jonathan, Williams and Davy Johnson in tow.

Mel stowed her handgun to avoid it being seen and questions being asked. She felt some relief that she hadn't permitted her fury to make her resort to murder. She suspected, too, that this might well be the man who had hit Joseph, but all of that would come to light now that they had him.

Derrin got up and allowed Williams and Jennings to get hold of the man. They dragged him to his feet, and despite the mud caked on his face, Jonathan recognised the culprit.

'Peters!'

'You know him?' said Derrin.

'Yes. He's Aidan Peters. My former butler. The one I sacked several months ago.'

'Hmmm. I take it you didn't know he was Lord Stanley's driver, then?' Derrin said.

'What? He's been working for Richard?' Jonathan said. 'But no. Richard often drives himself on our meet-ups.'

Derrin searched Peters. He pulled a bunch of keys from one of his pockets.

'They look like the keys Mrs Felman and Mr Williams have for the house,' Mel said, and another piece of the puzzle fell into place.

Derrin nodded. 'He's had access to Avonby all along.'

As Peters was bundled into the police van, Jonathan, Mel and Derrin stood and watched him go.

'When I sacked him for being a thief, I didn't think he was capable of murder,' Jonathan said. Then he turned and went inside the house, looking for all the world like a man who didn't understand people at all.

'I'm going to need you to come and give a statement,' Derrin said. 'Are you up to it?'

Mel nodded.

'Nothing a dram of French cognac wouldn't cure. How did you know where I was?' Mel said.

'I came to the house and Williams told me you'd gone to the cottage, so I went there as I wanted to speak to you. I found the back door wide open and a box smashed on the floor in the kitchen. As I went outside again, I saw Farmer Johnson. He told me he had seen Jonathan's former butler, Peters, heading in the direction of the woods and he was in a hurry. He also said you'd gone that way. I feared the worst.'

'So, you came after me?'

'Yes. I already suspected there was a problem, so I sent the farmer to the house in my car to get help,' Derrin said.

'I could have taken any direction back to the house,' Mel said. 'You were lucky to have come the same route.'

'I heard you yelp and followed the sound. I'm glad I guessed right,' Derrin said. 'But I've more to tell you.'

She followed him to his parked car, and he opened the passenger door for her.

'The station?' she said.

'I've a lot to tell you on the way,' Derrin said.

# 30

*Earlier that day*

DERRIN ARRIVED AT THE STANLEY ESTATE AFTER hearing from a source that Lord Stanley had returned from whatever trip he'd taken. He took Constable Jennings with him, and as they reached the main house, he pulled the Jowett Javelin in at the front. As they arrived, Derrin observed Stanley's chauffeur cleaning the black Rolls-Royce. The man scowled at Derrin as if he was a very unwelcome visitor, but continued to do his work without comment.

Derrin and Jennings rang the doorbell, and they were soon invited inside by Stanley's butler and led into the huge house and to the drawing room.

Lord Stanley came in soon after and Derrin began to question the man about his former girlfriend.

'Her name is Elsie Summers,' Stanley said. 'And I know she's not the woman you found at Avonby, because my driver took her some money from me a few weeks ago.'

'Your driver?'

'Yes. I have made sure she was taken care of,' Stanley said.

'But you haven't seen her, or your child?' Derrin asked.

'No. Why would I?' Stanley said. 'Besides, the baby hasn't arrived yet as far as I'm aware.'

Derrin raised an eyebrow in surprise. 'Surely it was due some time ago?'

Stanley frowned. 'Well, I haven't been keeping count of the months…'

'So, your driver saw her? Can you call him inside please? I'd like to speak to him.'

Stanley pulled the cord and somewhere in the distance a bell rang, summoning the butler to the room.

'Can you get Peter in here, please?' he said.

The butler returned a few minutes later. 'We can't find him, Your Lordship...'

Derrin's suspicions about the driver were raised. 'Go with him to look, Jennings,' he said.

Then, as the butler and constable both left the room, Derrin turned back to Stanley.

'When was the last time you saw Elsie Summers?' he asked.

'Just when she told me she was pregnant,' Stanley said.

'And you didn't think to make her an honest woman at that point?'

'Well, I can see you judging me, Inspector, but you don't know what you're talking about. Elsie was already married. But she claimed her husband wasn't the father of her child because he'd been working away. She hadn't gone to live with him after they'd married as she had an elderly mother to care for, but he'd offered her security, and she'd taken it at the time but sorely regretted it afterwards. From what she told me the man was... a bit of a brute...'

'She could have divorced him,' Derrin said.

'Yes. But after her mother died, she used a small inheritance to get away from the man. Then I met her. She was still wearing the ring, so it made our association a little nicer because I wasn't looking for a wife at the time,' Stanley explained.

'You had a fling that resulted in the pregnancy? So, what's this man Summers' first name?'

'Oh, he wasn't called that. I believe she never changed her name after they married. I never asked her husband's name. It didn't come up.'

'So, the husband is off the scene. And you haven't seen her since the time she told you she was expecting? Instead, you send Lord Jonathan Greenway to pay her off for you?' Derrin said. 'Why not take the money yourself?'

'I didn't want a scene. She was a little clingy. I thought it was over until she sent me a letter, asking for more money. She needed to set herself up in a house, buy stuff for the baby. I did want to do right by her, but didn't want to ask Jonathan again. It didn't seem fair to keep involving him.'

Derrin watched Stanley closely as he spoke, looking for the tells that might show a lie, but Lord Stanley was telling the truth. Then he revealed that he had sent the chauffeur to see Elsie the next time.

'Peter set up a regular payment with her that he would take every month. I said I'd review that after the baby was born and agreed to help with any expenses as the child grew up,' Stanley said.

Derrin observed how smug Stanley was with his explanation of doing what was right for the girl, when it would have been so much more considerate to have avoided a pregnancy in the first place.

'Inspector...' Jennings came running into the drawing room. 'The driver, Peter Sandi, has gone. He's taken a few things from his room, and His Lordship's car...'

'Peter Sandi is your driver?' Derrin asked.

'Yes,' Stanley said. 'He's been working for me for a few months now. Why?'

'Jennings, let's get after him...' Derrin said without answering.

Derrin and Jennings ran to the car, leaving a bemused Lord Stanley staring after them.

'He must have done a runner as soon as he saw us arrive,' Jennings said.

Derrin started his car and they raced down the lane and off the estate. About a mile or two down the road they found the Rolls abandoned. Derrin pulled his car to a halt beside it, and they looked at the car for any sign of where Peter Sandi might have gone.

'There's some tyre tracks,' Derrin pointed out. 'He had another car waiting in case he needed it for a getaway, which means he always thought he'd get found out.'

'But why's he run?' asked Jennings.

Derrin didn't answer but he thought he knew.

With no way of knowing which direction Sandi had gone in, or what vehicle he was driving, Derrin and Jennings returned to the Stanley estate.

'I need Elsie's address,' he said.

A very pale Lord Stanley got a piece of paper from his writing desk and wrote down the address he had.

Derrin took the paper from the lord's trembling hands. Perhaps he now suspected what Derrin already knew.

'I hope she's all right,' Stanley said, and the guilt in his voice was evident.

Derrin and Jennings left the house without another word.

It didn't take long for Derrin to discover that Elsie Summers had disappeared from her address, a little over six months ago. The same time that Peter Sandi would have paid her a visit with the money from Lord Stanley. The landlady, Mrs Beeson, was keen to share that the girl had left her in the lurch.

'But did you see anyone visiting her?' Derrin asked.

'She left after her husband came to visit,' Mrs Beeson said.

'What did he look like?' Derrin asked.

'Tall, greying hair. A fair bit older than her. She wasn't too happy when she saw him, so I suppose she ran away after that. Some women don't have happy times in marriage. I have seen my fair share of those come through these rooms,' Mrs Beeson said.

'Did you ever see Elsie's husband again?' Derrin asked.

'Mmmm. Yes. I did, actually. Just the once. He was driving a big fancy Rolls-Royce, and wearing a uniform. She told me once he worked on an estate. But I thought he was a butler for some reason, not a chauffeur.'

The pieces were starting to come together for Derrin, and he recalled at that point a chauffeur being sacked from Avonby, around the time that Sandi started working for Lord Stanley.

Derrin began to suspect that Aidan Peters and Peter Sandi – another near-anagram – were one and the same, so he rang Mel and arranged to go over there to speak to Jonathan again.

# 31

'After catching Peter Sandi attacking you, and Lord Jonathan recognising him as Aidan Peters, I knew I was right,' Derrin said. 'Elsie Summers was our Jane Doe. And Aidan Peters was the husband she'd escaped from. Unfortunately for her, Lord Stanley hired Peters and then sent him to pay Elsie. Putting her right back in his clutches.'

'It is a piece of the puzzle for sure. Aiden Peters was sacked and had a big grudge against Jonathan for getting rid of him. He killed Elsie and buried her at Avonby, waiting for an opportunity to frame Jonathan, perhaps?' Mel said. 'All of this was made easier because he still had copies of the house keys in his possession. Something no one suspected.'

'I'm sure of it. I'll get some answers from him, I promise you. Maybe we'll even learn what happened to Ned,' Derrin said.

'Ah. I may have another clue on that score. I have some papers to show you.' She patted her jacket pocket, making sure that Ned's papers were still there.

As Derrin pulled the car into his parking space by the police station, Mel noticed a Rolls-Royce parked nearby.

'That's our car,' she said. 'That's strange, we left Jonathan behind at the house.'

When they got inside, Mel and Derrin found Henry sitting beside the same young woman she had seen him with several days earlier, right outside the police station. She'd observed him giving her something, which at the time she had thought might be money.

'Inspector!' said Henry, standing up. 'Lady Melinda. This is Ruby. Ruby Lewis. She has something to tell you.'

Derrin took Ruby away for questioning and Mel sank down on the bench beside Henry.

'You were the one who helped her,' she said.

'Yeah. Mr Peters was coming on thick and heavy. So much so, the poor girl was scared to death,' Henry explained. 'She said she was leaving and he threatened he could always find her. Then, one night, Peters came and gave her a ring. Ruby didn't want it and she tried to refuse, but she said he got so angry. Then he told her the last woman to mess with him "wasn't around any more". She took the ring, scared to say no, and she came to see me when everyone was in bed and told me what he'd said. The next day, though, His Lordship caught him stealing and Peters was sacked. Ruby stayed because she now thought things would be okay.'

'But they weren't?' Mel said.

'No. A few weeks after he went, Ruby came to find me. She was terrified. She had been getting letters from Peters which became increasingly more threatening. Then, she said, she'd seen him at Avonby. Though she wouldn't tell me what he was doing there. She told me she believed he was going to kill her, and then begged me to help her leave as I'd promised to before.'

'And you believed her?' Mel asked.

'She believed it. And she wasn't the type to get hysterical over nothing,' Henry said. 'So, I took her to stay with a friend of mine. Knowing she was safe there for a while and Peters wouldn't know where she was.'

'Does she still have the ring?' Mel asked.

'Yeah. I reckon she'll give it now to the inspector,' Henry said.

'Henry, you were very kind to help Ruby. Why did you?' Mel asked.

'She is a sweet girl. Reminds me of my sister, and I would hope, if she found herself in trouble, someone would do the same for her, too.'

Mel nodded to show she understood and she had a new respect for the chauffeur because of his kindness.

'So what changed?' Mel asked.

'Ruby was going by Lis Burey and was working in a local shop. But then, a week or two ago, she saw Peters in York and he saw her. He started chasing her through the streets, and after she ditched him, she rang Avonby and told me he had found her. She was scared he'd figured out where she was working and where she lived. His Lordship wanted to go shopping with Lady Laura, so I went and helped Ruby move again while they did that. She told me, then, what happened on the night she'd seen Peters at Avonby. He'd been putting something in the plot that had been dug to plant the new rose bed. She broke down and told me she thought it was a body. I got her to another safe house with a promise to come back and speak to her. I knew she was scared, but I also wanted to persuade her to come forward. Then, when I picked up His Lordship and brought him and Lady Laura home, we were all were told about Ned and I was a bit too shocked to say anything. I thought Peters had done for him too…'

Derrin came out of his office, having taken Ruby's statement. He sent Henry into the room with Constable Jennings and Sergeant Wakeman, who Mel hadn't seen since the day she found Elsie Summers' body.

'If I'm right, I suspect this is Lady Laura's missing ring,' said Derrin, holding up a beautiful gold band with a large ruby set in the middle of a ring of tiny diamonds.

Mel nodded. 'I think you're right. What now?'

'With Ruby's statement in hand, I'm going to interview Peters while Jennings and Wakeman take Henry's statement. I might be a while,' he warned. 'Should I get someone to take you home?'

'No. I'll wait. I want to know what Peters says,' Mel said.

'Okay. But no reading of my case files this time.'

Mel smiled. 'I should have known you had guessed.'

She knew deep down that Derrin had left them on the table for that very reason, leaving her alone long enough to snoop.

Derrin left Mel in his office again, as it was more comfortable than the reception area, and he went off to interview Peters. After a short time, he came out.

'He's confessed. He's claiming it's a crime of passion, that when he realised Elsie was faithless, and had been sleeping with Lord Stanley, he lost his temper,' Derrin said.

Shouting erupted from the corridor then, and Derrin opened his office door in time to see Peters struggling against the two officers who were taking him back to his cell.

'She was an adulteress. She got what was due,' Peters said.

As the constables dragged him past Derrin's office, Peters saw Mel and his face flared again with fury verging on insanity.

'Bitches! All of you are bitches!' Peters shouted.

One of the officers cuffed Peters across the head, and they half dragged, half carried him away.

'If I have my way he'll get the rope,' Derrin said.

He came back into the office and closed the door.

'Are you okay?' he asked.

Mel nodded. 'I was just thinking, Peters and Ned were friendly. Maybe Peters knew Ned's uncle too?'

While he was gone, Mel had laid out the papers she'd taken from Ned's cottage.

'Maybe, but I don't see why he would…'

'Didn't you tell me you found Ned's cottage door open, a box smashed? That box was what these were in.'

'And?'

'Peters was spotted leaving there by Davy, who recognised him and knew the man had been sacked and removed from the property. What if Peters was looking for those papers for Jimmy Soames?' Mel said. 'That would explain why he came after me so hard, because he knew I must have them.'

'You think they joined forces? But why would they?' Derrin asked.

'Money. Ned's money, legally. And Peters wasn't ashamed of ripping off Lord Stanley, taking money from him every month and pretending to give it to… Elsie. Hard to think of our Jane Doe with a proper name… who he'd killed already by then.'

'Mmmm. I might need to pull him back and question him again,' Derrin said.

Derrin went away to give the order. When he came back, Mel asked, 'Can I come into the interview with you?'

'No, Mel. It's not like the old days. This is straightforward police work and there are rules I have to follow,' Derrin explained.

They heard Peters being brought back.

'It upset him when he saw me. My presence may help you break him down sooner,' Mel said. 'He's involved with Ned's business, I'm sure of it. We still don't know if he somehow coerced Ned into helping him, too.'

Derrin shook his head again. 'No, you can't come in, but let's make sure he knows you're behind the two-way mirror in the interview room.'

They opened the door as Peters was being taken into the interview room. Mel and Derrin walked down the corridor towards the open door as Peters was dumped, still cuffed, into a chair.

'So, I watch from in here?' Mel said as they reached the door, loud enough for Peters to hear.

'Yes. Any questions you want answered, write them down.'

Derrin went into the room and closed the door, while Mel entered the observation room. She sat down in one of the chairs that were by the two-way mirror and found Peters staring at the glass, as though he could see her in there.

Derrin took a seat opposite Peters and he now placed the documents on the table.

'We know you were looking for these,' he said.

Peters glanced at the papers and his lips drew back into a sneer. 'So?'

'Do you know Jimmy Soames?' Derrin asked.

Peters didn't answer.

'Did Soames ask you to get these for him?'

'Who's watching us?' Peters asked.

'What do you know about the death of Ned Soames?' Derrin asked. 'Did you kill him for Soames?'

'Ned was the only person who ever did anything for me, so why would I hurt him?' Peters said, surprising both Mel and Derrin.

'Ned helped you? Did he set that tripwire for you? And plant the razor in Lady Melinda's room?' Derrin asked.

'No. Ned was blameless. He took me in when Greenway threw me out. Even gave me some of his savings to help me out until I got a job. Had to change my name, though, as Greenway was blotting my reputation all over the county,' Peters said. 'I had to fake references. It wasn't that hard to do. Eventually, I got the job with Lord Stanley. I thought I'd be okay until I saw Lord Greenway visiting him and had to hide so he wouldn't see me.'

'I know all this. You set Greenway up for revenge. But where does Soames come into it? Did Ned know what you were up to?'

Peters glanced at the mirror one more time, and then he began to talk.

Mel listened, shocked that the man was calm and different when talking about Ned – his only friend in the world – even though he killed his own wife. He admitted also to attacking Joseph when he saw him in the woods with Ned, because he thought he would recognise him – and, of course, he tried to kill Mel. But he still had a sense of honour where his friend was concerned.

'Ned didn't know anything. He wasn't involved. But he had said how Lady Mel was asking questions of everyone, so I set the tripwire and left the razor in her room. I didn't mind making sure one of the Greenways got hurt. She shoulda kept her nose out.'

He glared at the mirror to make his point stronger, knowing she was there watching. Then he told Derrin how he had applied for a job at a manor house in Sheffield, only to learn the owner was James Soames. Working there for a few days, Peters discovered that Soames was Ned's uncle. He found the box with the papers and realised Ned's fortune had been taken from him. So, he took the papers, and the locket and the ring, from Soames to give to Ned.

'After that, Ned spoke to a solicitor. He was making moves to get his money back and have Soames imprisoned,' Peters said. 'He promised to help me a little too when he did, so it was worth my while helping him. Ned was a good man.'

Mel realised, even before Peters summarised it, that Soames had noticed the papers were gone, along with his new butler who had left his employment without notice. He must have traced Ned from the orphanage, because they had been the ones to help him secure the job at Avonby some years before.

After assuming that Soames must have come to Ned, Peters claimed that Soames then killed him and tried to find the papers. It was supposition at this point, but Mel could tell that Peters believed what he was saying, and she knew it was plausible.

Derrin cast the mirror a glance, which Mel knew was for her. They would confer later about Peters' statement. But they both recalled that day when Soames calmly lied to them. Mel believed, now, that he had just murdered Ned and was at the cottage to search for the papers. As Ned had hidden them well, he didn't succeed in finding them, a fact that would be his downfall.

'Just one other thing,' Derrin asked Peters. 'Why attack Lady Melinda?'

'I knew she had the papers. There was nothing I could do for Ned, but I could use the information to get something more out of Soames… I saw her come out of the cottage, went in and found them gone. Had to get them back, didn't I?'

This proved that, despite his feelings for Ned, Peters was still corrupt and wholly motivated by money, and his dead friend was worth capitalising on. Mel saw that Peters was evil to the core, with very little to redeem him.

When the interview ended, Derrin was galvanised into action, sending a police squad to the house where Peters told them Soames lived.

A few hours later, Soames was brought into the station.

Faced with the evidence Derrin now had in his possession, and a gun they had found in Soames's possession, the man soon crumbled and confessed. Bringing a resolution to the troubles at Avonby.

It was past two in the morning when Derrin came out of the interview room for the final time. Soames was taken to a cell and he and Peters would be put before a judge at some point in the next few days.

'I think I owe you that cognac,' Derrin said to Mel.

## 32

Derrin pulled the car into the kerb in front of a little cottage in Avonby village. It had taken them around forty minutes to get there, and despite the late hour, he appeared to be alert. Mel understood this more than most, as she was pumped with adrenaline after the revelations of the day.

'You bought Mrs Rendal's old place?' Mel said. 'I've always thought this house rather sweet. Needs work, though.'

'Yes. She went to live with her daughter in York. It's a good location. Right in the heart of the village. In walking distance of the inn.'

They got out of the car, and Mel followed him inside.

The entrance opened onto a cosy sitting room. Mel looked around at the drab, old-fashioned furnishings left by the old lady.

'It's not my taste,' Derrin said. 'But I've hardly had a chance to decorate since moving in.'

Mel felt a moment of pleasure at knowing Derrin was in the village very near to Avonby Hall, but more from the thought of what his buying a house in the village meant. He was planning to stay in the area. She tried not to read too much into it, but the thought made her happy as she followed him into the kitchen.

Derrin took a bottle from the kitchen cupboard and poured some of the cognac into two teacups.

'Sorry, no glasses yet,' he said.

Mel sipped the drink, savouring the taste that had once been so familiar and represented both good and bad times to her. But more good, she thought, because they had meant time spent with Derrin.

Her hand trembled as she took the second sip. There was no getting away from it, the old trauma had been sparked by the close call that day. She put the teacup down hard on the kitchen table and slumped into the chair, wracked with tremors.

She was aware of Derrin holding her while the episode ran its course, but afterwards he pulled away and stood with his back leaning against one of the cupboards as he looked at her. His face was serious. She felt shame for the first time in years and hated that her weakness had manifested itself right then in front of him. Perhaps this was why he'd never really tried to find her, even after his letters went unanswered? Mel was frail in her own way, and perhaps he didn't want that in his life any more? But Mel didn't ask if this was how he felt, she was afraid of the response.

'I thought you were better,' he said.

'I am… was… I think…' She placed her hands to her throat. 'When he was strangling me, I had a flashback of sorts… but it wasn't a real memory…'

'You were triggered by the shock of the attack. I realise that. But Mel, what the *fuck* were you thinking? You put yourself in the line of fire again and again. Were you deliberately trying to get killed?'

She saw his anger now as it burst out of him with a further tirade.

'You were reckless! I told you not to go anywhere alone and there you were, crossing fields, too far from the house to be heard… If I hadn't come to find you…'

Mel's face flared in anger. 'You're the one who took your constables away from Avonby, claiming we would be all right. Don't blame me for responding to a call from one of our farmers. I didn't know where that would lead. I was just doing my job.'

'You didn't think! As usual! Blindly throwing yourself into everything. He could have killed you!'

'But he didn't. You arrived in time,' Mel said. Her voice softened. 'And anyway, I thought you liked it when I went off and followed my own hunches.'

'I might not be around next time. And the thought terrifies me,' Derrin said. 'But yes, point taken.'

He picked up his teacup and sipped some more cognac. Mel noticed his hand shook, too. And she knew then that Derrin wasn't immune to trauma any more than she was.

Derrin closed his eyes and took a deep sigh, forcing the anger to subside. When he opened them again, Mel was in front of him. She took the cup from his hands and moved into his embrace. Derrin resisted hugging her, though, even as her arms circled his waist and her fingernails rubbed his back under his jacket, something that had always soothed and relaxed him in the past. But holding his arms away began to feel awkward, so he wrapped them around her. As she looked up at him and smiled, Derrin remembered that sultry expression and the invitation on her lips was hard to resist. This close, he could smell her skin, and was reminded of her beautiful aroma, a scent that had always sent his passion into overdrive.

Mel stood on her toes to reach him, and it was her lips that touched his. He'd always let her lead, right from the start, and he wondered now if this was why they hadn't reconnected again, because she hadn't put herself out there in any way to suggest she wanted him still. A thought that still stung.

Derrin pulled her to him, and it felt so reminiscent of the first time they were together that it sent shockwaves of anxiety through Mel, but she pushed the feeling away, determined not to show any further weakness that night. She hadn't given in to the tremors for years now, and he'd been right to observe that it was the shock of the attack that caused it. She'd been doing well with the calm at Avonby, all thrown into turmoil by murder and mayhem.

Taking his hand, Mel led Derrin upstairs, finding his bedroom, where they both began to disrobe. Halfway through, Derrin pulled her into his arms again. His tongue explored her mouth as his hand slid under her blouse and unhooked her bra. His fingers traced a line over her nipple until Mel was gasping with pleasure. She was more aroused because of the lack of sexual contact over the past two years.

Still half-dressed, they fell onto the bed, clothing discarded as necessary. There was a sense of urgency about their coupling, like two alcoholics desperate for their next drink, and as they switched and turned and changed, so did the control shift; but when Mel was in charge again, after a brief scramble for a condom, which Derrin had to go and find, she positioned herself on top of him.

Mel rode Derrin, her hands down on his chest, played with his nipples as one of his hands cupped her breast and the other helped her rise and fall as he held her buttock. When they both climaxed, pounding together until the last spasms ended, Mel fell down on the bed beside him. Her eyes closed, body sated and mind peaceful for a while.

Derrin turned into her, cuddling up as though sleep was a foregone conclusion and they could stay together all night as they had before. At that point Mel opened her eyes and sat up.

'I have to get back. Staying out would be difficult to explain,' Mel said.

'Okay... I didn't think, sorry.'

Mel was the first to get up, and she pulled on her clothes as Derrin disposed of the condom. Then, without further discussion, they left the cottage, and Derrin drove the short distance back to Avonby to drop her home.

# Epilogue

Mel was exhausted when she finally got home to Avonby Hall. Her body ached, but more than anything her mind and spirit were shaken.

They had parted on reasonable terms, but despite their mutual passion, Derrin had been withdrawn when he dropped her off. She suspected that he regretted their reconnection. She thought she understood why, with them living so close to each other, and with no war to blame any indiscretion on, their association might mean something else. Might lead, indeed, to something serious.

Sex had always been good with them, but no words of love had ever been exchanged. Yet Derrin had shared so many close moments with her, that at one time, Mel had thought it was a given. That was until he disappeared from her life overnight without any goodbye or notice.

She was shaky as she entered the house, letting herself in because it was so late that even Williams had retired.

Feeling somewhat insecure about where she and Derrin stood, she told herself that it had been mutual gratification, something she had been more than willing to participate in. Had instigated, even. It might mean nothing else to Derrin, and she had to harden herself to that possibility.

The light was on in Jonathan's study and Mel knew that her cousin was still up, probably waiting for her. He would want to know that the villains behind their recent troubles had been caught, and so, despite being tired and feeling the need to think privately about the events of the day, she went to the study first.

Jonathan sat by the dying fire, looking up at the Turner painting above the fireplace.

'Hello,' she said, interrupting his thoughts.

'Hello, Mel. Do you know why I have always loved this painting?' Jonathan said.

Mel came closer. She sat down in the other chair and looked up at it with him.

'I've always been aware of how brutal nature is, and none more than the sea, a powerful force that no man truly masters. This ship, as it navigates those turbulent seas, has always made me think of how lucky we are for the calm and safety we have at Avonby,' he said.

Looking at it now, Mel saw the significance of what Jonathan was trying to say. The ship was Avonby, but the storm, created by recent events, had almost overwhelmed them.

'But we're here still, even if we're limping,' Mel said. 'And we'll make it back to shore, in time to do the repairs needed.'

'I knew you'd understand,' Jonathan said.

Keep reading for an excerpt of
Samantha Lee Howe's *Flight of the Turner*

## Prologue & Chapter 1

## Mel Greenway Investigates: Book 2

# Prologue

*London, September 1946*

Joan pulled off her heavy gloves, stuffing them into her coat pockets, before inserting the mortice key in the lock of the back door of the pub. It was five in the morning and she was weary. An autumn chill was nipping at her fingers, and dawn had barely peered through the darkness. It was dreary and unpleasant to be out this early but Joan had no choice. The pub cleaning job was the first of four she would do that day and Joan had to start early in order to make it through the next few gruelling hours.

She came into the kitchen, closing the door but finding little relief in the room, which was also cold. Even so, she removed her coat, hanging it up on the hook on the back of the door. She was cold, but she would soon work up a sweat and the bulky coat was restrictive when she was doing physical labour.

The small kitchen was in turmoil, with beer jugs and glasses stacked high and left unwashed. Joan sighed. The bar staff were supposed to wash up before they left at night but rarely ever did. She considered complaining to the day manager, but feared losing the job. The war hadn't been kind to her, and she had been left widowed, with three small mouths to feed, and no sign of the widow's pension she had been promised, which seemed to be tied up in red tape. She couldn't afford to lose even an hour of the work she did, which brought in just enough to make ends meet, but left nothing for emergencies.

Joan pushed away any irritation because it was pointless. There was nothing she could do. Her babies needed to be provided for, and it was the least she could do for all the bravery her stoic husband, John, had shown: he hadn't wanted to return to the western front on his last leave, it was almost as though he knew he would never return. Even now, Joan remembered the desperation of their last coupling – which had left her stranded with yet another mouth to feed. But little Betty gave her such delight, with the smile that so resembled her father's and the quiet acceptance in her young attitude, that was so like Joan's.

Joan gave a smile thinking of little Betty, Stevie and Mary, all still tucked up in bed, with Joan's mum there to sort everything for them when they woke.

Joan filled a kettle and a large pan, putting them on the stove. She would need plenty of hot water if she was to get these glasses and jugs pristine and, of course, there would be the bar and tables which were often stained with sticky remnants of beer. While the water came to the boil, she began to tidy the kitchen. But as she drew closer to the door leading to the bar, she became aware of music coming from inside. She paused: it was unusual to hear the Wurlitzer playing when the place was closed. Joan shrugged, then turned back to the sink.

Not my business, she thought.

From the storage cupboard Joan pulled out the mop and bucket and picked up a carton of detergent before pushing open the door again between the kitchen and the space behind the bar.

Once the door was open, she could make out the song and the singer: Surrender by Perry Como was one of her favourite records, but Joan paused and looked around the room, half expecting someone else to be there because the machine couldn't play on its own.

The bar area, however, was empty, as it should be at this time in the morning.

Joan went back in the kitchen and filled the bucket with the detergent and steaming hot water from the pan. She added a little cold water to the mix, enough to be able to put her hands in. The brass-covered bar surfaces would need a good clean, as would the tables around the room before she began to sweep and mop the floor.

Nothing but the hottest soapiest water could deal with that mess.

As she carried the bucket back into the bar, the song finished. There was silence but for the slight whirring of the machine as it stowed the record back in its bay, only to lift it again and place it back on the turnstile.

Joan placed down the bucket and came around the bar as Perry Como's voice echoed around the empty space. She reached the brightly lit machine – a dark brown imposing gadget that held 24 discs, the latest thing the owner had installed and she suspected it was popular among the youngsters who frequented the pub. She had never paid much attention to the jukebox beyond polishing the glass and now she was at a loss as to how to turn it off.

She waited until the record finished before pulling the plug. She would have to leave a note for Rob, the manager, to say the thing was broken and explain what she had done. Although she wasn't sure he would be too happy with her decision, especially when she noticed the record hadn't returned completely to its bay.

Joan turned away, shrugging. 'Not my fault,' she said realising that Rob must have left it that way, even as he locked up for the night. He must have known it was stuck so why hadn't he done something about it?

Behind the bar, Joan took out a clean cloth from under the sink and dipped it in the bucket, wringing out the cloth before she began to clean the spills from the counter. Her hands stung with the hot water, years of hard graft had caused thick callouses to form on her palms and fingers, leaving them looking so much older than Joan's real age. But there was no time for vanity, survival, for her and the children was all she cared about, and maybe soon, with the widow's pension forthcoming she would be able to ease off a little.

An hour later she was done in the main bar, She changed the water and made her way to the women's bathroom which would likely be an easier clean than the men's as it was little more than a single cubicle with a toilet in, but as she pressed down the handle, the door didn't budge. Joan pushed against it. This door was prone to swelling in the wet weather and it had been a damp month. She pressed her shoulder against the wood, giving every ounce of her slight weight until it shifted slightly.

Joan took a deep breath and tried one final push. The door gave; she fell forward into the cramped space.

A woman's body lay across the toilet, slumped against the wall.

'Oh good god!' Joan said, stepping back. Her shoe skidded slightly on the damp floor. She backed away, taking in what she saw, horrified by the sight, and not at all sure if the poor creature were alive or dead.

Turning and hurrying towards the front door to call for the local bobbies, Joan didn't even pause when she heard the jukebox firing up again and the sound of Perry Como filling the air. All she thought of was getting outside and raising the alarm.

She didn't see the figure behind her, a dark shadow emerging from the gentlemen's toilets, and only knew she wasn't alone when a hard object hit her in the back, followed by intense pain as the knife slid home.

A sharp shock. Almost, she thought, like the bite of a snake.

# 1

*South Yorkshire, October, 1946*

Lady Melinda Greenway came into the kitchen to find the cook, Mrs Weston, hard at work. Mel was soaked through from the unexpected downpour that had caught her and the gardener, Joseph, out on the lawn soon after they had finished deadheading the roses. The roses had survived so well that year because of this practice, and Mel was sure, that with the continuing mild weather, they may yet get another bloom.

'Good heavens!' Mrs Weston said. 'Get to the fire before you catch your death!'

Unperturbed by a little rain, Mel smiled at the cook and took the offered towel, wiping her face and hair of the excess water.

'I wanted to talk about the dinner party,' Mel said.

'Everything is just as you asked for. A simple three course dinner, consisting of vegetable soup, a main of roast chicken breast in a pepper and cream sauce and Daisy has just finished assembling the Victoria sponge cake. Mr Williams brought up some decent wines from the cellar and I think they are ready to be decanted in the dining room,' Mrs Weston said, speaking of the kitchen maid and the butler.

'Perfect,' said Mel, her mind immediately organising all the items into a pattern for dinner which made her stomach growl slightly. 'But time is galloping on and I didn't expect to get wet today so I had better go and change. I confirmed how many would be attending?'

Mrs Weston nodded. 'The table is set for six. The bedrooms are made up for four guests. And I'll send Ruby and Toby to light the fires and warm the rooms shortly. It's chilly up there and the damp weather doesn't help'

'You think of everything,' Mel said. 'I'm so grateful for you, especially with Mrs Felman in London with Laura and Jonathan.'

'When is his Lordship due back?' Mrs Weston asked. 'Only I thought it was soon.'

Mel's second cousin, Lord Jonathan Greenway and his wife, Lady Laura, were currently the custodians of Avonby, inheriting the title during the war after Mel's father, George, and her brother Valentine, were killed in the blitz, along with Mel's mother, leaving her an orphan. They were all now away with the chauffeur Henry, and the house keeper, Mrs Felman, at the Greenway London house.

'By all accounts the autumn season has been a lot of fun for them both. A proper introduction into society for their new status according to Jonathan's letters. It has especially been a triumph for Laura and they have decided to stay another week.'

Mrs Weston grew thoughtful, 'I'm glad you've reconnected with some old friends, but didn't you want to go with them? Do the balls and parties?'

'Oh no, none of that is for me. I'm much happier being at Avonby and it has been rather restful these last couple of months, especially after all that awful business with Ned and the poor wretch we found in the rose bed.'

'Indeed,' Mrs Weston said, recalling the former farmhand's murder by his own uncle, and Mel's part in solving the case with Inspector Derrin Bradley. Life had returned to normal despite these awful events on the estate.

'Talking of Ned,' Mrs Weston said now, 'have you heard anything from Nancy?'

Mel smiled at the mention of their former scullery maid and fiancée of the late farmworker. 'She's settled into her new life well. It's quite something how she has taken to being a "woman of means" and running her own household in Sheffield.'

'Fancy Ned leaving a will like that? Taking care of the woman he loved. It's so romantic!' said Daisy as she rounded the nook corner where the kitchen fireplace was positioned with an empty coal bucket in her hand.

'Is that fire stoked then?' Mrs Weston said. 'And stop eavesdropping girl and go and refill that bucket from the cellar.'

'Yes Mrs Weston,' said Daisy and, with a nod in Mel's direction, she hurried off towards the cellar door to take care of the task.

'I'm happy for Nancy,' Mel said.

Mrs Weston nodded, before turning her attention back to the pan on the stove. She scooped out a spoonful of the warm, vegetable soup and tasted it.

'A little more salt I think,' she said.

Mel picked an apple from the bowl in the centre of the huge kitchen table which served as both a communal eating place for the staff and an extra work surface when needed. Even now, the table held a pan of peeled potatoes and another with some green beans and carrots, ready to be made up for the main course. The fruit bowl was always kept full these days from the estate's own orchard which had now nicely recovered from the neglect of the war years and was yielding both cooking and eating apples. Therefore, Mel felt no guilt at biting into the apple and enjoying it as the first food she had eaten all day.

She experienced a twinge of nerves about the dinner. She hadn't asked Laura and Jonathan if she could have friends staying over, or host a small dinner party, but she didn't see why she shouldn't be able to, when they were in London enjoying themselves and Mel, as always, was left running Avonby single handed. Not that she had any less of a workload when they were home, since Jonathan had all but abandoned any show of an effort where the estate was concerned. Mel did everything, and it was, she realised, just how she liked it. She loved Avonby and was proud of the estate and all the hard work she had put in to make it what it was today. Better in some ways than the pre-war days, because it was now a working farm, selling their own produce as well as using it to feed the estate.

She thought now of her old school friends. Clara Taylor-Smith, Eleanor Parkinson and her fiancé Charles Harris, not to mention

Michael Chase whom she hadn't seen for years because he moved to India with his parents when he was in his teens. Before the war, hanging out with Clara and Eleanor was comfortable, easy. She didn't know Charles of course, but she trusted Eleanor's taste in men as she was always the most sensible of the group and Mel couldn't imagine her choosing a future husband without due care and consideration.

The fifth guest was Inspector Derrin Bradley who she hadn't seen for a few weeks. He had been busy since they last spoke, after an argument had ensued that left them both wondering where their relationship was going. But her invitation to dinner had been accepted showing that Derrin was open to receiving an olive branch.

It was such a stupid argument, Mel thought now. She couldn't even recall how it started.

They had been discussing a case he was working on and something about her response had hit a raw nerve. After that Derrin had shut both her, and the conversation, down. They'd always been fiery, Mel knew that, but he'd always valued her opinion during the war and Mel didn't understand why that changed. Perhaps it was an ego thing, or maybe because he didn't want to put her in harm's way again. Either way, since then, they hadn't seen each other, though Derrin had called the house phone a couple of times showing he was willing to talk. It was a shame that on both occasions she had been out of the estate and missed the calls and her returned phone calls had found him unavailable also.

Ships that pass in the night, she thought now recalling Henry Wadsworth Longfellow's poem The Theologian's Tale which appeared in "Tales of a Wayside Inn": a well-thumbed copy of which was in Avonby's library. The metaphor was not lost on Mel as she and Derrin failed so often to negotiate common ground in any normal capacity, but somehow managed to come together during adversity. Mel wanted to change this pattern and whatever happened between them, be they friends, or lovers, she did not want "them" to be just nothing. Better they be enemies than that.

But we're not enemies, she thought, even though she wasn't sure what they were.

'I had better go and change,' Mel said aloud to no one in particular, but Mrs Weston nodded and Daisy, returning with a full bucket of coal, gave her a smile in acknowledgement.

Mel left the kitchen then, going upstairs via the servants' staircase as she often did. It was, after all, the most convenient and discreet way of traversing the huge manor house.

Now on the second floor Mel passed her former bedroom, the old seamstress's room in which her cousin's wife, Laura, had placed her when she first arrived at Avonby in December 1945. So much had happened in those 10 months, but only recently Jonathan had offered her a change of room and Mel had taken the switch because of the sheer practicality of having her own ensuite bathroom. She had smiled when Jonathan had shown her the new room. Having her own bathroom was a luxury that she hadn't expected.

Her new room was in the North Wing and further away from the stairs, But Mel loved the privacy this afforded, though she still felt some fondness for her former room because it had offered some security for the first time since she had been demobbed and unable to find work. For this reason, she had left the room with some regret.

As the staff of Avonby had helped her move her few possessions into the bigger room, Mel had seen Laura lurking at the end of the corridor and she knew she was peeved. She had done so much along the way to maintain Mel's precarious position in the household, but Jonathan's decision changed her status and Mel was firmly ensconced as a valued member of the family by the move.

Even so, Mel's relationship with Laura remained tense. Mel had made many attempts to befriend Laura, win her over, but Laura was always distant and reserved. No matter how hard Mel tried, Laura never met her in the middle at any point, and so, Mel decided that she had to look outside of the household for some female friendship.

She had been considering how to do that, perhaps even to get more involved in the local parish, when she received the letter from Clara and Eleanor. They had communicated several more times, had a few phone calls and expressed a wish to meet up. With Jonathan and Laura away, it was the perfect opportunity to have a reunion dinner party.

Mel opened the door of her new room and glanced around. Jonathan had arranged for it to be decorated before he told her this would be hers. The walls were painted a pale blue and Mel had a big dressing table in solid oak with a huge mirror that had two side pieces of mirrored glass hinged to either side so that she could see her face from all angles. Despite this Mel rarely spent much time in front of the mirror and only occasionally used cosmetics, of which she did at least now have a few.

There was a tall and wide oak wardrobe that matched the dressing table and a chest of drawers in the room. Although the wardrobe was still quite empty, Mel had more clothing than she'd had even two months earlier as Jonathan's generosity now stretched to a clothing allowance. Mel didn't take any of this for granted, however, as she knew it was all part and parcel of being a member of the Greenway family and image to Jonathan – and especially Laura – was everything. They couldn't be seen to neglect this poor relation now that things were improving overall because of her help. Thanks to Mel, Avonby's farm was flourishing. There was a bounty of fresh produce that was now seasonally sold at the market and even sent out further afield to Sheffield and Manchester. Construction had started on a new bigger greenhouse to house the growth of even more. Lettuce, tomatoes, carrots, green beans and cucumbers were already in production and they were growing way more than Avonby's occupants could eat. This, Mel knew, would increase tenfold when the new structure was completed, and it meant that some produce could be grown year-round instead of just certain times of year as a result.

This was all possible because Jonathan had listened to Mel. She had pointed out that if Avonby was to survive, they had to diversify and do more. Mel, as the overseer, kept a tight rein on production and they had even hired some more full time workers to help their aged gardener, Joseph, and his wife, Rosa, in their endeavours now that they needed a more commercial yield. Post war, homegrown fresh products were even more in demand and Joseph's experience was needed to guide the younger, fitter, team. Fortunately, the old retainer loved to share his knowledge and was proving to be a very nurturing mentor for their new employees and Mel wasn't worried at all that he might be overdoing things, in fact, Joseph was showing a great deal of enthusiasm and energy for the task which had given him something of a new lease on life.

Mel stripped away her work clothes and went into the bathroom to wash, after which she began to prepare for the evening. Wrapped in a towel she sat down at her dressing table and ran a comb through her rapidly drying hair. Then she put a few curlers in to regain control, before applying a modicum of rouge to give her cheeks a warmer glow and her lips a little blush.

It wasn't a very formal affair, but Mel suspected that her guests, travelling all the way from London, would probably make some effort. Especially Clara and Eleanor who were always so fashionable before the war. At the very least the men would be in tuxedos and the women, evening dresses. With this in mind, Mel pulled out a sophisticated blue satin dress from her wardrobe and lay it on her new double bed. Would this be the thing to wear? She wasn't sure, not having done much in the line of socialising of late. But the dress was lovely, simple and elegant as she was not one for frills and flounces. Yes. It would be perfect and she would feel comfortable too.

Even in the north wing the distant echo of the doorbell ringing reached Mel. With a twinge of apprehension, Mel realised that the first of her guests had arrived. She had left instruction to show them to their rooms in the guest suites over in the south wing and knew that this would be actioned by Mr Williams, the butler, and the footman, Toby.

She took a deep breath, catching sight of herself in the mirror. Had she changed so much since they last saw her? Not that much physically, she realised, with the hard work on the farm keeping her figure from expanding, she still had that youthful look. But what of the others? She hadn't seen either of her friends since the night of the blitz when her parents and brother had died and she met Derrin for the first time.

*How the world continues to turn and somehow we come full circle,* she thought.

Despite her nerves, Mel continued getting ready, knowing that everything else was being taken care of by the very capable, and well-trained, employees of Avonby Hall.

# Acknowledgements

Huge thanks to my agent and friend, Camilla Shestopal, Editor, Maxim Jakubowski, Jamie Hodder-Williams, Claudia, Polly, Victoria and the fabulous team at Bedford Square Publishers for all of their time and dedication.

# About the Author

**Samantha Lee Howe** began her professional writing career in 2007 and has been working as a freelance writer for small, medium and large publishers ever since. She is a multi-award-winning screenwriter and a *USA Today* bestselling author.

Samantha's breakaway debut psychological thriller, *The Stranger in Our Bed*, was released in February 2020 with HarperCollins imprint, One More Chapter. The book rapidly became a *USA Today* bestseller, and has now been turned into a feature film for USA, Canada, China, the UK and various countries in Europe. It won Best Thriller at the *National Film Awards*.

Samantha lives in South Yorkshire with her husband, historian, writer and publisher, David J Howe, and their cat Skye. She is the proud mother of a lovely daughter called Linzi.

# NO EXIT PRESS
More than just the usual suspects

**— CWA DAGGER —**
**AWARDED BEST CRIME & MYSTERY PUBLISHER**

*'A very smart, independent publisher delivering the finest literary crime fiction'* **Big Issue**

MEET NO EXIT PRESS, an award-winning crime imprint bringing you the best in crime and suspense fiction. From classic detective novels, to page-turning spy thrillers and literary writing that grabs the attention. Our books are carefully crafted by some of the world's finest writers and delivered to you by a small, but passionate, team.

In over 30 years of business, we have published award-winning fiction and non-fiction including the work of a Pulitzer Prize winner, the British Crime Book of the Year, numerous CWA Dagger Awards, a British million-copy bestselling author, the winner of the Canadian Governor General's Award for Fiction and the Scotiabank Giller Prize, to name but a few. We are the home of many crime and noir legends from the USA whose work includes iconic film adaptations and TV sensations. We pride ourselves in uncovering the most exciting new or undiscovered talents. New and not so new – you know who you are!

We are a proactive team committed to delivering the very best, both for our authors and our readers.

Want to join the conversation and find out more about what we do?

Catch us on social media or sign up to our newsletter for all the latest news from No Exit Press.

**f** fb.me/noexitpress    𝕏 @noexitpress

**noexit.co.uk**